TIME BOUND

Micky O'Brady

Time Bound
Copyright © 2022 Micky O'Brady
Cover Design: www.KimG-Design.com
Interior Format: Dorothy Dreyer

Published by Snowy Wings Publishing
PO Box 1035, Turner, OR 97392

Paperback ISBN: 978-1-952667-73-2
eBook ISBN: 978-1-952667-72-5

Table of Contents

Chapter One -
DEJA VU

Somewhere, Somewhen

Waking up hurts.

Headache. Body ache.

Something hard and cold presses into my back, rough edges poke through my clothes.

A groan breaks from my throat. Ow. Even that hurt.

Forcing one eyelid open, I lift a hand to my head: In one piece, no blood. Good. Something slimy is stuck to my cheek. I brush it off with an uncoordinated swipe of my hand.

One by one, my senses come back to me:

Scent of rain. Of nature.

Sounds of birds. Animals. Rustling of leaves.

Something makes a loud screeching-squeaking noise—

Startled, I open my eyes as I jackknife up to sitting, heart hammering, breath coming out short, only to be rewarded by an onslaught of dizziness. Holy Sun and Stars—

A… forest?

I'm surrounded by trees, bushes, vines, lianas hanging off some of the trees, plants, all in various sizes, shapes and colors. The ground is covered in wet moss and leaves, a thick fog lifting up and drifting in slow tendrils toward the treetops. Some kind of small, furry animal stares at me, sitting on a fallen trunk, large claws dug into its decaying bark, no more than a meter to my right. I blink twice, but it doesn't change a thing.

I'm still in a freakin' forest.

"What the heck?" I mumble. "Where am I and what am I doing—?"

Mashaule!

Like a flash of lightning, the last minutes come back to me: Mashaule! A mere moment ago, I was in USEF central arrest together with Chase and Zio, the old version of them, my mentors, trying to get information out of that traitorous admiral, because *something* had changed in the timeline. Or rather, was going to change. Either way, it was connected to Mashaule and him planning to kill Kieran in the past. *The biggest pity is that history will never know the role his early death played. That it saved billions of people.* Nausea rises. Words of a mad man—or rather, a man under the influence of some upstream evil mastermind, trying to change the timeline to their advantage. That's where Mashaule must've obtained that disc-like device from, which opened a portal to the past that I followed him through to—

To where, exactly?

I scramble to my feet, only to stumble two steps forward when the dizziness cranks it up. Whoa. Holding out my arms like a figure skater, I regain some resemblance of balance. What the heck did Mashaule use to jump us? Not that I'm an expert in time-jumps, but this was my third and least pleasant, easily.

The distant memory of *something* flashing past me during the jump, of screams, distorted faces, sends a shudder down my spine. No, that wasn't pleasant at all.

And neither is the result of said jump, but hey, at least that constant pain and aching I felt since I popped back into my time is gone. It's nice to not feel like I'm being torn apart from the inside.

I force myself to stand straighter and bring my hands up, ready to defend against whatever. I'm here, which means I'm assuming so is Mashaule, which also means he could be trying to clock me over the head with a branch or something at any given time.

I whirl around, scanning my six.

Nothing.

Nothing besides trees, bushes, leaves, all wet to a degree.

It for sure explains my wet backside.

Checking a full three-sixty, there's no trace of the admiral-turned-traitor. No trace of the man who wants to alter the past to change the future, risking everybody's life and the flow of time with it. I blow out a frustrated puff of air. "Where is he?"

The fluffy, brown-coated animal sitting on the trunk blinks twice, then scurries off, leaving me alone in the middle of an unknown forest, on an unknown planet, and—

Ugh. You're such a newbie, Thorburn.

I sigh. In the grand scheme of things, the Federal Bureau of Temporal Investigation only recruited me, what—a mere fifteen minutes ago? But still, even with the events of the last weeks I haven't learned my lesson.

The most pressing question isn't where I am.

It's *when* I am.

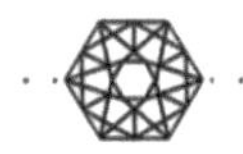

Some Forest Somewhere, Somewhen

About two hours later, I've made good headway through this pseudo-jungle. It bears a striking resemblance to a rainforest I was sent to for an SAR training during my second year at the academy, but given that two suns shine down on me here, this being Earth is out of the question. And speaking of: Looks like said two suns are going to set pretty soon. Got to speed it up if I don't want to be stuck in here when night falls.

That brings a whole motherlode of deja-vu, and none I want to revisit. Buzzwords: First Contact on T-12 and meeting Kieran.

Kieran.

My stomach cramps. I can only hope Mashaule hasn't gotten to him yet. Kieran's death will benefit absolutely nobody. My First Sense is—*I am*—sure of it. If anything, I feel like the timeline would've benefited from him still being alive in my time. Or, maybe that's just wishful thinking.

I rub a dirty hand across my eyes.

But now's not the time for self-pity. I have a job to do, and I can't do it stuck here, wherever that may be. I glance down at PADdy. "Distance to settlement?" I whisper to activate it.

My wrist PAD shows the outline of a crude map on its screen, complete with the forest I'm in, and hallelujah: a village not too far away. I'd rather use the holographic display, but until I know what time this is, I won't spring future technology on somebody who might be observing me. I'll stick to the small screen. And keep voice output disabled.

I tap PADdy once, acknowledging the information. Here's to at least limited environmental scanning functions, hallelujah. Otherwise, I wouldn't put it past me to run in circles for a day or two, no matter my SAR training at the Academy.

Keeping myself mostly hidden, I approach an area of the forest where the trees stand farther apart and the underbrush clears out. There, like PADdy promised, about two hundred meters straight ahead: houses!

And, even better. "Humans," I whisper, a weight the size of a boulder falling off my shoulders. That means I must be somewhen after 2150, which is when humans began to venture out into space and set up the first colonies. It also means I can blend in easier until I can get out of here, via time-jump or good old-fashioned shuttle.

My stomach cramps again, a nervous wave of nausea accompanying it.

Neither option is going to be easy. I have no means of opening a portal or whatever like Mashaule to jump back to the future—and my priority is finding Mashaule and keeping him from altering the past. If he succeeds, me jumping back to good ol' 2295 could mean I'd end up in a completely different future than the one I left. I think. Boy, how I wish I'd gotten my temporal mechanics brushed up before I got thrown back in time yet again. Alas, if wishes were fishes… I sigh and sneak forward some more.

It's a busy settlement, and large. The houses seem big and moderately modern, so I'm optimistic it's not the twenty-second century, but hopefully at least the twenty-third. And there's only one way to find out. I rub both palms over my face in an attempt to clean myself, to at least look not too suspicious. My outfit is dirty, so are my hands. I probably still look like something the cat dragged in, now more than after returning to my origin time. After all, I haven't even changed since I woke up this morning on the *Pioneer*.

"Damn Mashaule," I whisper, then take the first step out of the shadow of the trees and onto a small dirt road. Straightening my shoulders, I walk with a purpose, like I belong here and just had, I dunno, an unfortunate run-in with some creature in that forest.

Once I reach the houses, the road turns from dirt into pavement, including sidewalks. Fences separate the houses on both sides of it. In some front yards, children play, in others nothing's going on, and those I prefer, for obvious reasons. Some of the children stop their play and stare at me, which makes me self-conscious on a whole new level. Am I recognizable as an off-worlder? Or is it only because of my torn outfit? What if they call their parents?

After maybe five minutes of walking, the streets get busier. This seems to be more of a shopping area, with stores on either side of the street. The sidewalks are filled with people of all ages—and to say I'm drawing attention would be an understatement.

And just like that my priorities have changed order. Finding out where and when I am is important, but I won't be able to do any of that if I can't blend in.

I need clothing first. Fresh, clean, inconspicuous clothing. I mean, I knew that, but I had hoped I had more time.

Scanning my gaze over the store fronts and signs, it takes me less than twenty seconds to find one that looks promising. Okay. Let's speed this up, Thorburn. I weave through the masses until I reach the store. A wave of nausea washes over me when my approach triggers the sensor and the doors open. Good luck, Lieutenant.

I take a deep breath to sharpen my senses, then enter the store. The area straight ahead is filled with display cases for jewelry and sunglasses, while the left and right areas of the store are crowded with large shelves and clothing racks. Crowded is good. Makes it easier to hide.

Makes it easier to steal.

I cringe.

Sorry, owner of this shop. It's not a decision I made lightheartedly, but nobody's house I passed had old-fashioned clothes lines or clothing out. Would've still been stealing though, I know. I even considered burying my outfit and coming here in my underwear, the victim of a mugging or whatever—but while that would have solved the issue of my clothing being the problem, it then would have been my lack thereof causing me difficulties. Meaning, I nixed that idea as well.

Theft it is. Sigh.

Employees in this store are busy, serving several people. I catch parts of their conversation. Standard English, good. So, it's less likely to be twenty-second century, especially looking at the clothing styles offered. Not that I am an expert in fashion, but none of the shirts hanging from the racks or the pants displayed look like they're from over a century ago. I think.

Checking the area around me, I grab a black t-shirt from a pile, then keep on moving, like I was browsing, nothing more. No cameras as far as I can see—but that doesn't mean there aren't any.

Here goes nothing. I fake a violent sneeze, bend forward with it, and shove the shirt under my dirty one.

One down. Next, pants.

I take a pair of what looks like leggings from another pile. Usually, I wouldn't be caught dead wearing those, but—

"Anything I can help you find?"

I jerk when the voice coming from my right side startles me. "N-no. Thank you. Just looking around." I fake a smile at the middle-aged man in front of me, but it doesn't make him look at me any happier. Quite the opposite.

He presses his lips into an annoyed line, then folds his hands in front of his chest, which pushes his holographic name tag higher, the *MIKE* displayed on it throwing red-colored rays across his neck. "You're touching quite a bit for somebody who's just browsing."

Heat rises to my face. "I'm allergic to some materials. Gotta check. But alas," I add a theatrical sigh, "I don't think this will work for me. Thank you though." I take a step to the right to get past the man—when he mirrors my movement and blocks my way.

"Then I hope you won't mind removing that shirt from under yours." He points at my stomach area.

Crap.

Crap, crap, crap! I'm a lousy thief. I've been in here half a minute, and I've been made!

Unfortunately for me, Mike is blocking my way to the exit I can only see the very top part of, courtesy of being trapped between him and pretty high clothing racks, even for a half-Magellan. The door opens and closes, admitting another customer. A warm sensation rises in my chest, bringing a feeling of peace, which is ironic, because it looks like I'll have to tackle this guy to make it out of here.

As if he read my thoughts, he shoots one arm forward and captures me by the wrist. "Caleb! I caught us a thief!"

"Busy with a customer, Mike! Bring the son of a gun over, so we can book 'em," the other guy yells from the register, then lowers his voice to a normal speaking tone. "Are you looking for anything specific, sir?"

Double-crap. I can't get booked—I need to get out of here!

I raise my right hand for a wrist-release—

"Actually, yes. I'm looking for a crew member of mine."

That voice—

I freeze.

"Your crew member?"

"Yes. Not from here, young, about this high, female, red-brown hair—"

Mike's eyes widen when recognition strikes. "I got her!" He yanks me with him toward the register. "She was stealing a shirt!"

Now, I could still fight him. Getting out of his grip shouldn't be a problem.

But as he drags me with him fleeing from here is the last thing on my mind.

That voice—

We clear the last high racks of clothing, and there he is, standing in front of the register, in the same grey-and-blue uniform I saw him last in no more than two hours ago.

And yet it feels like it's been a lifetime.

His black hair is slightly longer now than before, and when he turns to look at me, a strand falls into his face.

For the longest second, his gaze connects with mine—warmth, relief, happiness, it's all there, and I swear I can breathe easier, like a weight was removed from my soul. He allows himself another second, exhaling slowly, like he felt the same weight gone, before he nods.

"That's her."

The man behind the register, Caleb, according to his name tag, looks from him to me and back. "This is your crew member?" He scratches his neck. "Aren't you… aren't you a USEF officer?" He points at the USEF patch on Kieran's shoulder.

"That I am. Captain Kieran Wildason from the *USEF Pioneer.*" He holds out a hand, and Caleb shakes it.

"The *Pioneer!*" Caleb smiles with honest enthusiasm as he shakes Kieran's hand. "Man, you guys kept the Quaneez away from us, much appreciated, really! You're heroes!"

Kieran gives a slight wave of his hand, his cheeks taking on the faintest trace of red. "Our pleasure. Glad we could help out. But we're on our way out of the system. If you don't mind, I'd like to take my Junior Ensign and go."

Caleb opens his mouth, but before he can say something, Mike takes over. "She stole a shirt! Stuffed it right under hers, I saw it!"

Awkward silence hovers.

"Well…" Caleb frowns, and Kieran levels me with an angry gaze.

"Ensign, what happened? You were supposed to be on an SAR exercise, and I find you here, stealing?" He jabs a finger at my stomach.

Honestly, I don't need to act. My reaction comes engrained from years of Academy training. I snap to attention. "Sir, I apologize. The SAR went awry—"

"No kidding, Ensign! No—I don't want to hear it." He holds out a hand, then uses the same one to pinch the bridge of his nose. "I apologize for the ensign. She was a transfer, and I hoped she'd do better in a nurturing environment, like the *Pioneer*, but..." He sighs, then sucks in his lower lip. "Could I convince you to not press charges, by any chance? I'd be quite embarrassed if this story came out."

Caleb opens his mouth and closes it again. "I—I don't know, we—"

"I caught her red-handed, Cal!" Mike yanks his hand up, and with it mine, waving it through the air as if he wanted to show said red hand. "Stealing is stealing!"

Kieran nods. "I agree. And I can promise you that her punishment will be appropriately served on the *Pioneer*. Maybe..." He drops his glance to the goods displayed in the class vitrine between him and Caleb. A short chuckle bursts from his throat, before he points at something in the glass case. "Maybe I could purchase something to make up for your trouble? This here would be perfect."

"I was about to sell that at the fair on Ortega One—"

"Where we're also going, but you'll save me having to find you there."

"Well—"

Mike pulls me forward. "Cal, she—"

"Never mind, fantastic," Cal answers, ignoring Mike and unlocking the vitrine for Kieran. "A very good choice, and also a satisfying solution." He takes out whatever Kieran bought his silence with, wraps it up, and holds a payPAD for Kieran. "If you wouldn't mind?"

Kieran presses his thumb into the indentation. "Not at all." He takes the little packaged item and stuffs it into his pocket. "Now, if you wouldn't mind?" He turns to Mike, an expectant look on his face.

"Hmpf," Mike grumbles and releases me. "You're banned from here, Missus. Good riddance." He adds a little shove that I sell with a head hung low and embarrassed expression.

"Thank you, Captain. Sorry, Captain. It won't happen again,

Captain." I catch a whiff of Kieran's aftershave—and boy, does it light me up on the inside. *Not* bursting out with the biggest grin ever, *not* throwing my arms around him, *not* jumping him and clinging to him like a love-hungry octopus is the biggest victory for self-control in the history of self-control.

Kieran swallows hard. "No, it won't happen again, ensign. Follow me. Gentlemen, good day, and thank you for your help."

"Any time, Captain! May the *Pioneer* stay victorious," Caleb calls out after us, before the doors close behind us.

Without hesitation Kieran walks to the left. "Ensign."

"Sir." I fall into step next to him, but because it's so crowded, I'm much closer than I would be under normal circumstances. As an ensign walking next to my captain, I mean.

"We'll demat up from the demat area. It's too busy here. Stay close."

"Yes, sir." Translation: Stay in character. Shouldn't be too hard, I—

Somebody bumps into me, and I compensate to the left—

My hand brushes over Kieran's. Like I touched a live wire, electricity shoots up my arm from this small contact. It zooms straight into my core, spreading into every fiber of my body, including my heart and soul, energizing me and recharging my batteries.

Blame it on my sensitive half-Magellan ears, blame it on being attuned to Kieran, but I hear him suck in the same sharp breath like I do.

Without breaking stride or acknowledging what just happened, he feels for my hand and squeezes it once.

My heart somersaults like an aerial gymnast on her best day.

This.

It's been two hours, but I've missed this.

I've missed *him.*

After two more minutes, we reach the demat area. Kieran stops at the mark for outgoing traffic and taps his Hablamate. "Wildason to Conolly."

"Conolly here. Ready to come back, Captain?"

"Got two words for you, Chase: Code Magenta."

I hear Chase suck in a harsh breath. "Be damned. Ready for demat."

"Ready."
Then, a warm, prickling sensation engulfs my chest—

Chapter Two -

SEVEN MONTHS OR SEVEN HOURS

USEF Pioneer, Demat Room, Somewhen

—And when my vision returns, I'm right back where I started, the *Pioneer*'s Demat room.

At the console, Chase whistles through his teeth. "Holy Sun and—"

"Nonie." Kieran says my name with a reverence that brings goosebumps to my skin. He turns to me, and like a magnet aligned to him I do the same. A myriad of emotions skate across his face, all eventually morphing into one: wonder.

Ever so slowly, he raises his hand and cups my face. "You're back. I— I—" He brushes his thumb across my cheek, and that touch, it releases a small gasp from my throat I had no chance to suppress.

Something lights up in Kieran's eyes, and like an invisible barrier was blown to pieces in that very moment, we're chest to chest before either of us can blink. He brings his second hand to my other cheek, tilts my head up, and crashes his lips to mine.

Whoa.

That's quite the welcoming.

One that I really appreciate.

I give in to the kiss, fingers digging into his shoulders, pulling him closer. A sound rumbles from his chest, a deep growl unleashing every bit of pent-up emotion I've been shlepping with me since I was thrown into the past, and turns it into something much warmer, much more wholesome. The kiss turns heated as he glides his tongue across my lips, coaxing them apart before he drives it inside my mouth. I'm losing myself in the sensation of him, of so many emotions scrambling together, gluing my soul to his. He tastes like hope, awe, wonder, and a whole lot like Kieran—

"Ahum. Really, keep on going, guys." Chase gives a small chuckle. "No reason to hold back."

Gliding his thumbs across my cheeks once more, Kieran breaks the kiss, but leans his forehead against mine. "I missed this. I missed you," he whispers, as if he had heard me think the same words a few minutes prior.

I reach up for his hands. "I missed you too." *I grieved you.* "Forty years are too long." I peel his hands off my face and place a kiss on each palm.

Chase steps us to the platform. "My turn. I'll be fine with a hug only though." He opens his arms wide, and I fall into them. Now that I have the direct comparison of a hug with Admiral and Commander Conolly within a day, I must say props to the older Conolly. He really kept in shape well.

Chase rocks me back and forth. Like with Kieran, the hug is loaded with emotions. "So happy to see you."

I hold on to him and his scent of familiarity. "Same here. What date is today, by the way?"

"December 14th, 2255." Nice of him to give me not only the day, but the year, because in my life details like that matter.

"Ouch." I cringe. "Seven months for you. That's long."

Chase freezes in mid-rocking motion. "Quite," he says after a short pause, and that word, it carries some kind of connotation.

I get it. Unwrapping myself from his embrace I straighten up and look at him, then Kieran. "I'm sorry I didn't say goodbye. I had no clue the Quaneez would trigger the Marmelite and that there was a chance of me jumping back. I would've said good-bye otherwise." My voice breaks at the end. It was hard enough to fly out there to fix the *Pioneer*, knowing there was a possibility I wouldn't come back. History said the *Pioneer* came out victorious, but it unfortunately neglected to mention me. Or rather, fortunately, but either way it didn't help me.

Kieran and Chase exchange a short glance that brings Kieran to a blush, before he looks at me sheepishly from under his lashes. "I think we made up for it."

Chase laughs out once. "Oh, heck you have. But anyway, let's go. I guess a little discussion is in order." He claps Kieran's shoulder, then walks toward the door, tapping his Hablamate. "Conolly to Upinga. Conference room."

"Acknowledged," Zio's voice comes back through the device.

Chase waits at the door and lets Kieran and me enter the hallway first. Considering I just walked this same path a mere few hours ago, it feels much better this time. More alive, less creepy. Even though…

I turn and look behind us down the empty hallway. "Where is everybody? Is it nightshift?" Because usually I would expect some foot traffic, cue the reason for me staying inside my quarters for most of my time on the *Pioneer*.

"It's actually the middle of dayshift." Kieran reaches for my hand and weaves his fingers between mine, like it was the most natural thing in the world.

Which I feel it should be.

But which for us, it isn't.

I try to pull my hand free. "People might see us!" And then they're wondering who the captain is holding hands with, leading to them memorizing my face and a whole buttload of trouble forty years down the stream of time.

Kieran squeezes my hand tighter, keeping it trapped. "Nobody will see us. We're free to do whatever we want." He lifts my hand up to his mouth and places a kiss onto its back, all without breaking his stride.

Not me though. I'm being thrown into a stumble, literally.

"What— How can you—"

"We implemented some precautions. You know, seemed like a good idea after we had a visitor from the future. You heard me call Code Magenta to Chase before we dematted?" Kieran waits for my reaction, so I nod. "That's a new code specific to the *Pioneer*. Under Code Magenta all personnel are to stay on their posts as much as possible. The admin and higher-deck hallways are off limits for everybody besides senior officers, and all video surveillance cancels out your presence. Same goes for demat logs and computer entries. We have a fake backstory for the crew about you, so it's all good."

Sun and Stars! That's like… "Wow." I blink. "That's fantastic." It gives me a whole lot more freedom than during the last visit, and considering they did this without knowing whether I would ever return… it gives me all the feels, really. "What a great idea, thank you!" I look up to Kieran, who smiles and winks at me.

"Our pleasure."

"Ah, Captain, you're just the smartest." Chase keeps his face so straight, I can't tell whether he's serious or— No, I don't think he is. In fact, I'm sure he's pulling Kieran's leg—because Kieran reaches back with the hand not holding on to mine and slaps him over the back of the head.

"You suck, Commander."

Chase ducks and chuckles.

I shake my head. "You guys are weird today."

That gets them on the same page again, both their faces splitting into a wide grin. Chase lifts both hands. "Nonie, since we met you, weird has been our middle name."

I huff. Well, they're not alone with that.

We arrive at the conference room, the doors opening automatically when they recognize Kieran approaching, revealing Zio waiting right behind them.

Like Kieran and Chase, he wraps me in a hug that I'm more than happy to return. "It's good to see you again, Nonie." As he lets go of me, I realize I never hugged Chase or Zio before, no matter if we're talking about the admiral- or commander-version—until today. Today

I've hugged the admirals *and* the commanders.

Which reminds me. "It's been a long day." I rub my eyes and let myself fall into the same chair I sat in on the day of the Battle of Balthar. So, earlier today for me, and seven long months ago for the guys.

Zio takes a seat, like the other two. He regards me up and down. "I can tell. Aren't those the same clothes you wore when you left us?"

Kudos for Magellan observation. "Yeah. But I upgraded. Ta-daah!" Reaching under my shirt I pull out the corpus delicti, otherwise known as *the shirt I stole.*

Eying the shirt, Zio crunches his brows. "I don't understand."

"Never mind, Zee." Kieran takes that shirt and shoves it to the side. "But I'd like to know the story—or as much as you can give us, because… timeline, etc." He makes a wave-motion with his hand. "Zee is right, you're in the same clothing, and while you last saw us seven months ago, not much time seems to have passed for you."

For a moment, I get hung up on his phrasing: *You last saw us seven months ago.* Does that mean— Did they see me sooner? Was I, or rather, will I be back sooner? I scratch my head, then drop my hand. Asking is not going to lead to anything, of course they're not going to say what happened—will happen.

Still.

I narrow my eyes at them. "Y'all don't seem very freaked out or surprised to see me again." And quite well-prepared, actually.

"Have you met us? No way we're ever again going to be caught unaware by a time-traveling nomad." Chase places a hand across his heart. "We took some precautions. Our smart captain came up with that." He wiggles his eye brows at Kieran, who wrinkles his forehead.

"Really, Chase?"

"Just praising your inventiveness."

Kieran ignores him with a roll of his eyes, and turning toward me. "If I may ask, are you here on purpose or by accident?"

Ouch. Valid question though. "On purpose. To a degree." I cringe. "But as you know, I can't give you any details." Which feels so wrong. I want to scream it at them, *protect Kieran, watch out for a mad admiral trying to kill him*—but what then? Would it help keep Kieran safe?

Maybe, maybe not. But I'm sure being warned about a possible assassination carries a big impact on one's life, so what if those precautions then change the path of time? If Chase kept Kieran so safe and bubble-wrapped he doesn't get to do something he should be doing, like, make peace with a new species, or intervene in a Quaneez attack, or... I don't know, there are countless scenarios that could prove to be disastrous for the timeline.

Meaning, as much as I'd like to warn him, I can't. *I'm* his safety line.

I swallow dry and force an apologetic smile to Chase. "Sorry. Hate to be so secretive."

Chase gives an understanding nod, leans forward, and folds his hands on the table. "We get it. This isn't our first rodeo, remember?" He winks at me. "But you'll need a place to stay and some help, I assume?"

"That indeed would be much appreciated." My cheeks warm. "I feel like I should stay out of your daily business as much as possible, since—"

Click.

Since this is not a predetermination paradox.

Right?

My mind scrambles to follow the dizzying logic of time travel. From where I was coming from, me going back to the *Pioneer* had happened before. The admirals knew it, and they knew I'd be back to the past, presumably to save Kieran from some upstream force trying to kill him before he died on June 8ᵗʰ, 2257, like the Taro said would be my job. But now another upstream player—or the same, who knows—has recruited Mashaule to change that past, which is why I'm here.

Meaning, this is new. The timeline has veered off its path already. I pale. Here's hoping minor changes smooth themselves out, as the current theories go. But still, reducing my footprint is, as always, paramount.

"Since what?" Zio asks.

"Since, uhh, since you have that Code Magenta, that should be much easier." Gee, I really hope the FBTI will have some kind of training in time-travel etiquette. To say the back and forth was confusing would be an understatement.

"Agreed." He looks at Kieran, then me. "You both look well today."

"Minus the fact that Nonie's in dire need of a shower," Chase quips.

"Not what I was going for, and you know it, Trip." Zio cocks his head at Kieran. "You were right. You felt her."

Kieran chews on his lower lip and nods once. "Clear as day. Told you I was sure."

Wait, what? I lift a hand. "I'm feeling a tad left out here...?"

"Join the club, Nonie." Chase adds an eye roll and a sigh. "Here we are, patrolling the area, when this one"—he points at Kieran—"gets all antsy and asks us—sorry, *orders* us—to check out the Alvero Prime colony. Zio of course backs him up right away, while I'm stuck with the unthankful job of telling him why altering course is not a good idea. Alas, turns out he was right, and we got you back. It's a win, I'd say, but this whole being bonded thing is really hard to understand."

"Bonded?" My jaw drops. "Like the Magellans?"

"Chase." Zio gives him a stern look—and the other man actually blushes.

"Whoops. Ran ahead with that one."

"That you did." Zio directs his attention to me. "Do you remember us talking about unions between Magellans, how they bond for life?"

Is a sun flare hot? "Yes, of course I do." Had made me wonder if Dad, since he never even had the shortest relationship since my mom's death, was in truth Magellan as well: Magellans choose one partner, and that one for life. Zio described it as a connection on a mental and physical-chemical level. "It sounded all pretty ominous though." Especially with the part where it altered physiology.

"It becomes much clearer when you put it into context. You're half-Magellan. As you know that comes with certain features, like your sensitivity for the timeline, but also with certain other add-ons."

I hug my elbows. No need to spell it out, because the math is pretty clear, unbelievable as it is. "You're telling me— That Kieran and I—" It sounds too private to say it out loud.

"That you're bonded, yes. To be honest, I didn't expect it. We assumed the bond would be weaker for humans, and with you being only half-Magellan, I was under the assumption bonding was out of the question, especially with a human. But when you traveled back and were cut from our timeline the effects on Kieran were immediate."

I whip my head around to stare at him. "In which way?"

He grimaces. "Let's just say when you left, I felt it in my very bones. Like I was torn apart from the inside."

"Whoa." Air whistles between my teeth as I inhale sharply. "That was the Bond?" When I arrived back in my time, I didn't feel good at all. Couldn't explain it, this continuous ache, like I was drained and couldn't stop it. *Like somebody had cut my soul in two.* And it's gone now. Has been, since I arrived back here. Holy Sun and Stars— Was that— was that us? Kieran and me?

Zio lowers his chin in a nod. "The separation of the Bond, to be precise." He makes a ripping motion with his hands that causes Kieran to flinch.

"It was the second most painful event in my life, and I think you know what the first one was."

Of course, I do. The day he was shot by his nanny and almost died. I cringe. "That's horrible." And so much worse than what I felt. I felt bad for sure, but not... not close to dying.

Zio gives his friend a supporting smile. "As a Magellan, I of course recognize the signs of a disrupted bond, so when Kieran was close to collapsing on the bridge after you vanished, I was able to stabilize him."

"I wasn't collaps—"

"And boy, it freaked me out," Chase adds. "We're retreating from an exploding planet, shaken around, shields punctured by shrapnel and debris, and our captain collapses."

"Guys! I didn't *collapse!*" Kieran glares at him. "I might've had a hard time to stay upright, but I didn't collapse!"

"Right. You would've done so well without Zio's meds." Chase cuts his eyes at him. "What did Zio say you'd go through? He called it acute withdrawal, so that would've been fun."

"Whatever," Kieran grumbles. "Point is, now I'm feeling better. And my second point is, when you came back, today, I mean..." He drops his gaze, then looks right back at me, warmth shining in his eyes. "I would like to say I felt you the second you were back in this time. Like a weight had been lifted off my shoulders. Breathing was easier. Living was easier. While that was a sensation I wish everybody could experience, I'm glad you didn't have to go through the first part of it."

It takes me a full two seconds to understand the implication behind his last sentence, and when I do, it's like a punch in the gut. From his point of view, I didn't have any withdrawal, because for all he knows he's still alive in my time.

Only he isn't.

I slap both hands in front of my face to hide what surely must be obvious to see and would give away the future. "That experience sounds horrible. I'm so sorry you had to go through this, Kieran." I lower my hands once I feel I can control my expression.

"Zio helped. The meds made it bearable." He shrugs, like it was no big deal.

"And we'll have them ready the next time." Zio nods.

The next time.

Because we all know I'll need to return to my time eventually. At least once I figure out how to do so.

And when I do, I'll leave Kieran broken.

Chapter Three –

ROLLERCOASTER

"Y ou really don't want a little bite now?" Kieran dings the wooden spatula against the Dutch oven, then puts the lid back on. Doubt it's going to keep that delicious aroma contained though. Synth meat, veggies, all sautéed… The scent alone is making it hard to focus, but boy, do I need to focus.

"No, thank you," I call back. "I'm *really* trying to concentrate here." As in: I've got to get *something* done if I ever want to get back to my time—or find Mashaule. And while my to-do list only contains two things, none of them are easy-peasy to check off.

Problem number one, find Mashaule—how? If I assume we're currently in the same time, how can I look for him? Facial rec via the USEF's systems? Yes, PADdy and me have hacked the *Pioneer*'s and the M-3's systems before, but installing a virus of the kind I'd need to find old Mashaule… tricky, to say the least. Risky, too. I have no good means to search for him—and that's saying he didn't activate his device and jump to another time period.

Which brings me to problem number two, initiating a time-jump. Taro Magona said a burst of Setayashi-radiation should do the trick, and who knows, maybe she would've given me a device similar to the one Mashaule has. Fact is, it exists—after all, he used it and here I am, which means I should somehow be able to build one. Right? Right? How hard can it—

"Who's distracting you?" Kieran's voice sounds so close to my ear I squeak and jump.

"Kieran!" That could've been a heart attack!

Kieran laughs, then presses a quick kiss against my neck, before he strides back to the kitchen area, leaving me alone at the desk. "Don't worry, I didn't look at what you're doing. I just couldn't resist teasing you a bit." He grins and winks at me, and I can't help but laugh.

I've been in this time for eight hours. I've been unsuccessfully working on trying to design a Setayashi-device for about five of them, make that six if it includes getting the material for my trials, but during those hours, Kieran has done his best to distract me. He has sat across from me like he wanted to hypnotize me, has taken off his shirt in extra slo-mo and put on a new one twice, has kissed my neck three times, and now started to cook dinner for us, including Zio and Chase, which means he only asked me every, oh, I don't know, every minute or so if I wanted to sample what he was prepping.

Point in case: He needs attention. Since I dematted on board, he's been like a playful puppy, happy, excited and joyful, and I've got to say, I've tried long enough to be mature. Funny thing is, once I get a Setayashi-radiation device built and can control it and my time-jumps, I can hopefully jump to whenever. So, technically speaking, I can take my sweet time right now.

And on a side note, since I have no means to find Mashaule, but Mashaule wants to kill Kieran, it's reasonable to assume their paths will cross eventually. The closer I stay with Kieran, the better my chances of preventing the assassination and catching Mashaule.

See? Just doing my job.

I turn the large box I brought upside down over my fruitless handiwork. Low key, but considering I'm staying in Kieran's quarters, I don't think I need to lock this away. He ain't gonna peek.

Stretching my arms, I stand up. "When are Chase and Zio coming?"

"Dinner will be ready in about an hour. It's gotta spend some time in the oven." As he says it, he places the heavy, cast-iron pot into the oven and closes the door.

"It smells beyond delicious." I sniff the air on my way over to the kitchen corner. Whoever designed the *Pioneer*, I doubt they had in mind the captain was truly going to cook in this tiny area, but he's making it work.

"Thank you." Kieran takes off the oven mitts and apron. "I went all out today, since we've something to celebrate." He wiggles his eyebrows at me as he steps closer, wrapping his arms around me. "Somehow, I'm really happy today. No idea why." I get a tiny kiss onto the tip of my nose, and call me a softie, but that teensy-tiny kiss brings tingles and warmth and *everything*.

"Me, too." I cuddle myself into his embrace. "I—"

Sirens blare, red lights flash—

"Red alert. Captain to the bridge. Quaneez battle ship within weapons' range!"

Kieran curses once, already sprinting to the door, tapping his Hablamate. "Wildason to Bridge—shields up, keep your distance. Do not engage! I'll be—"

The doors close behind him and cut him off, leaving me behind with a load of unease in my stomach, a very real reminder that while history is already written from my point of view, it is still being written at this very moment. We're already deep into the Quaneez War—what did I expect? All unicorns and rainbows? I let go of a deep breath and stride over to the couch. "*Pioneer*, display bridge view."

"Acknowledged. Live bridge view displayed."

I fall into the couch and stare onto the screen rising from the couch table. Several cameras monitor the events on the bridge, and while usually the recordings will be deleted after twenty-four hours, during Red Alert they won't. Must've been one heck of a job to edit me out after my last visit here, despite my little virus.

I stare at the little video tiles displaying the bridge from all possible angles.

The doors open, admitting Kieran. "Report!"

"One battleship, within weapons' range. They're hot, but haven't engaged yet. Our shields are at a hundred percent, weapons charged." Chase jumps out of the command chair and makes room for Kieran.

"Where the heck were they coming from?" Kieran sits down and signs into the system by pressing his palm against the reader on his right.

Manazari from Ops turns to face him. "It's that silent propulsion drive, sir. Tracking is close to an impossibility and so is getting a heads-up."

Kieran grumbles. "Tell me about it. Chocho—"

Chase looks over from the seat to Kieran's right. "Captain, Admiral Rozell's orders—"

"Admiral Rozell can go and shoot down the Quaneez himself, Commander." Kieran presses his lips into a tight line as his fingers wrap around and dig into the armrest.

"But—"

"Chase." Kieran shakes his head. "As long as the tactical decision about the admiral's request isn't made, as long as I don't have a standing order from the Fleet Admiral, I will not fire first."

Something passes between them, and after a second or two Chase nods. "Understood."

Kieran focuses back onto the view screen. "As I was about to say, Chocho, have you initiated contact protocol?"

"Not yet, sir. I know you're not a fan of it—"

"I'm not, but command is. I bet you if we retreated, they wouldn't shoot."

A bet I would join in on. Adrenaline spikes. Having an outsider position and forty years of history more stored in my brain might've given me the edge, but I swear there's something to my theory: the Quaneez don't like our hails. Maybe they misunderstand them, maybe we're saying something rude, or maybe they perceive them as an attack, but in the end, they take them as an invitation to fire on us. When I was on the *Pioneer* the first time, their behavior threw me off. History teaches Quaneez always fire first.

Only they didn't. They don't.

At first, I thought I got that wrong, but no. It turns out to be a repeating pattern. We hail, they shoot. Or, maybe their weapons take forever to load, and my theory is bull, but it's the only one I have.

Kieran leans forward in the captain's chair as if he could read the Quaneez better if he closed the distance to them. "Alas, my hands are tied, and that *is* a standing order. Peace greetings on all channels, Chocho."

"On it, sir."

We still do the peace greetings with every Quaneez encounter in my time, if for nothing else than our own peace of mind, to say, *hey, we're trying.* Only that it's a wee bit hypocritical to blast a message of peace at them followed by a few well-placed shots smack in their face, but maybe that's just me.

I lean forward, just like Kieran. Makes it easier to see details— Yes, there we are: as expected, the Quaneez' weapons are beginning to glow red, making them pop out from the background of a gaseous nebula.

Chase looks up from his console "Captain, enemy preparing to fire!"

Point proven. I sigh. That's as good a confirmation of my theory as any, and the pattern stands: doing nothing equals no attack, hailing them equals them opening fire.

I wish I had had the time to tell Admiral Conolly and Upinga that crucial detail.

"Thaler, evasive!" Kieran barks.

The *Pioneer* pulls into a tight left yawn. "On it, sir."

"Incoming!"

BOOM! BOOM!

Pioneer shakes, as a flash of light illuminates Kieran's quarters through the windows. Sun and Stars—that must be our shields deflecting those weapons! I swallow hard. I know I'm safe. The *Pioneer* has won this battle, not that I remember every single confrontation they had with the Quaneez, but I know she never lost. She never got destroyed. So yes, I'm safe, but that reassurance doesn't change how terrifying it is to be shot at.

"Thaler, can you do that somersault maneuver you did last time and get us in position to aim at their drive?"

"Yes, sir!" Thaler dances her fingers over the controls, pulling the ship into a tight, hard, backwards roll.

"Tactical, get ready, you know the drill! Chase, disable them! I want them limping enough to stop fighting, but able to limp home!"

"Yes, sir!" Chase keeps his attention glued to his station and readouts. "Firing!"

I could swear I feel a slight vibration when the *Pioneer* fires—

"Direct hit! You were right, the shields have a weak spot around the drives!"

For now, in this ever-changing race of destruction.

BOOM! BOOMBOOM!

"They didn't like that," Manazari calls out. "Firing from all—*ugh!*" *BOOM!*

Every impact lights up Kieran's quarters, every impact shakes us, despite the shields being up.

"Shields down to forty percent, Captain!"

"Acknowledged. Return fire, aim for their aft weapons! Let's do the same thing again, other side!"

The view on the main screen shows the Quaneez aft right in front of us, shields glowing with the impact from our shots.

"Weapons locked and loaded!"

"Fire!"

Chase fires—

A bright flash of light—

For a short moment nobody speaks. Then, Chase looks up from his readings. "Both drives disabled, sir! They're dead in space!"

The crew breaks out in short *woo* and *yay* sounds—

BOOM!

Another hit lights up our shields.

"Dead in space, but still firing, Captain!" Chase rechecks something. "But their aft weapons are down on both sides!"

Kieran points at the screen and the projection of the battleship. "Thaler, glue us to their butt!"

"Gluing to their butt, sir!"

"Chocho, hail them and offer our help with the repairs if they stop firing. It's not as if they could get us without maneuvering power and us behind them!"

"Yes, sir!"

"Maybe we're going to be lucky today and—"

"Sir! High energy spike like—"

Kieran has jumped out of his chair before Chase can complete the sentence. "Get us out of here, *now*! Move her, Thaler, *move*!"

To Thaler's credit, she doesn't bother with a reply. Within two seconds I feel the *Pioneer* move so fast, internal grav stabilizers lag behind and I get thrown into the couch's cushion.

Kieran stumbles, but catches himself. "Hundred percent energy to forward shiel—"

BOOM!

With the most gigantic flash, the Quaneez ship explodes, rattling the *Pioneer* when shrapnel and debris hit its shields.

Silence.

Kieran visibly deflates. He rubs a palm across his forehead. "Damage report." It comes out resigned.

"Shields holding at seventy percent. No hull damage sustained, no casualties," Manazari reads out.

For the longest five seconds Kieran doesn't respond, but keeps looking at the screen and the eerie image of a beautiful nebula marred by drifting components of what once was a spaceship with over five hundred living souls on board.

Slowly, he nods. "Acknowledged. Thaler, resume original course. You all know what do to." And with that, he walks off the bridge into his ready room, his shoulders hunched over and his head hung low, the epitome of misery.

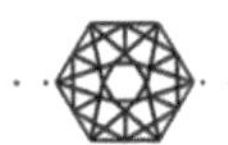

USEF Pioneer, Captain's Quarters, December 14ᵗʰ 2255, 1925hrs

The door to Kieran's quarters opens, admitting Commanders Upinga and Conolly.

"Evening, Kieran. Nonie." Chase waves, while Zio lifts a hand in greeting.

"Hey, you two." An interesting sense of deja vu hits me. Last time we had dinner together, Chase grilled me about crashing my shuttle and my involvement with the Quaneez. I'm optimistic today is going to be a more relaxed dinner. Knock on wood all the excitement of the day lies behind us already.

"You made it, guys." Kieran adds a pinch of seasoning to the pot and stirs. "Chocho was okay with bridge duty?"

"You know, you're being way too nice, *Captain*. You're giving him bridge duty, he's on bridge duty, end of story." Chase makes a slicing motion with his hand.

Kieran grimaces. "I know. But he's freshly engaged—"

"Which means he's set to have many more evenings with his fiancée and later on, his wife. This one night he's got the bridge."

"I *know*, but a good work-life balance is important. We're seeing too many traumatizing things and not enough good stuff, so I'm happy he's got her. I might make it up to him by scheduling them both off next weekend."

Zio lowers himself into his seat at the table. "I'm sure they'd both appreciate the gesture. And before you say something about duty coming first, Trip, a depressed, demotivated crew performs below their means. Keeping them happy therefore will increase their efficiency."

"Such a romantic, Zee." Kieran lifts the cast iron pot out of the oven and sets it onto the table. "Dinner might be a tad overcooked, but oh well." He shrugs, peeking under the lid, avoiding the steam rising from the content. "Could still be okay. Probably edible."

"Your food usually qualifies as edible." Chase sets a bottle onto the table. "But in case it isn't, I brought something to wash it down with. You should recognize it, Nonie."

I laugh out. "No way. You made the drink I mixed last time I was on board?"

"I thought I'd give it a try. Saw you do it, so—"

"So, of course, he has patented it," Zio deadpans

"Have not."

"Right."

"Well, I might've researched soda-production companies and invested in one or two that seemed promising. One of them had something pretty similar in development."

I groan. "Please tell me you're not going to go against all reason and give them my recipe. I don't need the timeline disrupted thanks to soda."

"He'll call it Nonade." Kieran grins, putting a baguette into the oven to reheat. "Nonie-lemonade. And right now, Old Trip sits somewhere in the future and counts his millions, while history discarded us poor souls. Thanks for nothing, Trip." He chuckles, and Chase blushes.

"You're exaggerating greatly. I'm just working on a little passion project. And if—that's a gigantic if—they should ever go into mass production, we came up with a name already. Hint: it's not going to be Nonade."

"*We* came up with a name?" Zio raises one eye brow, while my main question would be: what the heck? While soda doesn't seem a reason big enough for history to change, maybe it is! Lubbeck's is huge in my time! What if Chase's company is too strong a competition—

"*We* as in the company and its main sponsor, me." Trip pulls out a chair and falls into the same spot he sat in the last time we had dinner in Kieran's quarters.

"All right, spill it, brother." Kieran brings over a ladle and a pepper mill.

Chase rubs his neck. "Don't laugh, okay?"

"No.

"Would never."

Chase gives his fiends a critical glance and harrumphs. "Well, anyway. I asked them to consider naming it after my grandpa. He was a cool guy, and… I think I got my sweet tooth from him. So yeah, if—

again, *if*—this ever goes into mass production, you can raise a glass of Lubbeck's to my grandpa Joe."

Glass of—

My jaw drops.

Another freakin' predestination paradox! I introduced Chase to my version of Lubbeck's, got him hooked on it, and then he decides to invest in a soda company that happens to come up with the biggest soda flavor of my time.

I look down at PADdy. He was right when he gifted this to me. He won't go hungry. Admiral Conolly must be loaded!

Kieran catches my expression. "You okay, Nonie?"

"Y-yeah." Just trying to figure out whom to punch for this. The commander, the admiral, or myself. Sigh.

"Time to eat then." Kieran brings the heated baguette from the oven and sets it on the table. "Help yourselves."

For a moment, everybody is busy serving some of the French-style stew Kieran made, or tearing off some baguette. Or pouring some pre-Lubbeck's. Double-sigh.

Chase takes a bite of the food. "Mh. Nice. I'm glad the Quaneez didn't ruin dinner. Would've been another item to add to the list of things they destroyed."

Kieran puts his fork down. "Chase, come on."

The other man looks up. "I know. Sorry. It's my way of dealing with it."

With a big sigh, Kieran leans back. "Today sucked."

"Today sucked." Chase lowers his gaze to the table.

Zio looks from one to the other.

"And it will suck until we understand them better. Maybe we need to apologize for whatever we did when we first encountered them."

"Maybe." Kieran drops his gaze to the table and chews on the inside of his cheek. "Five-hundred lives. Gone. For what? I didn't want to kill them—and I wouldn't have destroyed them. Why self-destruct and kill everybody on board?"

Chase frowns. "Well, I'm not sure it's intentional—"

"It has happened several times, including when they destroyed their colony and ignited the Marmelite that brought Nonie home," Zio says. "It would seem like a tactical move on their part."

"But have you looked at what we know about their drive? That thing is basically built to explode! Can't get it close to atmosphere-bearing planets or it'll blow up and ignite the atmosphere! It very well could be an error in design, who knows, so there's that, but if you're right, then maybe they self-destruct to avoid capture." Chase wipes his mouth with the napkin. "It's making finding more about them much harder though."

Kieran plays with his napkin. "You know, I've been wishing we wouldn't run into them so often. Every time we do, we end up firing at each other, and I don't want that. Trip, can you find me a way to never ever run across a single Quaneez ship again? Or find something that keeps them from blowing themselves up? And I'm only half-joking." He picks up his fork again and shoves his food from left to right on the plate.

Chase looks up to the ceiling in mock annoyance. "If I could track them, sure. Or if I knew how that drive of theirs gets them to right in front of our noses so fast. From all I know about it, it should be impossible. And you know what I've been saying for the last few months. I'm—"

"—personally offended that somebody with such disastrous engineering skills is keeping us on our toes," Kieran and Zio finish the sentence for him.

All three guys start laughing at the same time, the somber mood broken.

Chase swallows another bite, then points his fork at me. "Hearing us talk like this must be weird for you."

Well… sad and at the same scary would be more like it. I straighten the napkin on my lap. "Because this is history? I wouldn't call it weird. I'm mainly trying to sit here with a very neutral expression on my face so I don't accidentally ruin the future. You know, no pressure."

Chase chuckles. "Absolutely none. But as long as Uncle doesn't get all nervous because of his Spidey-senses, we should be fine."

Zio cuts him an eye. "Still not the biggest fan of the nickname."

Chase rubs a finger across his chin. "Huh, I remember saying the same when you guys started calling me Trip, and what did you all say?"

"We said suck it up, Trip," Kieran says before popping another piece of bread into his mouth.

"That's indeed what you said, so…" He shrugs in a good-hearted manner. "You'll be fine, Uncle."

Zio harrumphs, but lets it go. "Changing the topic. We should probably go over the next few days with Nonie."

Chase groans. "The trade fair."

"Good idea, Zee." Kieran swallows and clears his throat. "We're on our way to the Ortega system and the annual trade fair. *Pioneer* is expected as the guest of honor, and we're expected to strengthen our bonds with our allies."

"Which is finally a mission up our alley," Chase adds.

"A hundred percent agreed." Kieran gives him a thumbs up. "And it's an away mission that's completely fine for the captain to be on." He pauses, as if he waited for me to say something. When I stay silent, he continues. "But here's the problem: We might have to go down from Code Magenta for a few hours to allow crew members to either visit the fair or to fulfill their duties, which means… It would be appreciated if you stayed in our quarters for that time. Since we're off Code Magenta then." He looks at me sheepishly. "Sorry."

Our quarters. I'm hung up on those two words. "N-no problem. I can stay here or come down with you, whatever works best." No, actually, wrong. I should go down to the fair with them. If Mashaule is truly in this time, what better place to attempt to kill Kieran than a crowded fair? What worse place for me to look for him?

I cringe, then swipe a strand of hair behind my ear to hide the expression. "Actually, would it be okay if I came with you? That way you can go off Code Magenta. Would make it easier for the crew on board, right?" And I'd be in civilian garb and less noticeable or memorable than in a uniform.

The guys exchange a glance, then, Trip nods. "Much, actually. *Pioneer* will cancel Code Magenta as soon as you disembark and the moment you're back up, she'll resume it automatically."

Oh, how convenient. "Because it recognizes my signature when dematting?"

Chase shakes his head. "No, because she's scanning continuously for traces of Setayashi-radiation."

Holy Sun and Stars, what? "Setayashi-radiation? As an indicator for time travel?" Could it be that easy?

"Correct." Zio places his fork next to his spoon and folds his hands in his lap. "It disperses slowly and leaves a measurable trace, like on your shuttle when you first came to us. It doesn't naturally occur very often, so it is a good way for us to scan for time travel. To scan for you."

To not facepalm myself, to not groan, to not roll my eyes at my own near-sightedness is a win for self-control, because *duh*. That's how I can look for Mashaule: traces of Setayashi radiation! I mean, I was only trying to build a Setayashi-emitting *device* for the last half day, so I couldn't have been expected to come up with that idea myself.

Never ever am I going to tell anybody that story, or they're going to make me return my lieutenant's pips.

Triple-sigh.

But at least now I have a means to find Mashaule, and to keep Kieran safe.

Chapter Four –
DELICIOUS NEWS

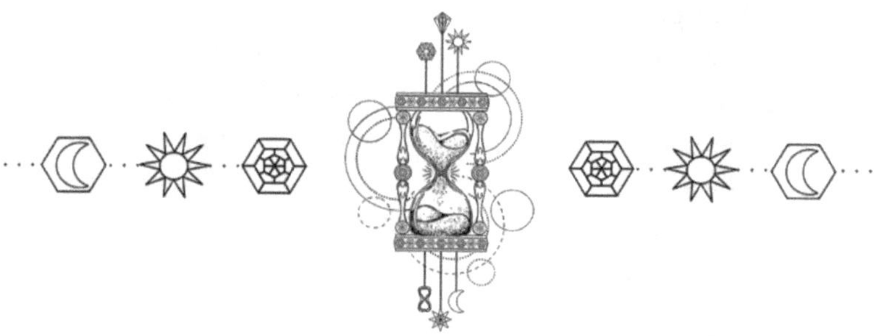

I t's fascinating how much progress one can make when the path is clear. Yesterday around this time I was desperately trying to develop a Setayashi *emitter*, and now I have a portable Setayashi *scanner* already up and running. True, it's not an emitter, but I'm counting it as a success. Boo-yeah, nailed it.

About thirty minutes ago, *Pioneer* pulled into an orbit above the Ortega System's main inhabited planet, Ortega One. Now, I'm not suffering from delusions of grandeur, thinking my self-built scanner was better than the *Pioneer's*, so…. "*Pioneer*, scan for traces of Setayashi radiation on Ortega One and report with location. Also, track movement of radiation source."

"*No Setayashi-radiation detected.*"

I frown. That's good, right? Means Mashaule isn't down on Ortega One. But why did he jump to this time then? Or, maybe he didn't? Maybe he just kicked me out of the stream and travelled on to wherever his destination was. I drum my fingers on the desk surface. Annoying.

"*Pioneer*, increase sensitivity to two-hundred percent and include faint exotic radiation signals as well." Maybe the trace is degrading already. This way I'll get a better overview.

"*No Setayashi-radiation detected. Minuscule traces of Tau-ration are found throughout the northern hemisphere. Pattern available upon request.*"

I wave a hand. "Cancel." I don't need to crowd my brain with Tau-radiation patterns nobody has any interest in. "*Pioneer*, how long until my Setayashi trace will have decayed?"

"*Your Setayashi-trace will have degraded completely in two more days, fifteen hours, and twenty—*"

"Thank you." Yay for physics and math. If Mashaule arrived on Ortega One the same time I arrived here, on the *Pioneer*, his Setayashi-trace should still be present, so at least now I can be sure Mashaule isn't down there. Yet, maybe. Meaning, I'll keep my eyes open.

"*Pioneer*, perform continuous planetary scans for Setayashi-radiation, transmit positive results to my PAD." I enter a quick succession of codes into PADdy to set up the connection. Boy, is this easier than last time, or what? Full access to the *Pioneer*'s systems, no worries about anything being recorded or tracked under Code Magenta… Life would be good if I could initiate a time-jump or successfully find—and preferably apprehend—Mashaule.

I rub a palm across my eyes and yawn. Didn't sleep well. Should have, as exhausted as I was from the longest day in history, but didn't happen, which feels like such a waste of a perfectly good night next to Kieran. Here I am, in his quarters—in his bed!—and I sleep. And it's not even best sleep of my life, but some crappy, time-travel nightmare stuff. Quite disappointing, considering the setup. Kieran was tossing and turning even more than I did, so it's fair to say neither of us had a great night.

I glance at the clock. Half past five in the afternoon. I expected him off a while ago, but then, a captain is never off, I know that much.

As if he had heard me, a soft, acknowledging beep comes from the doors before they open.

"Surprise!" Kieran walks in, balancing a large insulated bag in front of his chest.

I move my trusty anti-spyware box to cover my assembled device and jump out of my chair. "Surprise?"

He sets the bag on the kitchen counter and meets me half-way, wrapping his arms around me and pulling me in tight. "Yes. Surprise. If I've learned one thing lately it's to live every day to its best potential. Don't put things off. Do them. Time is… time is not really on our side."

I feel his chest heave up and down with a deep sigh, and for a moment, I allow myself to let the unfairness of it wash over me—the audacity of fate to bond Kieran to me and me to him, when we don't even live in the same time period. Falling for him felt unfair before I knew we were bonded, but now, with this little additional fact, it's like fate was showing us the middle finger: Yeah, you're bonded. Tough luck. Deal with it.

Swallowing hard, I bury myself closer into his embrace. Screw those thoughts. Kieran is right, we're going to turn that around and show fate the middle finger ourselves, because we'll be happy whenever we can. Screw you, fate!

"I love the way you think," I murmur into his hold.

He places a quick peck onto my cheek before he lets me go. "And I hope you're going to love this even more." Kieran points at the bag.

I sniff the air. "Is there food in there?"

"You bet there's food in there. Got off shift a bit earlier today and took over Zee's place to cook and prep. Wanted this to be a surprise." He zips the bag open. "Thought about using Chase's place and messing it up, but he gives me more crap about being all gooey about you, so Zee's it was."

I capture my lower lip between my teeth. "You did all that at Zio's to keep it a secret?" That's so… cute. Romantic. Adorable. Warmth builds in my chest, radiating through every fiber of my body.

"Well, I wanted to make it right. And speaking of." He takes me by the shoulders and directs me backward to the couch, until the hollows of my knees hit the cushion. "Sit. Stay. Don't look. Do I need to cover your eyes? Because I will, if you're prone to cheating." He emphasizes his words by brushing his palms down over my eyes for me to close.

Anticipation spikes. I slap both hands in front of my face. "I'll be good. And sitting right here."

"Perfect. *Pioneer*, music, level seven, something by Taw."

"Acknowledged." A second later music begins to play, some orchestral string piece of the kind that floats through the air and fills a room, no matter if you're into classic music or not. Level seven is also loud enough for me to not pick up much of what Kieran is doing, which was probably the point. Whatever he's unpacking though, it smells delicious.

After about three or four minutes, he peels one of my hands off my face, then the other. "*Pioneer*, music level three, lights level two, please."

Pioneer lowers the music, and when I open my eyes, Kieran is standing in front of me, the dimmed light in his quarters barely above complete darkness.

"Ready when you are," he whispers.

"Always." I leave my hands in his as he helps me up and guides me—

"Whoa." My jaw drops. Not what I expected. *So* not what I expected. There, in front of the large, floor-to-ceiling window, he spread out several blankets on top of each other, threw in at least ten pillows, and set the most delicious-looking spread of food on a large rustic wooden board in the center.

"You like it?" Kieran lets go of one of my hands and scratches his neck. "Romantic options are a bit limited on a starship and with our unique, uhh, set-up."

"Do I like it? I love it!" I step closer to the window. My heart swells into such gigantic proportions I could use it as a floatation device. Kieran has made us a picnic.

I throw my arms around his neck. "It's wonderful, Kieran! What a great idea."

He chuckles. "Well, taste the food first before you praise me too much."

I unwrap myself from him and lightly punch his shoulder. "As if you'd mess up food."

"I try not to. Food is good for your soul." He guides me to the heap of blankets, and we sit down across from each other.

My gaze drifts across the spread, amazed. "You even thought of candles."

"Holographic. But better than nothing." He motions at the food. "Help yourself. Everything is pretty self-explanatory."

That it is. Chocolate dipped strawberries. Crackers and dips. Slices of synth-meat. Ravioli with creamed mushrooms and asparagus. Fruits. Veggies. "It looks wonderful." My stomach grumbles.

Kieran smiles and serves himself. "Made several trips during my shift today to make sure everything was marinating and doing its thing so it would be ready. The bridge crew probably thought I had the runs or something with me leaving every thirty minutes."

I laugh. "They probably think the captain is odd under Code Magenta."

"Oh, please, they know the captain's odd, period." He takes a bite from a chocolate-dipped strawberry. "Mmh. Good. I hope Zio sees the chocolate wrapper in the trash and gets a heart attack. A little one, but still."

I'm sure he will. And I'm sure Kieran left it on the very top just to tease his friend. Wouldn't put it past him.

We enjoy the food and the moment. The view to my left is spectacular with Ortega One down below, its two moons in an irregular orbit, and the system's sun behind us, since we're in a stable locked position above the planet. The tendrils of a small nebula are visible behind the larger of the two moons, nothing more than thin, purple and pink hues of color, but in contrast with the blue-green planet with purple specks below us, it looks spectacular.

Not as spectacular as the man sitting across from me though.

Kieran is attractive, period. I'm neither the first nor the last person to think so, no matter the time period. But seeing him like this, in a leisure uniform he must've changed into at Zio's place, the black hair slightly tousled from a long day, eyes closed as he's enjoying another bite of food… it fills my heart to the brim with happiness.

As if he'd felt me watch him, he swallows, then slowly opens his eyes. "What?"

Heat rises to my cheeks. "Nothing. Just enjoying the view."

He wiggles an eyebrow. "Glad you are. Was trying to distract you with the view yesterday when you were building your *thing*, but it didn't work. I was worried there for a bit." Humor shines from his eyes, but I still ball up my napkin and throw it at him.

"I was trying to work!"

"And I was trying to distract you." He catches the napkin and hands it back to me. "And by the way, I… I didn't mean to fall asleep that fast last night." He lowers his gaze, the slightest hue of red coloring his cheeks. "I haven't been sleeping well." The apple in his throat moves up and down.

I can take a wild guess why. "Nightmares? You were tossing quite a bit."

He flinches. "Sorry. Wow, that makes it even more embarrassing." He rakes a hand through his hair and shakes his head.

"Not at all. Why?"

After a pause, Kieran keeps his gaze locked to the food in front of him. "Because ever since *they* took me, I've had nightmares. The last seven months I haven't had a night without them. And I know I'm not the calmest sleeper because of them, but having my weakness so obvious on display…"

I throw my napkin again. "Weakness? Hello? The Quaneez captured and mind-tortured you, Kieran! And you survived! I think you're entitled to some PTSD and nightmares from that—not that I want you to have them, but still." Not many people have survived mind torture. And if they did, they were broken. At this point in time, we had no idea how deadly their torture was and how incredibly lucky Kieran was to have survived with a useable brain. His might be the only recorded case of somebody not going insane after.

He picks up my napkin-turned-projectile and turns it in his hands. "Yeah, okay. But you're back and I fall asleep like a baby as soon as my head hits the pillow. Also a tad embarrassing."

I give him a bland glance. "Nuh-uh. I think I fell asleep first. It'd been a rough day, for both of us." Mine lasted a good forty years. Or eighty, if you do the math.

Kieran looks at me from under his lashes, the hint of a smile playing around his lips. "True, but I intended for the evening to end differently. Much differently."

Heat rushes to my face and some other very important body parts. "Well, today we're better rested, right?" I for one am optimistic I don't need any sleep at all tonight. Not the way I'm feeling right now, with my heart skipping every other beat in anticipation.

His gaze meets mine with such intensity, my breath gets stuck inside my chest.

In one smooth motion Kieran picks up the board with the food on and sets it aside, clearing the space in front of us. "Nonie?" He scoots closer, until our knees touch.

"Yeah?"

His thick lashes lower as he takes my hand and weaves his fingers through mine. "Remember when I picked you up in that store yesterday?"

"I wouldn't call it picking up, more like saving me from jail, but yes, I do." The moment when I realized the voice I heard was his... angels singing couldn't have been more beautiful.

Kieran plays with my fingers. "I bought something down there."

"You bought my freedom."

"Well, the owner just needed something to convince him to make the right choice. But anyway, when I saw this I had to get it for you. It's *you*, and... well, it's *you*." He reaches into his right front pocket and pulls out a small black box, then hesitates. "I know this comes with a lot of symbolism. And, while it's not intended, it still feels right, so..." He draws in a big breath. "I would like for you to have this."

He opens the box—

My heart stills.

Dizziness sweeps over me, making my head spin and my heart stumble back to speed, then into overdrive.

It—

It's—

It's a ring.

No.

Wrong.

So wrong.

So unbelievably wrong.

It's not a ring. It's *the* ring.

In the box, shimmering in a multitude of colors is a simple band-style ring.

A ring I've known since *that day* when I was nine years old.

She wore that ring.

The officer with the rainbow-swirl patch on her shoulder.

The officer who wasn't afraid of my dad.

The officer—

The officer who must have been—who will be—me. *She was my operative*, Taro Magona said, and boy, was she right with that.

Holy Sun and Stars—

"You're scaring me a bit," Kieran whispers. "Too much, too soon? I'm sorry, I—"

"No." I shoot one hand out and lay a finger across his lips. "It's perfect. I love it, from the bottom of my heart." Dragging it over his lips, I drop my finger again.

A relieved smile crosses his face. "I thought you'd like it. Like I said it's *you*. I had to get it for you, even if I didn't have to bribe the owner. Or, if I'd seen it on Ortega One, where he wanted to sell it. You would only have gotten it later then." He winks and takes the ring out of the box and my left hand in his. "Here we go again with the symbolism, but to be honest, we're not the traditional couple. Everything's different for us, and I would love for you to wear that as a reminder of that. Maybe as a visible sign of our bond. We both feel it, but I want you to see it whenever we're separated by space or time, and know that I'm here. That I'm yours. We didn't draw the short end of the stick, Nonie. We were the lucky ones." And with that he slides the ring over my left fourth finger and regards it with a calm serenity. "Now it is where it belongs."

My blood is zipping through my veins, as if powered by lightning. It's unlike anything I've ever felt, and maybe it's extra-special because we're bonded, but it is as if my self has expanded to not just me, but also Kieran. Like we're one, when obviously we're two people, like we're connected, our essence combined. It's the weirdest, most fulfilling sensation I've ever experienced.

"I love it, Kieran. Thank you. I…" *I love you*. I want to say it, but it's hard. It shouldn't be, not in our situation, not as two people being bonded, not with the magnitude of feelings I have for him, but saying it out loud…

Kieran closes his eyes for one eternal second. "Yeah," he whispers, voice hoarse. "Same here." He skims his fingers from my hand up my arm, then cups my cheek. In the little light coming in from the window I see his pulse jump in his throat.

No idea who moves first, but we're both leaning in. Our lips meet in the middle, and right away, Kieran deepens the kiss with a thrust of his tongue. Every nerve ending in my body fires at once from so many emotions blending together, even the one we refuse to name so far. His fingers tangle through my hair as he draws me closer, the kiss becoming more intense. We're gasping for air yet refusing to let go. Breathing is overrated. I grab his shoulders, his shirt, whatever I can get, because he's still not close enough, I'm still not feeling enough of him.

The feeling seems mutual.

With a little growl, Kieran breaks the kiss long enough to yank his shirt over his head and discard it to the side. Then he wraps his arms around me, lets himself fall back and takes me with him, so that I'm lying on top of him. Not wasting any time, he crashes his lips back to mine, as if a second without our lips connected would be a wasted second.

I agree with his assessment.

I place both my hands on his naked chest, right above the scar in its center and the one on the right side we share, and Kieran jerks like shocked. A soft moan leaves his throat, and all of a sudden, it's not just warm in here, it's hot. I don't know when or how, but my shirt is off in no time, leaving me in a bra only. And Sun and Stars, our bodies flush together is he most perfect thing I've ever experienced.

Bond or not, this is real. Raw. *Everything*.

Sparks shoot across my skin and sizzle in my core as he presses his hips into mine.

Yeah.

Nobody's going to fall asleep early tonight.

Chapter Five –

FAIR

The moment my vision is back online from the demat, my visual cortex is assaulted by an onslaught of colors.

"Whoa." No matter where I look, there's no boring spot to be seen.

Kieran turns toward me. "I take it you've never been to Ortega One?"

"No." I shake my head. "Haven't had the pleasure yet." Mainly because in my time, Ortega One is uninhabitable, destroyed by the Quaneez. I forgot when exactly, but not today, so for now we're safe. To know this planet's fate is like a load of lead sitting in my stomach. It's the same ethical dilemma I was in the last time I was thrown into this time period, only last time I was tempted to prevent humans from entering a war with the Quaneez. Now I'm tempted to warn the inhabitants of the upcoming attack so they can save themselves.

Alas, I know I can't do that.

It still makes for a very interesting ethical conundrum.

Kieran steps away from the Demat area. "Trip, where do you want to start?"

Chase grumbles and shields his eyes. "I can't think with all these colors."

I see his point, quite literally. The inhabitants of Ortega One terraformed and colonized a planet with a rich natural flora and fauna, and by that I don't only mean diverse, I'm talking about rich as in *intense*. Most of the grass here, a few kilometers in front of the main city, is green. Bright green, like close to neon green. Some patches of purple, higher grasses are strewn in here and there, and the trees... well, let's just say if you're offended by clashing bright colors, this is not the colony for you. Mother Nature must've been high on something when she created this planet with our help.

Kieran slaps his shoulder. "Good thing then that I have a to-do list for us. We'll start by checking what the colonists from Palmieri Prime have to offer in terms of that new ultra-fast recharging battery we could use for our shuttles, and then move to..." He glances at the PAD he brought. "Then move over to quadrant Omega-five for the weapons' display. Hm." He frowns. "Oh, well."

Chase takes the PAD. "Why did we have to be here again? Why can't the engineering corps check out the battery? Etc., etc.? This is huge." He taps onto the schematic display of the fairgrounds—and yes, it's huge. There's a reason why these fairs are held on colonized planets: space. The whole fairground is at least three by three kilometers large, designed like any modern city in a grid-layout, A-P and 1-15.

But, because Ortega One is an agricultural colony, they kept the trees and grass and erected the exhibition pavilions nestled into the nature. Just scanning over the first structures from the demat area, it looks really nice, especially with the high-rise buildings from the city in the background. Add the busy traffic of who knows how many Private Airborne Pods in the air, and the contrast between nature on one side and city on the other couldn't be any bigger.

Kieran snatches the PAD out of his friend's hands. "We're here because we're the USEF's flagship and we're representing all of the fleet. And like I said earlier, Chase. You don't have to babysit me. "

"Oh no, that's fine." Chase stuffs both hands in his pockets and rocks back on his heels. "I love to be the third wheel, really." He puts on a fake, exaggerated smile, then bumps Kieran into the shoulder with his, like, *hint-hint.*

Kieran closes his eyes for one long second. "All right then." He sighs. "Probably better if I'm not seen out too much alone with my girlfriend." He gives me an apologetic smile.

Girlfriend. Squee!

"Hey, no worries." I lift both hands. "There's a reason I'm in civilian garb, and it's to not be so memorable and, I dunno, to—" A buzzing sensation in my right pockets gets the last word stuck in my throat. My Setayashi-scanner!

"To what? Check out the grains in aisle thirteen?" Chase gives a dramatic hand wave in the direction of the fair as we step away from the demat area.

I glide one hand into the pocket of my black cargo pants and wrap it around the device. "Y-yeah. Grains. Totally my thing."

Kieran chuckles. "Let's get this party started. Chase, you got the list, Nonie, you do you." He walks ahead, head held high, shoulders straight, in captain mode.

Me?

I'm in borderline panic mode.

The scanner went off, so what or who else could it be other than Mashaule? Falling back behind Kieran and Chase, I unlock PADdy to check the read-outs transmitted by the scanner. My stomach cramps. There, smack in the center of the fair, PADdy displays a red dot besides the one at my location. And it's moving. That's not a natural, coincidental occurrence of Setayashi radiation. That's a moving source.

It's him.

I swallow down the sharp spike of panic. Easy to forget my job description when I'm high on hormones and having a picnic with Kieran, but this is why I'm here, to keep him alive.

For now, a little annoying, morbid voice whispers that I ignore. Shush.

Kieran and Chase led the way to the first pavillon. Mashaule must've dug deep in USEF records to find out exactly where Kieran would be, not protected by the *Pioneer,* served on a silver platter.

Unease makes me hypervigilant and shifts my mind into emergency mode. Everything is way clearer than 20/20, every detail heightened, every piece of information analyzed as a potential risk factor. How is he going to try to kill Kieran? I doubt he's going to strangle him with his bare hands. Do it himself? Hire somebody?

I work on a dry swallow. Unlikely, but it would be the worst-case scenario, since I don't know what or whom I'm looking for.

Commotion coming from the left brings a rush of adrenaline. A group of maybe ten people has lined up around a pop-up stand, its banner reading "Humanity First." Some of them yell slogans others just hold their own banners up, but either way, they make me nervous. For many reasons, given that we're still dealing with them in my time, but mainly because I wouldn't say an assassination was beneath them if it fulfilled a purpose to them.

Ugh.

Chase turns around. "Hey Nonie—" He frowns when his gaze falls on me. "You okay?" he mouths.

I give him a tight nod. Can't afford to lose focus. At one point, dear FBTI, I'd like to know protocol. Could I have told Chase to keep an eye out for Kieran? Would that have endangered the timeline?

As it is, I don't need to say anything. Chase turns forward again, but he's walking taller, more coiled, and moving his right hand closer to his weapon.

He read me just fine.

I throw a quick glance at PADdy. We're passing lanes G and H on Second Street. Mashaule is one block over, coming closer.

At this point, it's fair to say he'll try to do the job himself—why be so close otherwise and risk getting caught?

My heart thumps triple-time, harder with every meter we're getting closer to the red dot.

There—the red dot stopped at the next intersection we're heading toward. All tiny hairs on my body rise in response. Showtime.

With three fast steps, I'm in front of Kieran, my weapon drawn, but pointed down. Too crowded to shoot. Where is he?

"Nonie?" Tension creeps into Kieran's voice. "What's going on?" Not sure if he's surprised about my behavior, or that I have a weapon on me.

My gaze darts from person to person at the intersection. Not him, not him, not him, not—

Him.

Like a punch in the gut, I recognize the face of the man who looks like Santa, but behaves like the Devil. Not having the advantage of a scanner, only of knowing history, the very same he's trying to change, he's looking for his target. He hasn't seen us yet.

And I'm not going to wait for him to make the first move.

"Down!" I yell and turn into Kieran, tackling him like in a blast take-down. The force of the impact drives him back and to the ground—

I twist to aim my gun in Mashaule's direction—

PEW! PEWPEW!

He shot!

People scream, cry out, start fleeing aimlessly—

Chase moves to shield Kieran, dropped into a fighting stance, his gun drawn and at the ready, his face set hard. "Move, people!" he yells, trying to locate the shooter, but with all this chaos, he can't figure out where the danger is coming from, or who the assassin is.

I can.

I keep my body and weight on top of Kieran. "Chase! Protect the captain!" It's not like I needed to say it, after all, it's as much in his job description as in mine, but he gets the part I couldn't say loud: let me deal with this.

Within a second, Chase is grabbing Kieran him by the arm, keeping himself between his captain and the attacker. "Conolly to *Pioneer*! Emergency demat, captain and me, *now*!"

I push off Kieran and without a look back sprint toward where Mashaule was standing when he shot.

"Nonie, watch—!"

I don't let Kieran distract me. Looking back, as much as I want to, could be deadly for either of us. Two seconds later, the temptation is literally gone, as the hum of the *Pioneer*'s dematerializer is only barely audible over the panicked screams and cries of the masses, all scrambling to get away from this corner, which makes it so much harder to see—

There!

A white head of hair, white beard—Mashaule!

Powered by anger, I dart forward, weaving through the onslaught of people. Mashaule is walking fast, trying to blend in, but no chance. To me he stands out like a zit on clear skin. He looks back over his shoulder—

And that's when he sees me.

Surprise, confusion, irritation—it's all there for about a second or two, clearly written in his face. Then, as if his brain needed a moment to make sense of what he's seeing, his expression morphs into mad anger.

Somebody bumps into me in their headless dash away. I grunt and stumble, but catch myself. Where is—?

Got him.

He's running from me, but having a hard time getting out of the chaos he caused.

Anger fuels me, the determination to not let him get away. I can end this right here, right now—

Mashaule looks back for me, curses when he sees me—and stops.

Ten meters, max.

I duck, I weave, I dash through the sea of obstacles as fast as I can—

He pulls out a grey, oval device from his pocket.

My heart stops. No.

No, no no.

He can't leave. I have no means—

Six meters.

Mashaule presses his thumb into the device, yells something—

Four meters.

A flash of light, ultra-bright, every cell in my nerves screaming out loud—

Two meters—

Mashaule flickers in and out of reality—

I jump, and let the stream of time take me with him.

Chapter Six -
WRONG STOP

Somewhere, Somewhen. Again.

Whirlwind of colors—
Events. Faces of people. Pictures of things—
Quiet. Loud. Hot. Cold.
Confusing.
Something brushes into me—
Screams—
Somebody screams, screams, SCREAMS—
Kieran! That's Kieran—
Desperation.
Confusion.
I fall on through time and space— More screams, not Kieran's, somebody else's, lots of people—
I twitch—
Something hooks on to me. Get thrown off course, I tumble, head over heels, fall—

And land on both feet on solid, soft ground, only with such a speed, I fall forward onto my knees. At least I get my hands out before I faceplant. "Gee," I wheeze, bent over on all fours. Holy everything—what a ride! Where's—

A chair is being pushed back and brushes over carpeted floor. "*Liona*, mute alert." A screeching alarm sound snuffs out.

I jerk up and around. That voice—

My gaze falls onto the person standing up behind a desk in front of floor-to-ceiling windows: Me.

Me.

Same height. Same hair. Same everything. Only I'm—she's—wearing a uniform I've never seen before, red with black stripes on the side. What in the name of—

"Uhh, hi?" She smiles and wiggles her fingers, then silences another beeping and flashing alert on her wristPAD. "Need a hand?" With three quick steps, she crosses the room and extends an arm toward me. "Looks like the Maelstrom gave you a hard time." She grabs me by the arm and helps me up—correction, pulls me up. I'm too stumped to move.

"You're me." I blink, then feel my cheeks heat up. Astute observation, Lieutenant. Really.

The other me narrows her eyes and cocks her head to the side. "Uhh, yes? Shouldn't you know that?" She releases my arm, and look at that, I can stand on my own.

I straighten my shirt. "Well, excuse me—literally—that I'm a tad confused. I've never jumped into the future before." Even though it can't be too far ahead, looking at her-slash-me. We seem to be about the same age. And this place, the office… I throw a quick glance out the window. Yup. Admirals' Tower, USEF Academy. Close to Grazer's office, I'd say. The view is similar. Could even be Grazer's office. Ugh. Don't tell me future me is working for him. Never mind I wanted to do exactly that only a few weeks ago, but you live, you learn.

The other Nonie's brows pull down. "Not the future. I'm in your past."

"Huh?" Nope. *So* not my past. "You'd think I'd remember working in this office. You're my future. This hasn't happened to me yet." I let my gaze drift over the desk close to the window, the hastily pushed back chair, the PADs stacked the way I like to stack them… Yeah, I work here. Seriously? What about the FBTI? What did I do to my future to end up a desk jockey for Grazer, of all people?

All color leaves the other Nonie's face. "You can't be me in the past. This never happened, I never jumped into the future. I—" Her eyes glass over, then widen. "The admiral. You may want to hide."

"I do?" I squeak. Why? Where?

She points to the couch I materialized next to and waves an impatient hand. "Hop behind it. Now!"

Within a second max, I've vaulted behind the couch and crouched, barely in time before the doors to the office slide open.

"Good morning, Lieutenant."

I suck in a harsh breath so sharp it would've given me away, had my counterpart not answered right in that instant.

"Good morning, Admiral. You're early today."

"Couldn't sleep last night. Figured you'd be up and working already, so… joining you seemed to be the more appealing option."

Blood swooshes in my ears. No doubt about it. It's *him*. The voice seems deeper and a little bit off, but there's no mistaking it. It can't possibly be, yet it's *him*. My stomach cramps as silence hovers. Not awkward silence, but comfortable silence. Silence that carries exactly the emotion it would carry in my time and place if what I was hearing wasn't completely impossible.

I squeeze my eyes shut. What the hell is going on here?

Stretching my neck, I peek around the edge of the couch, and my entire body tenses.

Kieran.

Admiral Kieran Wildason is in this very room. With me—another me. He's alive, and that one word runs on repeat through my mind. *Alive. Alive. Alive. Alive. Alive. Alive.*

He stops close to the other Nonie. "Also, I was wondering if you'd like to start the day by going over some of your self-defense." Kieran gives her a mischievous half-smirk, one I happen to know really well—only I have never seen it in a Kieran older than early twenties.

This Kieran… is definitely over that age. Most of his hair is still black and in the same cut I know him to carry it, but along the temples grey is shining through. His body is wider, not from weight, but from muscle, like Admiral Conolly looks wider than Commander Conolly. A few wrinkles pop up around his lips and eyes when he smiles. This Kieran is what, Admiral Conolly's age? No, definitely younger. Way younger, right? I dunno. Still older than I've ever seen him.

But he's alive.

Emotion chokes my next breath. Kieran is alive. Will be alive.

Why? How? When are we? My heart beats double-time. When will I see him again in my time?

The other Nonie groans. "Sir, there's a reason I'm working from behind a desk and not in the field. I have two left hands when it comes to self-defense. Dad took me out of Krav Maga after two weeks, and you know how focused he was to get me into the academy."

I jerk back. Excuse me? Two left hands in self-defense? I'd never say that about myself, I worked too hard to *not* call myself a pro, mental issues aside. And what the absolute—! Dad was *so* not focused getting me into the academy, quite the opposite! What bull am I telling Kieran?

Other Nonie lets her head hang, then looks at him from under her lashes. "We could start with an analysis report instead?" Hope swings in her voice, together with something else, something more suggestive than an analysis report.

Kieran chuckles. "That's for later. You know I want you field ready, so stop pretending, Lieutenant. You love working out with me. We could—"

His Hablamate lights up and beeps. *"Chocho to Wildason."*

Kieran taps it. "All ears, Leonardo."

"Suzie and I were wondering if we could join you for the fundraiser tomorrow evening, if you don't mind."

Wait: Chocho—like, Chocho from the *Pioneer*'s bridge?

"I'd be honored to have you both there. Lieutenant Thorburn will contact you with the details. Wildason out." He taps the Hablamate once more. "Anyway. Where were we?"

Nonie sighs. "Thinking about how Captain Chocho will at one

point wonder why you always cut him off short when you're here." She folds her hands behind her back, fingers interlocked and cramped together, but even though her body posture looks like she's being tortured, her cheeks are flushed.

Kieran grins and steps closer, closer than I have ever been to any admiral besides my dad, which is weird, because she has been calling him *sir*, and he has been calling her *lieutenant*. A feeling of tightness grows in my throat. This isn't good. Something is wrong here, quite wrong.

"If he ever stopped swooning about that wife of his long enough to realize that's what I'm doing, I'd be happy to tell him he's right."

"Admiral—"

"Nonie." He says it so softly, this one word sucks the oxygen right out of the room. Other Nonie and I both bite onto our lower lip.

Kieran's gaze darts across her face for a long two or three seconds. Then, he slowly raises his hand and brushes a strand of her hair out of her face. The way he keeps his gaze glued to hers, how she doesn't even blink, her chest heaves up and falls heavily just like his… This isn't the first time this—or something like it—is happening.

And yet they call each other *admiral* and *lieutenant*.

He drops his hands, and his next words to a low whisper. "I know." He clears his throat and steps back. "But, all distractions aside, I'd like to reemphasize my previous statement. You do love working out with me." He winks and turns to leave. "I'll see you in Gym Three in a few minutes, okay?"

"Yes, sir."

Kieran walks out, and as the door closes, Nonie exhales a big puff of air. Holy Sun and Stars, that felt intense. I stand up behind the couch, while she has her gaze still glued where Kieran left, her cheeks flushed, chewing on her lower lip. "I do love working out with him," she whispers. "Damn him."

Our gazes meet, and for a moment neither of us speaks. If my expression mirrors hers though, we both know something isn't right.

I clear my throat. "Dad wanted you in the academy?"

"Since I was little. Proudest moment when I got accepted as the youngest cadet ever." She pauses, the apple in her throat moving up and down. "Are you saying… it was different for you?" Her voice cracks at the end.

I nod. "He tried to keep me out with all he had. I snuck into the entrance exam and aced it." The next breath sounds wheezy. "You don't do Krav Maga?"

"I suck at it. Almost failed the academy's self-defense classes. You?"

"Excel at it," I whisper. My heart skips a beat when I look her in the eye. "We're not the same."

"No." She shakes her head. "We're not. But how can that be? What's your native time?"

"My what?"

She makes an impatient gesture with her hand. "Your native time—like, when are you from? When is your present?"

Ah, okay, got it. "2295."

She cringes. "That's the year now. It's January."

A wave of dizziness crashes over me. January of 2295—I was at the academy, not yet a lieutenant, and a good three months away from being thrown through time to the *Pioneer*. "That's not good then. We're from the same time, yet completely different people. Well, not *that* different, but you know what I mean."

Sinking down onto the couch, the other Nonie swipes a strand of hair from her face, the same one Admiral-Kieran tugged behind her ear a minute earlier. "There's only one explanation, and it's giving me a headache already."

I let myself fall down into the couch at the other end, keeping a good distance between us. Who knows, the world might implode if we came too close. "It means… we are from different timelines."

Together we suck in a breath—and hold it at the same time.

"Gee, that's so weird," other Nonie says, then releases that breath through pursed lips.

"No kidding." I give a dry chuckle and shake my head. "So, I jumped into the past, yay me, but into the wrong timeline. I thought—and no offense—alternate timelines would cease to exist after they split off, leaving only one dominant, remaining branch?"

She gives me a funny look from under her lashes. "Ah, I see you have an FBTI as well, don't you? You just quoted the handbook."

My jaw drops. "There's a handbook?" I want that!

Other Nonie grins. "Yeah, but it's basically written as we go along. I'm the only operative who can travel through time, so…" She shrugs.

"So, has anything like this ever happened to you? And if so, how did you get back home?" Because let's face it, I'm not the master of the timestream or any jump. I have no idea how I landed here, or how to get back. I swallow hard. If I were trapped here, at least Kieran is ali—

Oh.

Grief hits, even though it has no business showing up. I know Kieran doesn't survive in my timeline. I know. And yet, seeing Kieran, as an admiral, here, I allowed hope to spring free—hope, that Kieran would be alive in my time.

Alas, no such luck.

I drop my gaze and allow myself one tiny second of regret, then pull my shoulders back and lift my chin. Nothing has changed. Suck it up, Thorburn.

Other Nonie leans forward and glides a finger over her PADdy in thought. "Well… No. I've done many jumps, and I'd say I'm pretty good at arriving when and where I need to go. It's all about visualizing your destination. But I've never ended up in a timeline that wasn't supposed to exist."

"Like yours."

She grins and shakes her head. "Nu-uh. Yours. Obviously, mine is the dominant one."

I give her a look that's supposed to say *oh really*, but ignore her comment. "Either way, I'd be quite happy if I could make it home to my time—and timeline." Wait a second. I meet her gaze. "You said you jumped. How? How do you initiate the jump?"

She looks at me like, *duh.* "I got a portable Setayashi emitter. Why? How do you jump?"

Holy Sun and Stars—a portable emitter like Mashaule's, the solution to all my problems! I could be proactive and chase that bastard, instead of following him and failing, and I could be doing that like right now. Making the decisions and calling the shots would be one heck of a game changer. I jump up and start to pace in front of the couch. "First, I don't jump myself. All jumps so far have been passive, meaning, there was Setayashi radiation that triggered me, and I…" I shrug. "Like, I got here because I followed somebody. And took the wrong turn or something." Quite heroic, right? I stop in front of other Nonie. "But if you could give me one of those emitters… And before you say anything, you're not changing the timeline. Yours, at least. But I would have a chance to complete my mission. Because right now… I don't know how to pull it off. I landed here, of all times and places. And no offense to your native time, but that's really not helping me." Lifting and dropping my arms, I deflate. If I let myself think about where I am, like, really think about it, I might start rocking in a corner somewhere and never come out again. Can't focus on that. All energy must go into finding my way home and protecting Kieran.

Other Nonie tilts her head. "Considering we're the same, you're quite the rule bender." Then, a mischievous grin spreads across her face. "I like it."

Hope springs alive. "Does that mean you can give me one of those emitters?"

She stands up and walks over to her desk. "I don't have a million of them just lying around, but you can have mine. I'll come up with something and get the FBTI to issue a new one for me."

I rush over to her and hug her from the side. "Thank you. Thank you, thank you, thank you! You don't even know how much that helps me!"

She pats my back in an awkward manner. "Given that I'm not a hugger and I assume neither are you, this is proof how much it helps you. So yeah, I can imagine."

We both chuckle as I let her go. She leans over the desk and opens a drawer, not unlike Kieran's secret drawer in his desk, with her palm print.

"You can put this in your pocket and tether it to your wrist PAD. I mean, if they're compatible, which I hope they are. Nothing about you seems that different, so chances are our tech won't be either. If it doesn't, it works via print recognition on this button here." She points to a central indentation on the Setayashi emitter, which really just looks like somebody hard-boiled an egg and smushed it flat. Minus the mess, of course. "Really convenient we're the same person." Throwing the transmitter up and catching it, her face falls. "Better set it up, it appears I'm expected in the gym."

It's not so much the words, more the way she says them, fake frown or not. I might not understand most of what's going on here, but I understand *her*. I know the way I look when I look at Kieran. I heard what they said. Saw what he did.

"You like him," I say. "The… *admiral*." And it looked like he likes her too.

Her cheeks turn red. "It's obvious, isn't it? It's also complicated, even without the USEF's fraternization regulations. He's twenty years older. And I know nothing can—or will—happen between us, I mean, we're working together, he's an admiral, I'm a lieutenant, then there's the age difference—" She stops herself, closing her eyes for a short second. "I'm rambling. But even though it's doomed, I can't help the way I feel. Like there was a connection between us that doesn't care about his rank or his age." Her shoulder droop forward. "Is there an Admiral Wildason in your universe?"

Like she twisted the knife in the wound, pain shoots through my heart. "No. No, there isn't. Captain Wildason died at twenty-three." I lower my gaze. If he hadn't, I'd know his older version. I might even be exactly where this Nonie is now, crushing hard on a man who is way older than me. Maybe, judging by what I just witnessed, maybe even with the feelings being returned, but with no option to pursue.

Not with this age gap.

Never with this age gap and the hierarchy between them. Us.

Nonie's brows scrunch down for a split second before she has her facial muscles back under control and a sad, knowing smile tips up one side of her lips. "Ah. I take it we're both in love with a man we can't have, albeit for different reasons. Pity some things stay the same across the timelines."

"Yeah, pity," I whisper. Pity.

When I look at her, her eyes are glistening, but she covers it with a quick clap of her hands. "Well, anyway, since I am apparently scheduled to practice my self-defense skills with the man of my unfulfilled dreams, I gotta go. So, let's get you back home."

"That sounds fantastic. Thank you for letting me take your emitter."

"Meh, we're family, right?" She winks. "Take the emitter and try it— Oh, wait. Do you want me to set you a marker ten seconds before you entered the Maelstrom that got you here? Would that work?"

I stare at her. "A marker?"

"A signal in the time stream for you to arrive ten seconds before you left off. Since I think you were following somebody else through their portal it might be convenient."

My eyes widen. "Convenient? You have no idea! I really need to stay on that person's butt!" Even though I'll have the other Nonie's emitter, I need to follow Mashaule. Him running amok somewhere— anywhere—in the past is not what I would consider optimal. If I could pop up at the right time and at the fairgrounds, I could follow Mashaule again, only this time do it right and not get distracted.

"Okay, then it's a plan. Let me scan your temporal signature and set it…" She sticks her tongue out of the corner of her mouth as she moves the disk over my body and enters something in her wrist PAD. "If I assume your timeline—"

A loud, rapid banging comes from the door, the urgent kind.

We both twitch—

"Manual FBTI override accepted," a female computer voice announces as the doors begin to slide open, a man dressed in black tactical gear squeezing through.

"FBTI! Temporal violation! Everybody, hands up, nobody move!"

My insides freeze. No. It doesn't take rocket science to figure out I'm the temporal violation, and that they're not happy about it. I whip my head to look at my counterpart. "Nonie, what—?"

The guy spills through the door as it opens further, followed by three more men, all dressed in the same uniform as the other Nonie, red with black stripes at the side. "Nobody move, hands up! Up! Up, I said!"

For one eternal part of a second the other Nonie's and my gaze connect.

It's enough. I read her as well as she reads me.

Steely resolve glues my shattered soul together. We got this.

The other Nonie yanks up both her hands with a little yelp. "Sun and Stars, you scared me, I—" She adds another squeak. "I'm so sorry, I pressed—" She lowers her hands, checking the disk. A bright light erupts—

"Hands up, I said! Abort the burst!" The men are coming closer as my vision tunnels—

"I can't, it's initiated, I'm so sorry, you startled me, and I just pressed it—"

The first guy darts forward and rips it out of her hands. "Lieutenants, restrain the violation!" He throws the device on the floor and stomps on it.

The three other men rush me, reach for me—

My vision darkens around the edges, my body begins to vibrate and tingle as it feels the pull of the timeline.

And just before the jump takes over, I see the other Nonie grin behind the guys' backs, giving me a thumbs up.

Then—

Chapter Seven -
SWEET TWIST

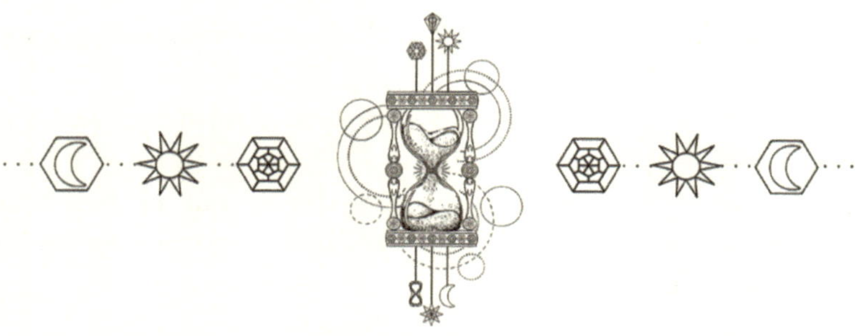

Somewhere, Somewhen

Floating through time. Through events.
Too tough to trace it all. Some seem clear-ish, most don't.
Overwhelming. Too much.
Chaos, colors, screams, screams, SCREAMS—
One voice is Kieran's, I know it.
I don't want to hear—
Something draws my attention, like a shiny ruby in a sea of dark. The Marker?
I look at it and come closer, closer—
BAM!

Panting like I'd run a marathon, I land in a half-crouch on the most neon colored gras I've ever seen. *Not* the other Nonie's office, but potentially at the Fair on Ortega One, potentially in my time. All I see are legs and feet of people walking fast.

My heart stumbles over its fast beats. Holy Sun and Stars—I made it. She brought me here, minus the emitter, but beggars can't be choosers. Air whistles between my teeth as I suck a desperate breath in. Somebody remind me to never time-jump for fun. What the heck is happening during these jumps? It's like a nightmare come to life. Those screams—

Somebody bumps into me. "Hey, watch it," they yell at somebody with shimmering hair running, darting, after an older man—

Mashaule! Me! That was me running after Mashaule1

I stumble up and take off, sprinting as hard as I can. I've literally just been in this situation about twenty minutes ago.

Mashaule stops, pulls out the oval device, and activates it. It's too crowded for me to shoot, since my younger me is so tantalizingly close to him. I'm hot on their heels as well. If anybody wonders why two people looking very much alike are running for their life in the same direction I have no clue, and I wouldn't stop to find out.

In a flash of light, Mashaule vanishes, followed a second later by the other me, until I'm close enough to—

Screams, worse than before, horror, pain, desperation, more screams, screamsscreasscreamsSCREAMSSCREEAAA—

Thrown around like in a hurricane, head whipping left and right and left and ri—

Must focus. Follow Mashaule. Follow—

I hit the ground with a thud, landing smack on my back, the sound of Kieran's screams echoing in my mind. "Nggh." A grunt breaks from my throat. Ow. What—

Twigs. Leaves. Grass. The smell of fresh air, a fruity tang—

I force my eyes open—

Sun. Clouds.

Crap—Mashaule! Is he here?

I force my body to roll on my tummy, then scramble off the ground, hands up, wobbly like a newborn deer—

He isn't here.

"Damn it!" I stomp one foot and lose balance. Stumbling to catch myself, I curse again. Am I where he is? *When* he is? Is this even the right universe, for crying out loud?

I turn a full three-sixty, hands still up, just in case, since my body is having a hard time with these transitions. I feel like I've been high on adrenaline since the fairgrounds, but on the other hand, tackling Kieran to protect him from Mashaule feels already like an eternity ago.

Okay, business: I'm on a dirt road, which seems to be a preferred pattern for me after a time-jump, but this time at least no forest. Only rows and rows of green plants, strung up to head height, and loaded with—

"Raspberries," I whisper.

Sun and Stars.

When I'm back in my time, we need to upgrade PADdy to use the star constellations to find out the current time and date, or at least the date, but for this jump, I think I know where and when I am, or at least where and when Mashaule wanted to go. Today must be the day Kieran's nanny shot him and he was saved by a medic. It's not a hard conclusion to make that Mashaule will want to make sure little Kieran dies for real this time.

Taking out a child. Despicable.

No time to give in to panic, nausea, or anything distracting me. It's imperative I find Kieran and his nanny. And the medic saving him, so that I can make sure she's there to do her job. Mashaule could be trying to take out both, to be on the safe side.

Adrenaline spikes some more as I tap PADdy. "Location scan, fast. Corelate with scanner." Because that thing's vibrating in my pocket and it's not supposed to be alarming for my own radiation trace, only on others', i.e., Mashaule's.

Two seconds later, a rough layout of my environment pops up on PADdy's display. The entrance lies about four hundred meters to the north, following this path—and one of two red dots is moving right in that direction.

I break into a sprint, dust flying from my boots with every hasty, hurried step. My breath comes out harsh and short. The farm is huge. Judging by the sun, it's mid-morning. Meaning, there are people going to be here, people who can see me, who can recognize me—

Who can get caught up in Mashaule's spiel and get hurt.

After about three hundred meters, I slow down to a fast, hurried stride, before the first customers see and memorize me. The entrance is right there, maybe a hundred meters ahead: grassy, a barn with a white picket fence in front of it, some goats grazing in that area, some kids playing on the playground, laughing and squealing. It's getting busier in this area, with families in every row, no matter whether I check to the left or the right side. Some of them must've been here for a while, if the amount of raspberries in their baskets is any indication.

According to PADdy and the scanner, Mashaule is somewhere to the left, a few rows ahead.

Which means Kieran is probably close by.

I draw my hand up to my hip—

What the—

No weapon! I suppress a curse. No clue what happened to it, and it doesn't matter. I don't have it, which is all I need to know.

Just great.

The closer I get to the area with the red dot, the more I feel… calm, to a degree. Like my soul knew more than my frantically beating heart. Like a pull. A yearning. Like—

I enter the row on my left, following my intuition. Kieran said he felt me, when I came back. Maybe I'm feeling him? Would that work? Even though we're not bonded yet, at this point in time?

Sneaking forward, I keep one eye on the readout and one on the ground. Last thing I need is twigs breaking and announcing me to Mashaule. The plants are taller than me on both sides, each tied up to their own vertical wooden pole and loaded with red, plump raspberries. Bees are busy flying between the plants, looking for pollen. If I wasn't here to catch a crazy man, I'd enjoy this place, like everybody else, if the far-off laughter and conversations are any indication.

"Can we go home, Addi? My basket is already full."

I stop dead in my tracks. That voice—younger, pre-adolescent, but unmistakably *his*. Magellan hearing FTW!

"Addi?" Young-Kieran's voice turns whiny.

"Soon," a female voice replies.

Kieran groans. "But I'm done already."

I sneak to the right, through one of the rows of bushes. They must be one more row over. I can see their feet. And Mashaule—

I check PADdy. Mashaule is on the other side, two rows over from where I am. I bet he's getting ready to take Kieran in his cross hairs—or maybe getting ready to put the medic in there, because if I remember correctly, the sitter would've killed Kieran had the medic not shown up.

Problem is, no matter what he's surely keeping his eye on the row Kieran is in, and I need to cross said row to get to him. My heart's frantic thump-thump is rattling my ribcage. It's one thing knowing the story, but another waiting for it to happen, waiting for Kieran to get shot.

That's some messed up stuff, right there.

Carefully, I part some of the branches to peek through. As soon as my gaze falls onto young Kieran, I'm hit with the sledge hammer of emotions: Kieran is Kieran, even as a kid. His hair is slightly longer overall, but with the same waves he carried into adulthood. It looks messy, in a cool way. He's tall for his age, lean, and with an athletic build.

And very much annoyed at this moment.

"You're weird today, Addi." He kicks at some pebble on the ground. "Can we just go?"

The nanny, Addi, apparently, doesn't respond. She has her back to me, her head tilted up as if she was soaking up the sun, her right hand inside a large purse.

Kieran tries again. "We could play your favorite holo-novel, you know? I still have it bookmarked to where we left—"

BANG!

In one fluid motion, Addi has drawn a gun from the purse and shot Kieran straight in the chest.

My outcry comes simultaneously with hers. Kieran! A wave of agonizing pain tears through my heart—

Like somebody cut a puppet's strings, Kieran collapses to the ground, coming to lay on his side, right cheek smushed into the spilled raspberries from his basket, blood gushing out from the wound in his chest.

A choking sound leaves his throat, weak—

Addi wails. "I'm sorry, so sorry, they made me, I'm so sorry—"

Another eardrum splitting BANG tears through the air, followed by the heavy thud of an adult body hitting the ground.

Kieran's chest lowers with a soft exhale—

And doesn't rise again.

Pain like fire shoots through my body, searing every cell in and turning them to ash. Holy Sun and Stars— I press both hands against my chest. Can't breathe. Like somebody's choking me, squeezing the blood out of my heart into a wide gap in my chest. Dizzy.

Somebody screams. "Oh my God, oh my god, somebody call 911, fast, somebody call!"

A man comes running down the row. "We need help here! Help!"

My vision turns blurry. Spotty. Blackish.

Three more people run over—

My next breath wheezes. Brings no oxygen.

The first man kneels next to Kieran. "Oh my god, that blood—"

"Does he have a pulse?"

"I don't know, I can't feel any—"

"Here, let me!"

Anguish racks through me, taking my sanity—

"I'm a medic, coming through! Make room, people!"

The medic! Through the soul-ripping agony, my mission regains priority. Must get Mashaule. Must protect the Medic. Now's as good a time as any.

I part the branches and stumble forward, every step a victory of mind over body. Something's tearing me apart from the inside out, one fiber at a time.

Passing the raspberry bushes into Kieran's row, I glance to the right, to the crowd of people standing around the two bodies on the ground— and at the female medic running in, dressed in black, with a slight limp to her left leg, choosing not the clearer path closer to the plants and Mashaule, but to force her way right through the middle of the assembled crowd. Something catches the light on her left ring finger and reflects it in a million colors.

For the blink of an eye, I doubt my sanity, but then, I've seen crazier, about five minutes ago.

Our gazes connect for no more than a second before she nods at me in acknowledgement. "Take care of *him*. I'll take care of Kieran. Oh, and keep this." She throws something small to me that I catch, the movement of my arms bringing the soul-tearing anguish to a whole new level.

Holy Sun and—

I bite down hard. Suck it up. Priorities. I pocket the data disk she threw to me while *she* kneels next to Kieran, several people around her at all sides. "I need space, people!" She checks his neck for a pulse. "Kieran!"

Kieran.

I jump into action. Despite the pain, despite the agony, I burst forward and through the next row of bushes. I turn to the right—and there he is. On his stomach behind a tall bush, distracted like a first-year ensign trying to get a clear shot aimed through the branches, unaware of his surroundings and waiting for the opportunity to shoot either Kieran or me. He jerks away from the bushes. "What the absolute—?" he whispers.

Judging by his reaction, I assume he saw me—the other me. Mashaule shakes his head, then readjusts his aim.

Oh, hell to the no! No matter if he wants to shoot Kieran again, the quote-unquote medic, or anybody else, it's not going to happen!

She calls out, "No heartbeat! Come on, Kieran, come on!"

I dart forward and throw myself onto Mashaule, reaching for his weapon with both hands. Deja vu hits—Mashaule and me fighting for a weapon—but today is different. He isn't ready. Mashaule grunts as my weight hits him full force and flattens him onto his stomach. Like him, I have two hands on the weapon—and I've got the better angle. As much as I can, I keep my weight forward, on my hands and therefore the gun, only lifting a knee to ram it into his head with all the power I can muster while feeling ripped apart from the inside. Again. Again. *Again!*

Mashaule roars and yanks his legs in and under his body, coming up to a turtle position. I slide off his back, but keep my hands on the gun—

"The woman is dead," somebody yells, followed by several shocked gasps.

Mashaule, now in a stronger position, draws his arms in, and me with it. I slide over the ground, twigs and pebbles biting into my skin, but it's not as bad as the pain inside, the fire eating me alive and leaving nothing but ash.

"Oh, my god, he's just a boy!" a woman wails. Some kid's panicky, crying—

I scramble to get onto both knees without the use of my hands—

"Heartbeat! I've got a heartbeat! 911, we—" The rest of the sentence is drowned out by the noise of the approaching Airborne Emergency Pod.

Mashaule growls like a wounded dog. "No! You little—" With all his power and body weight, he wrenches on the gun with so much force, I expect to go flying with it.

But I don't. Maybe I just needed a breather or something, but I resist. That pain inside my chest is gone, like the weakness and wobbliness. I feel like I could conquer the world and come out on top. I burst forward from my knees and ram my shoulder into his gut, taking care to keep the line of fire directed away from my body.

Mashaule falls back with an *oomph*, and without missing a second, I scramble on top of him, rip the weapon out of his hands, and throw it as far as I can. Will deal with it later.

"Make room for them to land, people! He's stable, but we've got to hurry—"

The hate flaring up in Mashaule's eyes makes up for the misery I just went through. He didn't get to kill Kieran or, well, me, but also, he doesn't seem to have gotten that message yet.

"I'm going to kill you, bi—"

Boom! I've rammed my fist into his face, and I'd be lying if I said it didn't feel good. Mashaule's head hits the ground and bounces once. His eyes roll back as he goes limp.

Yes! "Gotcha, sucker!" Relief and exhilaration of a magnitude never experienced before flood my system.

Over.

It's over.

A few rows behind us the Airborne Emergency Pod lands, if the crunching, sound of snapping branches and wooden support poles breaking is any indication.

Kieran will live.

I allow myself one more deep breath, then shift my weight to reach for—

Lightning fast, much faster than I'd assumed a man his age could move, Mashaule shoots one arm down to his thigh, and—

Sharp, burning, all-encompassing pain bursts from the left side of my chest—

I gasp, the breath cut short by—

Knife.

Knife stuck in my chest.

An evil grin spreads across Mashaule's face. "Your own trick. Idiot." He bucks his hips and topples me off his body like I was a rag doll.

Hit the ground.

Dizzy.

Vision turning black.

Can't breathe.

Can't—

Kicked into my side—

Excruciatingpainagony—

"—extraction, now! —good riddan—"

Bright light.

Feels good.

Must follow.

Kieran.

Chapter Eight –

BACK

Somewhere, Somewhen

Hard, cold floor.

Cool air—

"Holy—!"

Shuffling. Commotion. Chaos.

Hand on my pulse.

Palm cupping my cheek.

"Wildason to Upinga! Medical Emergency, Code Magenta! Speed the hell up, Zio!"

Then, nothing.

Chapter Nine -
OUT OF WHACK

Somewhere, Somewhen

The first thing I notice when I wake up is that I'm not in pain. Whole.

I feel whole.

The second thing I notice is that I'm not alone.

Somebody is holding my hand. Gliding a thumb over it. Playing with the ring on my finger.

A slow smile works on the corners of my lips. Smiling doesn't hurt either.

"Hey," Kieran whispers. "Are you awake?"

Opening my leaden eyelids takes the strength to move a mountain, but I get it done. "Yeah," I whisper back, voice horse.

Kieran closes his eyes, his shoulders heaving up and down in a silent breath. He lifts my hand to his mouth and places a kiss on my knuckles. "Thank the universe. It was touch and go there for more than a minute. And probably one of the more traumatic experiences of my adult life. You popping up on the bridge out of nowhere, a knife stuck in your

70

chest. You were in surgery for three hours."

Oh.

The memory returns, and with it shame, burning like a wildfire. What a beginner's mistake—and Mashaule was right, I fell for the same trick I used on him on board the *USEF Guardian*.

And by the sound of it, it close to killed me.

I throw a look around. "Sickbay." Shows how much my brain prioritized Kieran over everything else. Only now do I notice I'm in sickbay, an IV in my arm, a monitor beeping in a soothing rhythm behind me.

Kieran brushes his knuckles over my cheek. "You were in a coma for three days. Zio didn't sleep for two of them, and me..." He shrugs haphazardly. "Not much either. Or if, here. I—"

The doors open, and Zio strides in, a medical PAD in his hands. The relief on his face when he sees me is beyond obvious. "I was hoping my alerts were correct. You're awake." Stepping to the other side of my bed, he reaches for my pulse. A typical Zio-gesture. I'm most likely tethered to every monitoring device imaginable, but he still likes to go old-school. "How are you feeling?"

Truth? "Not bad at all. Much better than what I last remember." Obvs.

Zio nods while checking the display mounted to the wall at the head side of the bed. "Your vitals look good, especially considering you arrived here more dead than alive. I'm expecting you to be fully operational in a day or two." He gives Kieran a probing look. "And aside from the obvious lack of sleep, you look better, too."

Better? He still looks like he'd neither slept nor eaten in a while.

Kieran points one finger at me. "There's the reason. I think I'm good without your cocktail for a bit, Zee."

Cocktail? Oh. I flinch. "The Bond—"

"Yeah. It's never exactly pleasant. But we have a good routine, right, Zee?"

"Considering the Magellans rank loss of the Bond as a clear ten out of ten on the pain scale, I'd say we've been successfully keeping you functioning."

A clear ten out of ten… "Like being ripped apart on the inside," I whisper. That's what I felt at the farm, when Kieran died. And that's what was gone when *she* got his heartbeat back, and I felt invincible.

Invincible my butt.

Kieran makes a face, then playfully flicks a finger at my ear. "Meh, let's not make it so dramatic. Last thing I want is for you to feel guilty when you leave me. After all, what's another few decades of withdrawal pain until you're born? Zio says at that point, even though we're technically not bonded yet, it should be easier. So, it is what it is."

It is what it is until his official death in—

I look up. "What day is today?"

Kieran's brows move down into a confused V. "Date? Oh, yeah, right. July nineteenth, 2256.

The date hits me like a punch to the gut. Seven months. It's seven whole months after the fair on Ortega One. And that's not even what takes the cake: It's the date. Today is so unbelievably unremarkable as far as I know, I have no idea why Mashaule wanted to jump here. On the other hand… did he? Do I know for a fact I landed where he wanted to go? Because, my track record isn't exactly the greatest. The other jumps I remember bits and pieces from, like following a pull, and these screams and… this *horrific* feeling. This time, not so much.

Which translates to the very worst-case scenario possible, and it comes with the bitter taste of failure and deja vu: I'm stuck in this time with no means to leave and no idea when Mashaule is. Could I have ended up in this time on accident, and could he have done the same thing Other Nonie helped me to do—go back to where he started, just a few minutes earlier? Meaning, could he have returned to the raspberry farm, this time hidden somewhere else, and succeed to kill Kieran, while I'm busy fighting his other self? Would that even work?

I pinch my eyes shut until stars dance in front of my closed lids. My First Sense is quiet, and I'm still here. So is Kieran. That should mean Mashaule did not just go back to turn his failure into success. Why? Why didn't he? It's a great opportunity knowing where all the players are at that very moment. So why are we still here? Because he can't go back? Is there a limitation to the disk? A limitation to interference in a certain time period?

Frustration brings up nasty bile. I know way too little about the opponent I'm fighting, or his abilities.

But what stings like a stab to the heart—or the chest, as experience shows—is that even if I don't know when he is, I can protect Kieran.

After all, it's not even a year until he is supposed to die.

And that thought, it hits the hardest of them all.

Chapter Ten –

FUNK

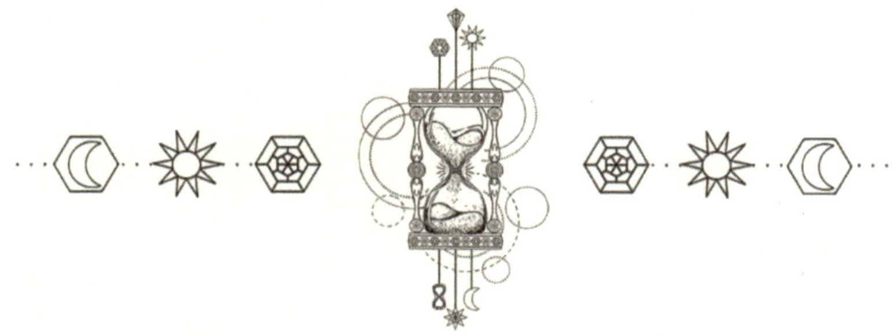

Kieran adjusts the pillow stuffed behind my back. "Are you sure you don't want anything to eat? I can fix you something, it's not a problem at all."

Before he can jump into another flurry of activities, I grab his hand. "No, thank you. I'm fine. Stop fussing over me."

Zio discharged me from sickbay after another night of observation and meds, and since I've been home, I.e., in Kieran's quarters, Kieran has been Mr. Mother hen personified. I don't think there's a single pillow in here he hasn't brought to the couch and added to my pile to make me comfy. The temperature has been adjusted to a perfect twenty degrees Celsius, the lights are dimmed, and the windows set on transparent. Still, he's been busy trying to make me even more comfortable.

And while his kindness is well-intended, it hurts.

He wouldn't need to do any of this if I hadn't been so overconfident and gotten myself stabbed. If I hadn't failed. Hadn't left him open and vulnerable for another attack by Mashaule, whom I have no way of following or finding, unless he's so close, it might be too late. He could be at any given time. Good luck sniffing him out, Lieutenant.

I got another chance courtesy of the other Nonie and I ruined it.

I'm a toothless kitten in a war fought between full-grown sabertooth tigers.

Kieran stills and deflates. "I can't stop fussing over you. I'm a captain of the USEF. It's not in my personality to let things happen without having a say in them. I'm used to being in control. Doing something is better than doing nothing, and with this whole time-travel drama, all I can do is nothing."

I grimace. Sounds like a description of my life.

He turns his hand over and weaves his fingers through mine, then sits next to me on the couch. "But speaking of time-travel drama. I never thanked you for saving my life during that fair on Ortega One. So, thank you. I know I can't ask you any details, but it still makes me a bit nervous that I needed a personal bodyguard. Gave me an extra adrenaline-kick every time I left the *Pioneer* since then, wondering who might try to shoot at me next," he tries to joke, but it falls flat when he sees my facial expression. "Not funny, I take it?"

Not even close. I pull myself together. "I like you in one piece, and preferably not injured or bleeding."

He gives me a pointed glance. "Ditto."

Heat rises to my cheeks. "Well, then you know what I mean. I really am not the biggest fan of you going on away missions." Fast-forward a decade or two, and no captain will be allowed on anything even remotely smelling of trouble. We learned our lessons.

After a short pause, he sucks in his lower lip and shrugs. "I'm not the biggest fan of you jumping through time and risking your life. Not in general, and especially not when I don't know if whatever you're doing is worth your risk." He softens his words with a stroke of his thumb across the back of my hand. "So, I guess neither of us gets what they want, do we?"

"I guess not." I drop my gaze. For the umpteenth time I wish I could talk about my job, about what's at stake—but that's the point: too much is at stake for me to risk it. Hello, weight of the world. You're heavy today.

Kieran lets go of a long, soft breath. "You don't seem your usual self." Using the index finger of his free hand, he boops my nose.

"I—" I snap my mouth shut. Mashaule, my responsibility to the timeline, my incompetence—it all gnaws on me. But what hurts like a knife to the chest—and I should know—is what will happen on June 8th, 2257. The day Kieran will die.

Since I heard the name Kieran Wildason for the very first time, I knew he died young, at the hand of the Quaneez. I knew it then, I knew it when I met him for the first time, I knew it when I fell for him. I always knew it.

But it never hurt as much as it does now.

Maybe it's because of my sadistic job description to keep him alive until he's supposed to die. Maybe it's because I've failed him so miserably at the raspberry fields, failed to capture Mashaule. Maybe it's everything together.

Fact is, he'll die, and there's not a thing I can do to prevent it. What does that make me if not an accessory to murder? Or the cruellest girlfriend in the universe? I'm letting Kieran die. I'm not telling him what's going to happen. Can't tell him.

And I'm. Letting. Him. Die.

Tears spring to my eyes. I raise one hand to wipe them away before they fall.

"Hey." Kieran scoots closer. "That bad?" And damn his empathy, damn the soft, caring tone of his, because it crumbles down my walls.

The first tear falls—and then another one. I squeeze my eyelids shut so hard, stars dance in front of my inner eyes. No crying, I wasn't raised to cry. No crying, no—

In one smooth motion, Kieran has scooped me up and pulled me onto his lap, holding me half-sitting, half-cradled, my head resting against his shoulder. He scoots himself with his back against the armrest and swings his leg up to stretch them out onto the couch. "Okay, no need to answer that question. I can take a guess."

He keeps me close, his left hand smoothing up and down my arm.

Every breath he takes is calm and soothing, every heart beat a reassurance he's still here. For now. I focus on the deep, rhythmic *dub-dub* sound, and bit by bit it calms me down. It gives me courage to talk and to open my heart, a tiny bit, at least.

"Everything's against us," I whisper into his chest. "Fate sucks."

My statement draws a small chuckle from Kieran. "Actually, I'm kind of thankful to fate."

That's because you don't know what she's got in store for you. "Why?"

"Well, duh. Because she brought me you." He stops the soothing motion across my arm to pull me in tighter and drop a small kiss onto my temple.

Aww… Heat rises to my cheeks, powered by the very recent knowledge that things could have worked out differently. Buzzwords Other Nonie and Old Kieran. I frown. "True. But she didn't play fair. First, she brings us together, then she tears us apart." And no, I don't mean separating us by time. I mean separating us by death.

I feel his chest lift up and lower with a deep breath. "Well, there's that, you've got a point. But you're here once again, and even though I worry about you jumping through time, in a wholly egoistical way I love that you do. You're *here*, in my arms. In my heart, Nonie. Normal isn't in the cards for us, I guess, if that's what you're going for. But I refuse to let that define us. I know we can't change the timeline, but hell, we can ride it out for all it's worth. Because the alternative is being miserable even when we're together, and I refuse to believe that's the way." His voice is soft, deep, and so full of confidence, it stirs something in me.

"You really believe that." I sit up and scoot back a tad to get a better look at his face, and yes, there's the same confidence I heard in his voice reflected in his eyes.

"I do. I feel like part of you is always with me, no matter where— or when—you are. I wouldn't want to trade that feeling for the world. I told you that before, most days, I consider myself the luckiest guy in the galaxy. But I get what you're saying. Some days I'm…" He shrugs with one shoulder. "Some days I'm just plain scared."

This admission, given so matter-of-factly, hits me right in the feels. "Me, too," I whisper. "Scared and angry at the same time. Scared I won't see you again, angry at life being so complicated for us. Angry that I can't see a happy ending." Because I know the ending, and it won't be a happy one on June 8th, next year. I drop my gaze.

"Ye of little faith. I can. I see that happy ending." Kieran takes me by the hips and moves me so that I'm facing him, then taps my legs and guides them to the left and right of his body. "I know that one day we'll have more time, that we'll be existing at the same time. And I get what you're saying, but even if I'm old then and we're just friends, I'll take it."

I would take that too. Like the other Nonie. In a heartbeat. If there was a deal I could strike with fate to keep Kieran alive, I would do it, even if it meant we wouldn't be together. A small price to pay in the grand scheme of things.

I angle my head so he doesn't see the new tears rising to my eyes.

Kieran takes my hand and plays with my fingers and the ring. "I'm not expecting you to continue *this*, us, with geezer-me, but just being at the same time, it'll be good for our souls to be living in the same time. So, to sum it up, I'm not mad at fate." He pauses, his voice flat with the next sentence. Hard. "Well, rephrasing. I'm not mad at fate for bringing us together. *That's* one thing I'm not mad at her for."

I look up. "But there's something else."

"You could say that." A muscle in his jaw thrums as he keeps his gaze glued to our hands. Lowering his chin makes the dark circles under his eyes even more obvious.

"No offense, Kieran, I know I'm the one who got herself stabbed, but you look like crap." Like he hadn't slept in days—no, weeks.

He huffs out dry. "I feel like crap. It's just— Never mind." He chews on his lower lip, a resignation in his expression so very much unlike him, it scares me.

"What's going on?" I brush a lock of his hair out of his face.

For the longest time, he stays silent, the muscles working in his jaw the only indication he heard me. Eventually, he closes his eyes and shakes his head once.

No need to say it out loud. I know. It's obvious. "The war."

"Yes. The war." When he opens his eyes again, they're wide and dark. "I shouldn't feel bad. They attack without mercy. They hunt us, they find us, they kill us. I shouldn't feel bad eliminating a single one of them. USEF tells me I should be proud of what we've done so far, how we've defended our colonies and avenged our dead. They say we're working on peace and we're doing everything we can. But are we? Because I don't think so. I don't think so." His voice trails off with the last word, but the pain stays, hovering between us like a third entity in the room.

War.

It's always the war.

The Quaneez War for Kieran. A temporal war for me. What's wrong with people?

I cup his face and brush my thumb over the bit of stubble on his cheek. "What do you want to do?" Not that we had figured that out forty years in the future.

He snuggles himself deeper into my hand. "What I *want* to do and what I *can* do are two completely diametrical things. I want to withdraw *Pioneer* from the front lines. I want to continue looking for allies, to make new friends, to gain new knowledge. I want to work on finding out how we can make peace with the Quaneez and keep it. And all I *can* do… is keep following orders and kill more of them. It's been over a year of this, Nonie. Over a year."

And it will be more years. Decades. Kieran sounds so defeated; I want to make him feel better. "I agree with you. Killing doesn't sound like the right solution."

"But you can't say in which direction I need to go, I get it." He works a hand through his hair, then peels my hand off his cheek, puts it down onto his chest and holds on to it. "But my subconscious is doing a good job with that already, according to my nightmares."

I grimace. "Ouch. Again?"

"Not again. Still. Never stopped. Whatever I do during the day, however well justified it seems, at night my brain turns on me. Every. Single. Night."

"Does Zio know?"

"To a degree."

"So that's a no."

The hint of a smile tugs on the corners of his lips. "You know me."

I give his head a little smack. "I do, and I also know that Zio might be able to help you. And don't forget, you were captured and tortured by them, so I think you're entitled to some PTSD."

He rolls his eyes. "Granted, but it's not real PTSD. It's different. Remember I told you about the day my nanny shot me?"

A loud BANG, young Kieran dropping to the ground, blood gushing out of the wound in his chest—

I squeeze my eyes shut. I don't want to ever see that image in my mind again. "Yeah, I do."

"One could argue that was a quite traumatic incident my life. From what I was told, my heart stopped."

So does mine with the memory.

He shrugs. "I can't say I didn't have nightmares afterwards, but it's nothing compared to now. I hear them scream, Nonie." His expression is full of dread and anguish. "I hear screams, see their masked faces, feel their pain. There's tons of confusing stuff in there, too, but overall, my subconscious has been making it quite clear it doesn't like my actions." A fine tremor courses through his large body, and my heart goes out to him. "And now USEF wants to give me the Golden Star of Combat in two days. For my *heroic* actions. Look at that, eh?" His voice is flat with the last two sentences.

The Golden Star of Combat. One of the highest military honors ever given by the USEF, and another chapter dedicated to Kieran in the history books. From what I remember it was not just a simple ceremony at headquarters, but a really, really big deal across Earth and all our colonies.

Yet, something tells me Kieran isn't exactly happy about it. Might be the tone of his voice, the rigid body posture, or the anger radiating off him. Point in case, I don't need a bond or training in psychology to pick up on his mood.

I slide off his lap and sit legs crossed facing him, keeping one of his hands in mine. "The Golden Star. That's… a big honor."

He huffs. "I don't know if I would call it that. It's nothing but a kill reward. How can I accept it? Accept an *honor* for my achievement in killing sentient beings? It's not an honor to have killed. It's a curse." He all but spits out the last part, jaw set tight. "You know, I'm thinking about declining it."

I sit up straighter. "Wait, what?"

"Declining it." He lowers his gaze to our entwined fingers. "I can't be forced to accept it. If I want them to work on a solution other than winning this war by force, how can I let myself get rewarded for something I don't believe in? Last thing I want is to become their poster boy for killing the Quaneez. I'm going to decline it."

Treading carefully, I stroke a finger along the vein on the back of his hand. "I understand why you want to decline it, but have you thought about what the Golden Star means to others?"

"To whom? In which way?" Confusion colors his voice, and I get it. Kieran doesn't have an outsider perspective. He is in the thick of the war, the very middle, the hotspot. His perception is a different one than ninety-nine percent of humanity's.

"The war came out of nowhere. People lost families, friends, loved ones. *Boom*, just like that. They don't know anything about the attacker, besides that they're merciless and that there's no escape. No warning. Their lives, or the lives of their families, could be extinguished any time, and in no time. They live in constant fear and state of insecurity. And here is the *USEF Pioneer* and Captain Wildason. Protecting them. Fighting to keep them alive, to avenge—no, hear me out," I say, when Kieran pinches his lips together and looks away. "And avenges their losses. Do I know you're not swooping in with revenge on your mind, trying to kill as many as possible? Yes, I do. Do I understand that to people who have been through unimaginable loss for no discernible reason someone fighting for them is like a guardian angel? Yes, I do."

"I'm not a guardian angel—"

"All I'm saying is that you give people hope, Kieran. And it's not the way you want to, but maybe that's the only good thing that comes out of the fighting and killing: that people get hope from it."

For the longest moment he is silent, gaze following my finger trailing over his veins. "I get that, but I wish they'd see the other side of it."

I shrug. "Then make them see it."

His gaze flies up to meet mine. "How?"

"By accepting the Golden Star and telling them how it really is."

Understanding flashes across his face. "My acceptance speech."

"Exactly." It was the speech that made his Golden Star special. I remember, I had a history quiz about it. Transmitted to all colonies. Thousands of people present at his speech, crowding the plaza—

Realization shoots through me. Thousands of people. A great place to hide. This could be what Mashaule was going for. Killing Kieran during the speech. Sun and Stars, it could be. I—

Kieran covers my hand with his and scoots on his cushion to face me. "The idea is only half bad, Nonie."

I fix a fast smile on my face. "Rousing endorsement, thank you."

Kieran chuckles. "Actually, it is. I think I can work with that. I get what you're saying, and maybe a bit of what you're not saying." He cuts me a glance "And for that, thank you."

Leaning forward and scooting closer, I bring our upper bodies flush together in a tight hug. Conflicting doesn't even begin to describe how I feel. What a good FBTI agent I am, getting Kieran to do what he's supposed to do, the speech. What a bad girlfriend I am, sending him out there even though I bet Mashaule will try to assassinate him. I hide my face on his shoulder and force my tone into a lighthearted one. "Hey, any time. I wish I could help with more than just vague phrases, but—"

"You're helping with way more than that." He hugs me back and snuggles his chin into my neck.

"I am?"

"Well, duh. Always. For one, whenever you're here, my Bond and I feel better, period. For another, you just opened my eyes to other means of warfare: communication. Popular opinion. Oh, and then there's this teeny-tiny fact that you kind of prove to me that humanity hasn't been wiped out by the Quaneez forty years in the future, which makes me hopeful that eventually we'll find peace. We're just not there yet."

Before I can come up with something that won't give away how miserably humanity has failed in building peace with the Quaneez, he kisses my neck. "But when we do, I want to be there. I want to make that peace, and I want to keep it, Nonie. Thank you for showing me a way."

He doesn't expect a reply. He knows I can't give one. But his words cut deep.

We won't have peace.

Or, if we ever will, Kieran won't be there, because Captain Kieran Wildason will die in a little more than a year, if I don't fail him and Mashaule kills him sooner.

Chapter Eleven –
HONORS

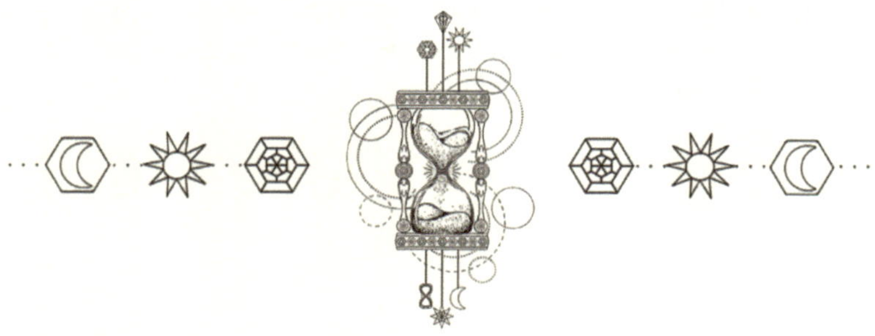

Gemini-Colony, Exploration Plaza, July 21ˢᵗ, 2256, 1500hrs

The last weeks have taught me enough about history to know it feels way different when experiencing it than reading about it. I've also learned it doesn't always seem like you're making history, even in the midst of it.

Today is not a day like that. Today feels momentous, grand even. Gemini is a beautiful natural colony to begin with—one that's still intact in my time, hallelujah—and their Exploration Plaza surrounded by a thick perimeter of large leaf-bearing trees is beyond beautiful. Where on Earth we would've used concrete or any other stone for an outdoor stage and the auditorium's ranks, they used a material found only on this planet, a hard, naturally growing substance reflecting light in iridescent colors. It looks a bit like marble covered with a pink-red-purplish oil sheen, and it might be the most beautiful thing I've ever seen. Depending on the angle, it shimmers and shines in different shades. Beyond pretty, really.

That being said, it's one thing to have a plaza that, if we're honest, should've been called an arena considering its size, made out of shiny glittery material. It's a completely different one to have every single seat of said arena filled.

We're talking about ten thousand people here.

Ten thousand plus waiting on one more who shouldn't be here, if I'm not mistaken.

I let my gaze roam over the rows and rows of people, searching. I sigh. As if I'd be so lucky to have Mashaule pop up right in front of me.

Alas, I'm doing the best I can. He wants Kieran, and I'm staying close to him. Dressed in the dark grey uniform of this time's security division, I at least have access to all areas without arising suspicion. Not even Kieran or Chase know what I'm up to.

Doesn't mean the latter wasn't suspicious.

"So, anything specific you're going to have an eye out for?" Chase tugs on the tight collar of his dress uniform, then drops his hand with a sigh. "Scratchy, that thing."

I grin. "I don't think they'd want you at your captain's Golden Star ceremony in regular day attire." And right they'd be—Chase is rocking this uniform. The cut emphasizes his wide shoulders and muscular build, plus, the dark blue contrasts nicely with his lighter blue eyes and blond hair. I've heard quite a few squeals and demands for autographs already, and we've only been down here a few minutes.

"They probably don't, but I wouldn't have minded it." He cuts me a frustrated glance from the side. "You didn't answer my question. Anything specific you're having an eye out for?" He gestures to the audience in front of us. As the guests of honor, the *Pioneer*'s bridge crew is seated in the very first row, which is given a wide berth of at least five or six meters until the second row, and a small, hip-high wall in-between the rows. To make the honor of sitting up front even more obvious, the seats for the *Pioneer* crew are cushioned in red velvet, while the rest of the audience sits on benches made out of that same iridescent material, more like in a Roman arena. Some of the crew look uncomfortable with the preferred treatment. Zio, for example. Thaler and Chocho on the other hand seem to be having a blast, judging by their excited looks around and engaged conversation. The woman next to Chocho— Ah, that must be the infamous Suzie, considering that she and Chocho are holding hands and giving each other these gooey-eyed looks every few seconds. Once in a while, he sneaks his other hand to either glide it over hers, or to play with the few strands of dark blonde hair that escaped her high bun. They look so… I don't know, so at peace and happy together, it makes me wish Kieran and I could be the same. This open about our relationship. This optimistic we'd have forever together.

"Hello, Earth to Nonie. Anything specific you're having an eye out for?" Chase waves a hand in front of my face, and I shrug, then fold my hands behind my back. Forever isn't an option in our life.

"You know, just really enjoying being part of history. Golden Star and everything, you know?"

"Yeah, right." Chase grumbles. "Sure. You activated a protective field around the stage before you dematted down. Quite sneaky, and quite sophisticated—and no, I didn't tell anybody," he adds when he sees me grimace. "But aside from that, you're right, I'm probably nervous for no good reason. Other than that you are here. For no good reason. Like last time, when somebody shot at Kieran. No good reason at all. Whatever happens, happens, right?" He says it in a sarcastic way, but it strikes home. *Whatever happens, happens.* In the end, Chase is right: my actions here are not going to prevent what's going to happen. Kieran is going to die. All I'm doing is giving him a few more months. Acid rises up my throat. A few more months. He should have had years. Decades. He should've gotten old, like Chase and Zio. Like the Kieran I saw with the other Nonie. The *Admiral* Wildason.

I'm doing nothing to help him in the grand scheme of things, and that futility, it's mind boggling. Why kill him a mere few months before his official death? How sick does somebody have to be to steal a dead man's last weeks?

Forcing my hands to stay calm and relaxed at my sides instead of balling into fists, I shrug. "Don't be nervous. Unless you're worried about Kieran forgetting his speech, then go ahead." I wish I could unload some of the burden placed upon my shoulders. *Watch out for Kieran, Chase, somebody wants to kill him.* So few words, such a big impact once spoken. I sigh. Won't be responsible for changing their reactions and the timeline.

I got this.

I hope.

Chase snorts. "Kieran forgetting his speech? I don't know if he even wrote one. Until a few days ago, I thought he wouldn't accept the medal. Shows what I know."

"Guess he had a change of heart."

"Guess so."

Comfortable silence falls between us as we both let our gaze roam across the audience. People are settling down; the ceremony is about to begin. Besides a disturbing amount of *Humanity First*-banners, I've seen about ten white haired men already, the discovery of each sending my heart into palpitation-territory, but for none of them PADdy vibrated. Meaning, none of them were Mashaule. Also meaning, it's time to crank it up.

I wave with one hand. "Excuse me. I'll be mingling and enjoying this historic moment."

He lifts one eye brow. "Watch out for your side. Zio tells me you're barely holding together."

"Pfft. Exaggerations. I'm as good as new." And with that, I slip away from Chase and follow the little path between the rows to the outside of the seating area. Hey, Zio cleared me. I would prefer to not do any hand-to-hand fighting today, but if I'd have to, I could.

Turning away from most of the audience, I shield PADdy when I activate its screen and check on the Setayashi-scanner. While generally I'd call its silence a good sign, it does nothing to reassure me. What if I'm overlooking something? What if the Setayashi signature changes over time, pun intended? I can't afford any mistakes, no matter the protective field around the stage.

The audio system springs alive, bathing the arena in perfect surround sound as an admiral steps onto the stage. At his first words, the audience turns quiet, like they rehearsed it. *"Welcome, citizens. Welcome, fellow humans. It is an honor to see so many of you in this very place and moment to celebrate the achievements of a man whose name has been in all our thoughts for the last months. Without further ado, please let me introduce Captain Kieran Wildason!"*

The admiral steps aside, clapping his hands as the audience breaks out into applause and cheers. Thousands of voices scream his name, others *wooo* and whistle, but it all results in a beautiful cacophony of noise, all for Kieran. Large screens show the reactions on the other worlds, where people have gathered in public viewing areas, celebrating the occasion. Goosebumps erupt and run down my spine. It feels... momentous.

Kieran walks onto the stage, looking more than spiffy in his dress uniform. He waves at the audience as he strides across the stage, and I swear his mere presence charges the atmosphere. The *wooos* get louder, the applause turns thunderous. Kieran shakes the admiral's hand, then turns to the audience again, bowing, waving, being celebrated like a pop star. No trace is left of the man who had to be convinced to accept the medal.

Eventually, the admiral begins to speak, most likely realizing this, the hero welcome, could go on for much longer than he thought. *"Captain Wildason, it is a pleasure to be here today with you. For the last months, you have been an inspiration—"*

PADdy vibrates. Such a small, soft motion, such a jolt to my system: Mashaule. Relief washes over me, chased away by a good old serving of adrenaline. I made it to the correct point in time. I can protect Kieran. I must protect Kieran.

Angling my body, I look at PADdy's screen: high up. Mashaule is all the way up. Dang it. No time to lose. I had assumed, falsely, obviously, that Mashaule would choose a location closer to the stage for an easier kill, but maybe he prioritized his way out of the venue over a secure shot.

Either way, it doesn't matter as long as my shield holds.

Like a madwoman, I sprint up the stairs at the side of the arena, taking two steps at a time. PADdy shows him all the way up, possibly hidden in the treeline behind the top rows.

"... so many families have faced hardship at the hand of our enemy, but also felt the support by you and your—"

Faster, faster! If Mashaule shoots, realizes Kieran is protected, and jumps to whenever in time, I have absolutely no chance of ever finding him again. So, I force my legs to speed it up and ignore the burn in my side as I shoulder past several men and women standing on the stairs who didn't find a seat. It slows me down, but I'm three-quarters up already, although it's steep, which doesn't exactly help me. Neither does having been stabbed a mere few days ago or my weaker left leg, but it's not as if I could change either. My heart hammers, not so much from the exertion, but from the fear of failing. I need that bastard in custody. Mine, preferably.

PADdy gives me a double haptic feedback: Target has stopped moving. Not slowing down the least, I glance at the screen. Yes! He's close, not even fifty meters, his position circled to be in the treeline behind the audience, a tad to the left from me, in the center.

"... an absolute pleasure to pin this to your chest: The Golden Star of Combat."

The audience erupts into cheers, applause, and even foot stomping, just as I reach the top of the stairs, darting to the left. If Mashaule plans to shoot Kieran when he's at the podium for maximum effect, it can't be much longer.

Behind the last row of seats is a walkway, maybe two meters wide, framed by a hip-high wall on the other side keeping the vegetation—trees, bushes—growing on its other side in check.

"Thank you, Admiral. It is an honor—"

There! In a tree, a mere twenty meters away from me, climbed up to the first thick branch sprouting off the trunk about three meters up, Mashaule clings to the limb, peering through the scope of a rifle lifted to his shoulder.

My heart stops, no matter I have the protective field in place, no matter he can't harm Kieran. The sheer visual image is enough to bring nausea to a rise—and so is the realization I might not make it.

"—but it also hurts me to have been considered for this honor. It means I killed thousands of beings, and frankly, I'm not okay with that. I—"

Kieran has begun his speech, and I swear I see Mashaule's finger curl around the trigger.

My decision is made in a heartbeat. Coming to a dead stop, I draw my weapon and aim it at the branch Mashaule is clinging to. Deep breath in—and a slow, controlled exhale. Aim—

I squeeze my trigger. A yellow beam streaks through the air, slicing the base of the big branch mostly away from the tree in a shower of sparks. Mashaule's weight breaks it the rest of the way. A startled grunt breaks from his throat as gravity gets an unexpected hold of him. The rifle falls from his grasp as he tries to avoid a fall—unsuccessfully so.

Mashaule crashes down onto the walkway, half on the branch, half under it, his rifle flung somewhere behind him. The people closest to him in the last rows of the audience jerk around at the sound of his impact, surprised gasps and a few yelps coming from them. Several spectators scramble to get over the back of their seats to help Mashaule—

"Freeze!" I yell and point my weapon at Mashaule. Funny enough, the men trying to help Mashaule do as I say.

Mashaule, on the other hand, doesn't.

Face distorted into an ugly grimace, he reaches down at his thigh—

I fire at the branch, missing him by mere inches. On purpose, I might add, since I want Mashaule alive and his portal-thing in one piece.

Anger fuels me as I stride closer, my gun steady and aimed at Mashaule. The warning shot worked; he's holding still. Luckily for me, his hate-filled glare won't kill me.

Some guy swings one leg over the back of his bench. "Is that really necessary? We are a gun-free colony. That man—"

"Is none of your business," I hiss, never breaking my stride. Thank you for the *Zivilcourage*, but it's misplaced. Mashaule doesn't need protection. The timeline, on the other hand, does.

The man huffs. "Look, I know you're wearing a uniform, and I get it, but that man is a civilian." He swings the other leg over the seat and reaches for my outstretched gun.

Oh, hell to the no! I swerve, but that slight movement, it costs me.

Mashaule, not one to waste a chance if it opens up, draws another gun from somewhere close to this thigh and fires.

Pew! Pewpew!

Call it instinct, call it reflexes, but I know Mashaule is aiming at the guy whose well-intentioned deed is about to blow up in his face. That's the only reason why I'm barely fast enough to push him out of harm's way. Tackling the guy with the speed of a professional footballer, we both hit the mesmerizing sparkling floors with a grunt.

"What—"

"Stay down, dammit!" I shove the guy into the shoulder as I pop up with my knee in his stomach, then jump up to my feet, aiming my gun at Mashaule—

Who shows me the middle finger of one hand, while pressing the button on his oval disk with the other. It sputters, its light flickers—

No!

Icy cold terror sweeps through my veins. No!

Bursting into the fastest sprint of my life I dash toward him. My skin prickles, like before a jump, as if time were getting a hold of me, Mashaule's image flickers, flickers more—

And flickers out of existence.

He's gone.

I'm not.

Skidding to a halt, I stare at the spot right next to the broken-off branch where Mashaule just stood a moment ago.

The guy I saved from an untimely death scrambles back to his feet, judging by the sounds with the help of some other people. They mutter and complain under their breath, but don't approach me. Don't challenge me. Did they even see what happened? Maybe they think he dematted out of here, and he kind of did.

"Soldiers. Typical. Shooting, shooting. Bringing their conflict to us."

"Yeah. Just because they're wearing a uniform—"

I swallow hard. It wasn't me who brought this drama here. All they see is a uniform. They don't see the responsibility behind it. The dues paid.

They also don't see the pallor on my face. The wide eyes.

Nobody notices my fast breathing, or that it's way too shallow to get enough oxygen to my lungs.

With wobbly knees, I walk past the trees and to the next flight of stairs leading toward the stage. When my legs can't support me anymore, I sit down, barely ten stairs from the top.

Mashaule's gone.

Gone.

And I have no idea to where or when.

He could be killing Kieran tomorrow right now, for all I know.

And, once again, I'm stuck here in the past.

"—I see your signs reading Humanity First. I hear your calls to protect humanity above everything else, and I get it. But if we don't reach out a hand to others in friendship and support, we're going to be very alone at one point. We—"

An older couple, in their late sixties, seated at the aisle close to me hugs. Like everybody else besides me, they're standing, mesmerized by Kieran's words.

I just wished they'd changed something.

Just like I wished I'd not failed at securing Mashaule. Again.

Chapter Twelve –

FUNK AGAIN

The *Pioneer* is cruising through uncharted space. Well, uncharted at this time. Very much charted, and very much inhabited by Quaneez in my time.

We soar past nebulas, meteorites, suns—it's all very pleasant to watch from behind the window in Kieran's quarters. Very pleasant, and very distracting.

It's what I need.

Kieran is on the bridge, and even though he didn't want to leave me alone, I made him go. Wouldn't that be ironic if I came here to save the timeline, but ended up altering it by keeping Kieran from his duties?

But then, I wouldn't call it saving the timeline. *Saving* implies an active involvement on my part, and I don't see that at all. I did nothing but let myself get pulled along by Mashaule back at USEF Central Jail. Okay, I made the decision to follow him when he jumped on Ortega One, but again, I merely followed. I myself didn't do a thing. Didn't even catch him. Add getting myself stabbed and ending up here—at a completely useless time—without any means to jump to anywhere or any idea, where or when Mashaule might be or try to kill Kieran again…

Yeah.

I'm not feeling well, and hint-hint, it's not, like Kieran thinks, from the remainders of said knife wound to my chest. The physical wound has healed, the psychological trauma my failure caused on the other hand…

Not.

For the last two hours, I've been standing right in this spot, glued to the view, and while it's pretty, it's nothing I haven't seen before.

But it's good.

Mind-numbing.

I was so happy when I arrived on the *Pioneer* the last time, after Kieran saved me from jail for shoplifting. Seeing him, even though we had only been apart for a few hours-slash-forty-years, was thrilling, and I was so optimistic. Build a Setayashi device and jump through time? Sure, let me get right to it. And I mean, the other Nonie has one, so must be a piece of cake, right?

I huff.

The only reason I could build a portable Setayashi *scanner* is because every ship even in this time period has full-scale Setayashi scanners. They're massive, far from portable and easily twenty times the size of the scanning equipment on modern ships, but the underlying technology is the same. Engineering has improved in the last forty years and Admiral Conolly is an engineering nerd. The information he stored on PADdy has been helpful times a million.

But when it comes to getting stuff done myself, like build a Setayashi radiation *emitting* device, I'm useless, especially when I'm on my own. Again, can't really ask Zio to help. Knowing how to initiate a time-jump is a biggie, so I better not share it.

Yeah. I'm absolutely, freaking use—

The doorbell chimes, followed right away by the doors opening. "What's up, traveler?" Chase walks in, smiling from ear to ear, a small fabric pouch in one of his hands.

"Hey." I add a small wave and turn back to the window. Sorry, that's all I'm capable of today.

Chase grimaces. "Well, a good morning to you, too. Excuse me if I'm happy to see you." He drops the pouch onto the couch table and comes to stand behind me, twisting his body to the left and right, checking out the view. "Anything exciting out there?"

I shake my head in slow-motion. "Absolutely nothing." Both our reflections show in the window, his tall, but not that much taller than me, thanks to my Magellan genes.

For a moment we both stay silent. Then, Chase cocks his head. "You're stuck."

I whip my head over my shoulder. "What?"

"You're stuck. You look like someone who's been thinking hard and can't come up with a solution."

Well. I open my mouth and close it again. Part of that assessment is correct. I'm stuck, in more ways than one. And I can't come up with a solution either, but I can't say I've been thinking hard. I've been wallowing in my misery is more like it. I shrug. "Maybe."

"Yeah, yeah, keeping the timeline intact, I know. You don't have to give me any details, but just looking at you I get the general direction." He moves his hand up and down at my face height. "I'll go out on a limb and say that since you came back with a knife in your chest and your mood hasn't improved since Kieran's ceremony yesterday, things aren't going so well for you."

I cross my hands in front of my chest. "Fair assessment."

"To be honest, I can see why that stab wound would throw any plan into chaos."

That's giving me too much credit. I didn't even *have* a plan.

When I stay silent, Chase tilts his head and smacks his lips. "Can't be easy to almost die for the second time."

I whirl around. "Second time?" Why does *Commander* Conolly even know about the first time?

Chase flinches. "Oops."

"*Oops* indeed. So, you know." I cross my arms in front of my chest. It's not a secret-secret. Not to him, anyway. *Admiral* Conolly is going to find out from Dad—

I close my eyes. Never mind. Admiral Conolly probably knew about my kidnapping before it even happened. Case in point, Chase rubbing his neck, looking at me sheepishly.

"Hey, don't be mad at Kieran. He can only talk to Zio and me about you, and believe me, while we try our best to not have him do that all the time, sometimes he's got to get stuff off his chest. So, your kidnapping story came out. Didn't sound like fun."

"No. No, it wasn't. Neither was getting stabbed—which, you're right, is a problem for me."

"In the sense of that you were close to dying? That it still affects you?"

I wish it was that simple. I chew on my lower lip. "No. Yes. Both. It's a wake-up call for sure, but…" I shake my head. Getting this close to being killed by Mashaule isn't what worries me most. It's in the past, quite literally, and I can deal with it. The true problem is what me being stabbed indicates. I meet his gaze in the reflection. "Since I was nine, I never wanted to be not in control. That's why I trained, to be ready. I joined USEF to be ready. And yet, in the moment…" In the moment I was too arrogant, too sure of myself, and I ruined the opportunity to secure Mashaule.

"In the moment things were different."

"Mildly put, yes." I acted like an amateur. Like a freakin' amateur when I got stabbed, and then again when I let Mashaule escape yesterday. Maybe I should just shoot him and deal with being trapped in this time later. Maybe I shouldn't care about his death. It wouldn't be an innocent person dying, let's put it that way.

Chase tilts his head, crossing his arms like me. "Have you thought about that without your training you wouldn't even have gotten this far?"

I cut my eyes at him, remembering we're talking about the stabbing, not Mashaule leaving this time in front of my very eyes. "I got stabbed, Chase."

"But you didn't die. And, while I neither presume to know what happened, nor do I want to know any details, but I assume you didn't just get into a bar brawl. Whatever the reason for the fight, was it worth it?" He regards me with earnest sincerity, his blue eyes staring right into my soul.

Was it worth it?

Young Kieran survived, because the other me survived to save him. Even yesterday wasn't a failure, not a complete one at least. Kieran wasn't shot. I lower my chin in a slow nod. "A hundred percent."

A small smile plays at his lips. "Then it's a win. You took one for the team, but you're alive. It seems to me that you're looking at things from the wrong angle. It's not a failure. It's a win. Just disguised itself a bit, you know. And the last thing you should do is give up on yourself." He reaches out and tousles my hair until I swat his hand away.

"Stop, it, you—"

Chase evades my half-hearted defense, takes me in a playful headlock, and noogies me until I burst out laughing. "Okay, okay, you win. I win. Whatever, everybody wins!"

He lets me go, straightens his uniform and peers down at me with soft eyes. "That sounds better, Lieutenant. And now chin up, stop deserting yourself, snap out of this funk, and get to work. Whatever that work may be—and no, I don't want to know."

I blow out a puff of air through pursed lips and tighten my ponytail again. "Okay. Okay. Will do. Can do." I pause. "Chase?"

"Yeah?"

"Thank you. Sometimes things get complicated. Outside perspective helps. It's just hard to come by."

"Any time." He holds up a hand, then grabs the bag from the coffee table. "Zio sent me to drop this off. That stuff was in the pockets of your bloody, dirty, and completely ruined clothing. We kind of forgot about it. Priorities. Oh, and we didn't even peek. Am kind of proud of us." He winks and throws the bag over to me. "Kieran will be back in a few hours. Make yourself useful."

And with that he turns around and leaves. Make yourself useful. Right he is. Question is just, how? It's not as if I'd had a mind-blowing idea in the last five minutes. I sigh and open the pouch, reaching inside. There's my scanner. And—

I pull out a data disk.

The data disk.

The disk *she* gave me—that I gave myself at the raspberry fields.

I had completely forgotten about it.

Hope surges like a dam had burst. Why would I give myself a data disk if not with important information on it? Clearly the raspberry-me was older than me—she had been where I was, or else she wouldn't have known where I'd be, and why.

I facepalm myself. I should've seen it. She's the sign that I won't be stuck here forever, but that something will happen that gets me to use my time-travel skills, or else older me couldn't be jumping through time, disguising herself as a medic and saving Kieran.

And maybe, just maybe, this will help. I close my fingers over the data disk and rush over to the desk, hope fueling me as I shove the disk into the reader. "*Pioneer*, transfer data to PADdy. Security protocol Nonie Alpha Echo Three."

"Acknowledged. Transfer complete."

I tap onto PADdy to access the data she gave me—

And suck in a sharp breath.

Sun and Stars, I might've just saved myself.

Chapter Thirteen -

GOODBYES

Amazing what a difference a day can make.

Yesterday around this time I was frustrated, hopeless, and more or less defeated by my own inactions, and now…

I whistle a tune as I walk down the *Pioneer*'s A-hallway toward the bridge. Now I have a Setayashi-emitting device and a plan. Thank you, future me. I'll pay the favor forward. Well, backward. But either way, the schematics helped. I wonder where I got them from. Maybe I got back to the other Nonie and got it from her? Or, we'll come up with something similar in our timeline? Mashaule? I guess I'll find out eventually. Maybe I've got to work on my patience.

Patience. A heaviness settles over my heart. Patience is tough to come by in the game I'm playing, and it's an odd bird. I might see Kieran again in a few hours—or never. And what if Mashaule jumped to before Kieran and I met? When he was at the academy, for example? Now, that would be a whole other mess to handle.

The heaviness turns into lead chains around my heart, but I refuse to let them strangle it. Self-pity and anxious worrying doesn't suit me, I've learned. I'm an active officer of the USEF's FBTI, well-trained, and outfitted with a few extra-features thanks to my Magellan heritage. All I need to do is get into the groove and figure them out. And I will.

I curl one hand into a fist. I will.

And once I do, Mashaule won't know what hit him. He might have the upper hand when it comes to the finer details, but heck, two can play this game. And I'm going to beat him at his.

If he hasn't figured out yet that I'm trying to track him down, I'd be surprised. Who knows what he knows about me, what the upstream-power has told him. And who knows what he can do, maybe he kicked me out of the time stream on purpose and landed himself at sometime else. It could be any time, literally. He could try to kill Kieran as an infant. Kill his dad or mom. Maybe I got quote-unquote lucky that he stayed within a certain range of time where I have backup, i.e, the *Pioneer*.

Or maybe… Or maybe his disk isn't as perfect as I thought it was. Honestly, it's been bugging me since the raspberry farm: why didn't he go back ten minutes and try a do-over? He called for an extraction before he vanished, maybe he wasn't precise enough and the upstream power sent him to the time of Kieran's medal ceremony? There though, his disk sputtered and flickered, not like before, where its light shone strong. Is it not working well, maybe? Made for a certain amount of jumps? Needs some charging? Some TLC?

I blow a raspberry to myself. All good questions, even though the answers don't really matter at this point: I lost Mashaule, and no matter what, he'll be on high alert after I spoiled two assassination attempts of his, and needless to say that's not going to make things easier for me, even if I knew when and where he was.

So, I'm changing my approach. In Krav Maga, they taught me to never fish for the end of the stick when disarming somebody. It moves too much, too fast and unpredictable. Instead, go to the source: grab the arm, and slide to the stick from there. And since I can't find Mashaule in this vast land of time and space, I'll have to go to the source. Somebody upstream has been in contact with Mashaule—and most likely still is. Somebody is telling him when to jump to, somebody is calling the shots, and that somebody he seems to contact before the jumps. *Extraction, now*, Mashaule yelled at the raspberry farm.

I want to know who the person is and what their game plan is. I want to listen in, if possible. Want to know which locations in time-space Mashaule is going to be sent to. It would give me a huge leg up. There must be a way to scan that thing or take it apart and find out its frequency, for a lack of a better term. I doubt communicating through time is like old-fashioned radio with hundreds of channels. It must be a fixed connection between the sender and devices, or else the signal would get lost in the time-space continuum.

Right?

That's the theory at least.

Ergo, I need to at least get a good look-slash-scan at that communication device he's using, and since I have no clue when Mashaule is, I've got to find said device or at least something similar in some other time, so I can get the quote-unquote frequency from that. Thanks to medic-me, PADdy has a few new tricks up its sleeve I'm eager to use, and I know just where to go. There are two points in history I know for sure the upstream powers have intervened in: my kidnapping and the events at Alpha Rubrum.

In the first, I already know from Taro Magona that I was saved by *an operative of the FBTI,* meaning, me. I brush my finger over the ring Kieran gave me. She/I could've said something, you know? Anyway. The kidnappers vanished from their jail cell, which drove my dad nuts. They must've had some kind of device, like Mashaule. I'm a hundred and ten percent sure all prisoners are searched before they're locked away, so however Mashaule got to hold on to his—

I stop dead in my tracks.

Idiot.

Idiot me.

I know how Mashaule got his. The older ensign we ran past in the hallway—he'd brought him food, food Mashaule hadn't touched. I bet it wasn't just his dinner. I bet it was the communicator-Setayashi-device thing as well.

A shudder brings goosebumps to my neck. The Temporal War… It runs deep.

I blow out a puff of air. Okay, thinking. In the second case, at Alpha Rubrum, something happened to the *Eclipse*'s systems and logs, which were altered, according to Zio, with the same particles he found on my shuttle, which Mashaule altered, presumably with help from the future to make me blow up the Quaneez' planet.

So, I should be able to find out something about the future in either location. I thought about jumping to the future—but heck, no. I don't know when, I don't know where, I don't know anything about it. That's not going to happen. Ended up in a different universe once already, so no, thank you. At least I have a rough road map for the past. I'll stay out of the future if I can.

PADdy vibrates once and I glance at the display.

SED fully loaded.

Nice. I expect it to take about ten minutes to recover after a burst, which is pretty good, I feel. And PADdy should still be able to give me my newly programmed landing scan, even while charging the SED. I did well over the last hours.

Now I need to do well when I jump, or my one beacon of hope to keep Kieran safe will go *poof.*

I arrive at the bridge, the doors automatically opening for me.

"—you had said next month, so no, I don't think we need to do that." Kieran sounds annoyed.

"But sir, all they want is a little inside story—"

"No, they don't, Lieutenant. All they want is gossip."

Nobody pays me any attention when I enter the bridge. Everybody's focused on Kieran, framed by Chase and Zio, and Chief Engineer Alyssa Lopez in front of them, a pleading look on her face.

"Captain, gossip is part of business. People want good news. Good stories. And hearing from the Hot—"

"If you say Hotshot Trio, I'm kicking you right off my bridge." Kieran's brows lower.

Chase lets his shoulders droop forward. "Man, I like that name."

"I also can't say I'm personally bothered by it," Zio adds.

Kieran groans. "Guys, you're not—" He notices me out of the corner of his eyes. "Nonie. Thank the universe, save me."

Coming to think about it, I don't know what exactly my cover story for Code Magenta and the senior bridge crew is, but the way Kieran's face lights up when he sees me, the way his body language changes from closed-off to open and welcoming, I'm sure they can come up with assumptions.

I gesture at Alyssa, her PAD in her hand. "From what? An interview?" Walking past Chase, I come to stand next to Alyssa. "I can tell it's going well."

Somebody snickers in the back, probably Chocho.

Kieran rolls his eyes. "Chocho, I heard that. Tell your wife I'm sorry, but you didn't behave. Nightshift on Saturday."

"Aww, man." The other man groans, then clears his throat. "Uhh, I mean, yes, Captain, sorry, Captain."

Alyssa wiggles her PAD. "It's just a few questions and a couple of pictures, since the captain nixed the idea of a two-D-hologram already." She points to something on the screen I see she crossed out.

"Hey, I really don't need to be a holo in people's homes. I've got a job to do, and this is not making it easier."

"Captain—"

I look up from the PAD— And holy Sun and Stars, recognition strikes.

The way they're standing there, Chase to Kieran's right, one foot up on the little step the captain's chair sits on, Zio to the left, hands crossed behind his back, and Kieran leaned forward—I know this. There's an image burned into my memory just like it.

I take the PAD from Alyssa. "Captain? If I may?"

Something in my voice makes him pause.

Cock his head.

Swallow.

"One picture," he says, and brings himself into the exact position I knew he was going to be in. After all, I've only looked at this very same picture about a million times.

I lift the PAD to take the picture, my heart skipping a confused beat. I don't know if it will ever make it into whatever news outlet, but I know it'll make it into a frame, to be hung over the entrance to Admiral Conolly and Upinga's simulation room. Without this picture... I dunno. It fixed my soul more times than I can count. "Smile."

No need to say it.

Kieran lets loose one of his trademark smiles, the one with the dimples, the one that gets me each and every time. His smile, the emotion that comes with it, is breathtaking to me.

I take the picture, then hand the PAD back to Alyssa.

She takes it and checks the photo. "Whoa. That's—" She looks from the captain to me and back. "—unexpected."

Kieran jumps up and out of the chair. "And that's all you're getting, Alyssa. Don't make me regret it. And Nonie, Trip, Zio—my office." He walks ahead, the three of us following like ducklings after their mother.

As soon as the doors have closed behind us, Kieran spins to face Chase. "Can you please make sure that picture never makes it anywhere?"

"Why? Camera shy? If I remember correctly, you had a blast posing for Chocho's wedding pictures."

"Because I officiated the wedding! Excuse me if I think having the power to marry two people is quite cool. That was my first wedding as a USEF captain, and it's different!"

Chase lifts both palms up. "All right, all right, no problem. Pity though, the picture seems to have been a good one."

"Too good. Do with it whatever you want, but I don't want to see it anywhere public."

"Sure, Captain." Chase sighs, but he knows when a battle is worth fighting, and when it isn't. "Could you at least let Chocho off nightshift?"

A mischievous smile sneaks onto Kieran's face. "I'll consider it." He looks over at me and his expression falls. "You're leaving." He says it calm, like a statement, not like a question.

"Yes." It comes out as a sigh.

"I guessed so. You have that look on your face."

I have a look for that? Anyway. "I wanted to say goodbye,

because…" I shrug. "Because you never know when it's going to be the next time." *Or if,* and while I don't say that, they all heard it.

Kieran glides a finger over his desk in thought. "We'll be ready for when you're back."

"Thank you." My voice breaks. This could be goodbye forever. We're not in a typical long-distance relationship where I can drop in whenever I want to. Every action comes with a consequence, and my actions here could alter the future. I clear my throat. "But I wanted you to be ready for when I leave this time." I look over at Zio, who gets the hint.

He takes two steps to the wall next to the door to the bridge and opens one of the drawers integrated into the wall. "Experience has shown that keeping the cocktail close to the captain is a wise plan of action." He takes out a medical pouch and nods at Kieran. "Since we know ahead of time, it won't be so bad."

Kieran blows out a puff of air through pursed lips. "I'm gonna be fine." His face has lost most of its color, calling him a liar. "But this visit wasn't long enough." Regret radiates from his body and rolls to me in palpable waves, hitting me right where it hurts.

Can't let that get to me.

"I know." I walk over to Kieran and wrap my arms around him, trying to convey all I can't say in my embrace. He snuggles into me, burying his face into the crook of my neck.

"I'll see you soon, okay?"

"I really hope so."

"And you'll watch out for yourself."

"You, too, please." Makes me feel like a hypocrite to say it, knowing the outcome of next year.

The biggest pity is that history will never know the role his early death played. That it saved billions of people.

We let go of each other, but his hand lingers around my waist. That touch, it reassures me. Gives me strength. Determination. Fate might be cruel to us, but I can make sure she isn't becoming overly cruel. I can protect Kieran from Mashaule. I can give him that year, even if I can't give him anything else.

His gaze shifts to me, ensnaring me with such intensity, it tears at my heart and rips it open. Crazy-insane emotions spill from it and rush through my body, all of them for the man in front of me. Regret. Hope. Sorrow. The strongest of them though lights me up, lifts me up, and builds me up.

I capture my upper lip with my teeth. "I—" *I love you.* The words catch in my throat. Why is it so hard to say? Why?

Kieran lowers his chin in a single, slow nod, eyes vibrant behind thick lashes. "Same here."

For one short, eternal moment, we savor the presence of the other. Then, I peel his fingers off my waist, weave mine in-between and squeeze once before letting go. It takes more than strength to tear myself away. Stepping into the center of the room I look at Chase, then Zio. "You ready?"

"We've got the captain." Zio pats his medical kit.

"I'm glad you found your mojo back," Chase adds with a little lift to his eyebrow.

"Me, too." I give everybody one last look. Feels final, somehow, but so far, I've thought that every time and fate has proven me wrong. Swallowing the lump in my throat, I lift a hand. "I'll see you, guys." But I also have to say, whenever I'll do this again—if I ever have the privilege to see them again in the past—I won't say goodbye when I leave. It's a major tearjerker.

Swallowing the lump in my throat, I step out into the hallway, their gazes follow me until the doors have closed behind me, adding more weight to my shoulders and reminding me of my responsibility to the timeline. To Kieran.

With three long strides, I step around the corner and palm my way into the conference room. Last thing I need is witnesses when I pop out of existence in this time. I take off my jacket and slide out of the large pair of pants I put on only for these few minutes, because… well, my outfit would've given away too much. I turn once, looking at my reflection in the window: Blue-and white uniform. Knee-high boots. One pip on my collar. I look like an ensign from a few years ago, which is exactly what I need if I want to blend in on the *Eclipse*.

I fold the clothing I just shed and place it on the table.

Here goes nothing. I slide my right hand into my pocket and press the button on my SED.

Bright, burning light bursts from my pocket, blinding me—

I focus on my destination: *USEF Eclipse.* Alpha—

Chapter Fourteen -
STUCK IN A HOLE

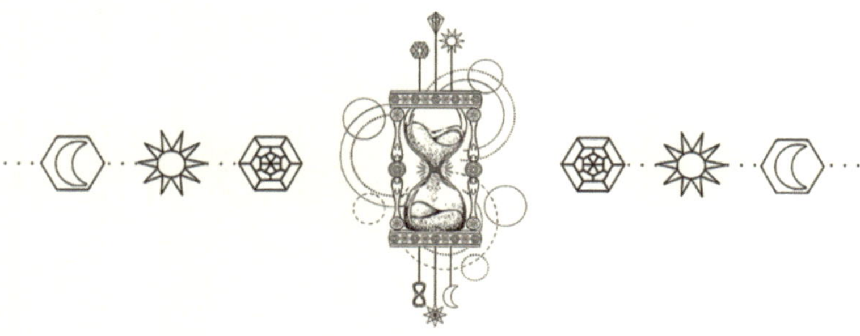

Somewhere, Somewhen

*D*ark. Cold. Hot. Bright. Dark. Tight—
Blur.
Confusing.
Past, future, present, all here, all mixed into one, whirlwind of colors and events—
Leftrightstraight—I can't tell where to—no, that way—
There! Can see my destination. Feels right.
Must go to—
A bright, shimmering cloud-thing rushes toward me.
Bump into it—
Soft and warm and—
Screams.
Screamsscreamsscreamscomingfromoverthere—
QuaneezQuaneezeverywhereeverywhereEVERYWHEREQUANEEZ—
KIERAN SCREAMS—
I hit the ground feet first and stumble forward, taking five or six

steps, before I catch my balance—

Whoa, what in the name…!

I bend over, supporting my weight on my knees, panting, gasping for air, heart racing, dizzy—

What in the name of the Universe was that? I shake my head to clear it and rub one hand across my forehead. Kieran. I heard Kieran scream. Like tortured, worse than I heard the last time I jumped. Goosebumps and shivers run down my back. He sounded so… afraid. Alone. Why the absolute heck do I hear nothing distinguishable, but Kieran screaming? Why is my subconscious making that up for me?

I shake my head. Can't make sense of anything happening during these jumps. To a degree, it feels like part of me knows what to do, while the other part is completely overwhelmed. Maybe it's an organ that I need to practice, only if I hear Kieran scream like that, I don't really want to. Guess my subconscious threw in some horror about the Quaneez to keep me on my toes.

Speaking of.

Priorities. I straighten up as if pulled by a string. I'm not on board the *Pioneer* anymore, which is good.

But neither am I on board the *Eclipse*, which is bad.

I groan. "Ugh. Of course, it wouldn't have worked out." Do people time travel and end up where they want to go or anywhere else but in remote areas? Maybe I should've taken classes with Nonie from the other universe. She seemed to have figured things out, while I materialized in the middle of a freakin' jungle. *A-freakin'-gain.* To be fair, it looks like it could be the same jungle I jumped to before, on the planet Kieran saved me from jail time. The plants look the same, the lianas, the moss on the ground, and I even see one of those scurrying, bug-eyed mammals from last time.

So, unless Alpha Rubrum has changed from what it looks like in our database, I'm in the wrong location.

"Super," I mumble to myself. I had two pinpoints: a place, and a time. Looks like I hit neither, if the distance between those two suns up in the sky is any indication to when I am.

But hey, on the upside: my Setayashi Emitter worked! Here's to small victories. And, besides that totally traumatic ending to my jump, I feel like I actually had some control. Was more awake, for a lack of a better term. It's weird, but I could *feel* my way through the timeline, could feel where I wanted to go. And given that other-timeline-Nonie knows how to maneuver through time, maybe I got that in me as well. I did better. Until I heard that scream, that is. That threw me off, and here I am.

"PADdy, landing scan." I tap the screen, waiting for the readout. I'm not walking around blind here. Heck, I'm not standing around blind here. The display lights up: no settlements, no biped-life signs, no Setayashi radiation besides my own, a few spots of Tau radiation, that's it.

I deactivate the screen. How can one live and go through Academy training and never hear about Tau radiation, and now it's popping up everywhere?

Anyway.

Drawing my SED from my pocket I check its battery status. Ten minutes until loaded, okay. Doable.

Something roars, not too far off, and I jump. "Sheesh." Yeah. Okay. That I didn't hear the last time I was here. With a few large strides around bushes and fallen trees, I walk toward the clearing at two o'clock. Whatever is growling, I'd like to see it before it attacks me from behind a tree.

I step out of the treeline— And jump right back, behind a large bush, entire body tense and coiled.

What the absolute— I had *no life signs* on my readings! And there's definitely a life form, one I'd have preferred to know about!

I peek around the foliage. A single, lone Quaneez has chosen the same clearing I did—and that Quaneez has definitely seen me, or else I wouldn't know why he'd stagger backwards, looking in my direction, and having his hands up by his face as if to protect himself. Surprisingly he isn't shooting—

A snapping sound— The Quaneez' right foot breaks into some kind of hole, and *slurp*, he sinks in down to his hip, struggling to free himself, trying to claw his way out, but nothing.

He's stuck.

I let go of a sigh of relief.

Heart hammering, I scan the area. No shuttle that I can see. And if this is the same planet I was on before—it's not Quaneez territory, no matter when we are. I think. What is a Quaneez doing here? Alone, apparently?

A knot lodges at the base of my throat.

I have less than ten minutes on the SED to recharge. Not much time at all, unless that Quaneez has friends around. Then, it could be the longest less-than-ten-minutes of my life.

Or, the last.

My stomach twists as I sneak one hand to my weapon. Better safe than sorry.

The Quaneez is grabbing for roots, grabbing for anything to pull himself out, motions frantic and panicky. No screams, no nothing—no shooting. Maybe he didn't carry a gun and didn't expect me, like I didn't expect him. To be fair, I wasn't here until few minutes ago.

Holding my right hand close to my holster, I keep an eye on the enemy.

Huh.

Something about him is odd.

I tilt my head. The hole is not that deep. Why doesn't he push out? How weak is that guy? And he's not the most coordinated either—

Another wild roar makes me twitch. "Holy Sun—" I whisper. That sounded big and close. I—

About thirty meters to my left a large feline-like furry animal prowls out of the forest and into the clearing. It bears some similarity to a lion in the way it moves with its stealthy soft steps, but it looks even more dangerous. Two large, curved tusks protrude from its snout, some kind of spikes sit on its back, and I'm not kidding, I can see its claws with every step. They're that thick.

With the slightest, slowest movement, I sneak farther behind the bushes. That guy I don't want to mess with. Fortunately, it hasn't seen me—but it has seen the Quaneez.

And the Quaneez has seen the predator.

For the shortest moment, he freezes, as if couldn't believe his bad luck, but then he breaks into frantic, panicky grabbing and rowing motions to pull himself out. His free leg is of no use at the angle he's stuck. Something in the way he moves—

Click. Ugh. Of course. "Sun and Stars," I whisper. "It's a kid!" Not an adult, a child! Now the uncoordinated movements make sense, why he looked so off—because the proportions are all messed up compared to an adult Quaneez.

A child. The whole-body armor threw me off, but then, the last kid I met inside the bunker also wore the armor. Like with the last one—or any Quaneez, really—it's impossible to tell whether they're male, female, old, young, or in-between for either or. The armor keeps those details hidden, if they even have them.

Unfortunately, I don't expect the armor to protect him from any kind of predator built like the one approaching him at this very moment. Those saber teeth will slice through it like a can opener.

My chest hollows out deeper and deeper with every step the lion-thing takes toward the Quaneez. The kid struggles, fights, scrambles, but to no avail. Only ten meters away from him the mammal speeds up—

Oh, screw it! I jump out from behind the bush, weapon drawn. "Hey, kitty!" I fire into the ground in front of it. Dirt bursts up from the energy impact, spraying everywhere and showering the mammal in debris. It jumps backward with a startled sound, while the Quaneez covers his head with both hands—

"Get away from him! Move! Move!" I run out into the clearing at the cat, making myself as big as I can, as loud as I can, as dangerous as I can. "Move, you annoying thing!" I fire again, to scare, not to hit. The beast recoils, but hesitates, probably weighing its options: the benefit of two juicy breakfasts versus the risk of one fiery blaster.

ZING! I fire again, again—

And the cat-thing gives up. Roaring once more, it turns around and sprints back to the forest, vanishing in-between the greenery, howling louder once its hidden. Complaining, I assume.

Which leaves me alone with the Quaneez child.

I slow down from my sprint to first a trot, then a fast walk, then to taking the next steps more carefully. I doubt he's alone. There must be adults. How would a kid end up on a planet by himself?

At least five other cat-things roar and howl, all of them quite close to the clearing.

Uh-oh.

Maybe that guy didn't complain, maybe he called for back-up.

And that child is in no better position than before, worse rather, I would say. He isn't even trying to get out anymore, but still covering his head with both hands, shaking like a leaf.

A louder, more menacing howl penetrates the air.

Well… I glance at my scanner. A few more minutes until I can jump.

Movement catches my attention in the corner of my eye. I whirl around—

"You! Stay away!" I fire another round at the cat, presumably the same as before, but crap, it's not the only one. Another one prowls forward from farther left.

And another one from farther right.

"Crap." My gaze darts across the underbrush lining the clearing as I turn a full three-sixty. Four cats. Four cats that I see.

Four cats, and one helpless Quaneez kid.

"Aww, dang it!" My decision is made before I've considered the potential consequences. If I hadn't materialized here and scared him, presumably he'd have never blindly stepped into this hole and gotten into this predicament. He's my responsibility, and I've got no time to lose. I dart forward, crossing the last meters to the child in a few seconds.

He doesn't scream, he doesn't try to escape—he just cowers deeper, shaking like crazy.

I kneel next to him. A whiff of decay and mold oozes off him, reminding me of the day in the bunker, when I freed Kieran. What is it with Quaneez and body hygiene? "Hey. Look, I know you're not happy to see me, but the tiger-things there are no fun." I holster my weapon, keeping my voice calm and even. "You probably don't understand me, because you guys never understand us, but just that you know, I'm going to grab your arms and try to pull, okay?"

Of course, I don't get an answer. Well, excuse me for trying.

I grab the kid by the wrists, and after a second, he gives in, letting me take his arms from his head. "Here goes nothing." I stand up and pullpullpull—

His leg moves out of the hole by a few inches—

And as soon as I let go, the progress is gone as he's sucked back into the earth.

Movement at my side—

I twist around, draw the gun and fire. "Bugger off, or I'll hit you for real!" The cat jumps back into the thick brush.

I really don't want to shoot them, but I will, if I have to.

"Come on, dude." Holstering the weapon, I fall to my knees and dig around his leg. The stench is so unbearable, I've got to breathe through my mouth.

A growl, a blur of motion—

"Crap!" Just in time I pull out the gun, fire—and hit one of those lion-things straight in the chest. It collapses, stunned, no more than three meters to my right.

"Crap," I wheeze again. Not cool. And there are at least five more at this point. We're outnumbered, in case that wasn't clear before.

Definitely gotta speed it up. "Let's go." I jump up to standing, grab the kid again and pull with all my might. He moves… moves… moves… and pops out of the hole onto the grassy surface like a cork from a bottle of Lubbeck's.

No time to celebrate, because those cats have just gotten their breakfast freed and served. Like they practiced it, or as if they communicated—which is totally a possibility, what do I know about this species—seven of them prowl out of the bushes and into the clearing. *Seven.*

My stomach cramps. I shoot one, I could be lucky and the others run. Or I shoot one, and the others attack, making that six fast moving targets I have to hit.

It's a gamble.

Step by step, I sneak back until I have the child behind me. "Stay where you are, kiddo. We're going to take care of those guys, okay?" I hope I sound more confident than I feel. Chances are I can protect us, but—

The first cat attacks.

I whirl in that direction, fire—

Missed it.

Fire again—

It collapses in a heap of fur and tangled extremities—

The other beasts ready themselves to attack in the universal language of aggression: bodies coiled, teeth bared, a low, menacing growl coming from all of them.

One of them howls out in a goose bump-inducing cry, and all six of them burst forward—

I wrap one arm around the kid, keeping him close, shoot at the first cat, hit him, shoot at the second, miss that one, shoot again—

ZINGZINGZING!

Yellow beams slice through the air, felling three of the cats at the same time—

ZINGZINGZING!

The last mammals collapse, two sliding several feet through the grass until inertia releases its grip on their bodies.

Silence hovers, only disrupted by my heavy breathing. A short moment of relief lifts the heavy weight of responsibility off my shoulders, at least until four adult Quaneez soldiers step out into the clearing.

Four.

Against one.

Out of the rain, into the storm.

A bundle of nerves form in my belly. My next breath in comes with a whiff of something sweet and flowery before it gets cut short. I don't want to fight. I don't want to shoot. I also don't want to *get* shot, please.

Ever so slowly, I lower my weapon and drop it on the ground, then brush a finger over PADdy and whisper, "Time to full charge." Angling my wrist, I glance at the display: two minutes.

Way too long.

A strong smell of soap wafts over, as if the Quaneez all just stepped out of the shower. They come closer, tension in every step, their weapons aimed at me, but not shooting.

I repeat: Not shooting.

In the great scheme of Quaneez-human relations, this is huge.

But then, I probably shouldn't let that go to my head, because I still quote-unquote have the kid. A trickle of fear moves through my veins when I give him a little nudge. "Come on, buddy. Go." The kid looks up at me, then the adults—and runs over to the closest approaching Quaneez, leaving me open for them to shoot at me without risking hitting their little one.

A risky move, but I'm outnumbered either way. Showing I mean no harm to them is the right step to take, even if it removes my one security, the kid.

The adult wraps the kid into an embrace, and no matter the species, no matter the armor, no matter we know nothing about these people, the body language is clear. Universal, I dare to say.

The adult looks up and at me, and as if on command, they all lower their weapons. Holy Sun and Stars…! I let go of a breath I didn't know I held. This moment is… momentous.

I cringe. I'm so eloquent. PADdy vibrates two times, translating to twenty seconds to jump capacity. Even though this is indeed momentous, I don't mind getting out of here. Who knows if they're just checking if the kid is in one piece before they decide they'd really rather see me dead than alive?

As it is, the adult in charge glides both gloved, armored hands over the child's helmet down to the neck, like he was checking for injuries. He makes a short twisting motion, and the child's armor begins to glow, bright, brighter—

"No!" I yell out, stepping forward, because I know what that means, I've seen it!

With a little *poof* I might've imagined, the kid's gone.

Gone.

I saved him from that lion-thing, and they killed him.

They killed him.

For what—because he misbehaved and was here alone? What could he possibly have done that warrants death as punishment?

Anger rises, together with tears.

What a waste. What a cruel, unnecessary—

PADdy vibrates once, then again—

And bright, white light shoots from my pocket. I focus on—

Chapter Fifteen -
ALPHA RUBRUM

This time it's different.
I feel where I am.
When I am.
Time passes leftrightabovebeneatheverywhere—
Blurry.
If I focus, I can see—
Screams. They're there. ScreamsscreamsscreamsKieran'svoicescreams—
No. No, no, no. Ignoring what my mind makes up for me. Focussing.
Alpha Rubrum. Eclipse.
Alpha Rubum. Eclipse.
Feels like it's close. Feels like—
Right there. Right—

I hit the ground in a crouch, the impact driving the air out of my lungs. "Ugh." I grunt. Hard landing—but I landed, and I didn't feel like a play ball in the timestream! I saw where I needed to go! If that isn't progress, I don't know what is.

Straightening up with a smile on my face, I look around—

Aaand the smile fizzles out.

Right.

So much for progress. Clearly, I'm not on board the *USEF Eclipse.* A groan breaks from my throat. Why can't I get this right—?

Wait.

Hope spikes up. Maybe I'm not that far off the target. Excitement shoots through me when I think I recognize where I am: a tundra-esque landscape, two moons, one sun—this must be Alpha Rubrum! Hey, that would be fantastic! Not bad at all, in the grand scheme of things! Now, if only the time is right… "PADdy, landing scan."

PADdy does its thing, then displays the verdict for me: 450 human life signs, scattered over a few square kilometers, and several thousand Magellan life signs within the same area.

Relief sweeps over me, washing away the weight from my shoulders. I've jumped to the right time and somewhat to the right location. Considering I never landed this precisely before, being on the planet the *Eclipse* is orbiting equals a bull's eye. I can work with that.

Plus, this time around doesn't look like I'm running into another unsuspecting Quaneez.

Pressure builds in my chest. I could have sworn we were off to a good start. Call me crazy, but the vibes I picked up from the adult Quaneez, for a lack of a better term, were good. Until they killed that kid, for exactly what reason? Not a huge leap, given that cold-blooded murder and the history of our people, that I'd been next.

A cold numbness seeps into my bones. This close. I was this close to making real progress.

Speaking of: Alpha Rubrum. Priorities. Taking a deep breath to clear my mind, I throw a closer look around and compare it to PADdy's readout. Huh. All inaccuracies with my jump aside, I don't think I can complain too much. Over there, at one o'clock from my current location, the outlines of houses are visible against the horizon, partly hidden by the rolling hills typical for Alpha Rubrum. Most life signs register within that area, and so do two shuttles. I cringe. I'd prefer to not have to walk into the thick of it.

A small smile tugs on my lips.

Which is why I won't.

A third shuttle registers much closer to me, about two hundred meters behind those hills at ten o'clock, with only four life signs close to it.

Four people versus several thousand. Not a tough decision to make. And if the mission logs saved on PADdy are correct, this shuttle is supposed to bring equipment down from the *Eclipse*, while Kieran will need those other two shuttles later today to save the Magellans with his *heroic acts* that got him promoted to captain.

I fumble the cargo pocket on my uniform pants open and take out a cap, embroidered with *USEF Eclipse*. Ah, the stuff one can do with time for preparations. I won't have time to access the *Eclipse*'s systems and delete myself out of there, so it's good, old-fashioned low-key disguises instead.

After straightening my uniform, I start hiking. The terrain isn't bad at all, no high bushes, not many trees, but mostly grasses and smaller plants. It's a quite beautiful planet—especially considering with this jump no Quaneez are popping up out of the blue—with great potential for colonization, if it wasn't for those seismic shifts.

Once I reach the top of the little hill, the shuttle comes into view, next to a small hut made from wood, one that definitely has seen better times. It must be one of the first ones the Magellans built when their scouts had just discovered this planet. It looks more makeshift than anything else, some planks or boards missing, leaving gaps in the walls. Wouldn't call this weatherproof at all.

Glancing down at PADdy, I get the confirmation: four people are in there, two humans, two Magellans, probably loading something they need to bring up to the *Eclipse* via shuttle, who knows. And sorry, guys, you'll have to wait with that, because I intend to borrow this one for a short trip.

I'm a mere ten meters away from the hut. For a moment I consider crouching and sneaking closer, but if they saw me, it would just be suspicious. Instead, I own my role. If I were an ensign here and had a job to do, I'd do it, period. *Fake it until you make it* has served me well so far. If they see me and ask… well, I'll give them my fake orders. I can wing it. This is USEF-stuff. My home turf.

I move a bit to the right and onto the little path coming from the main settlement, I assume, and speed up a tad. Just because I have a Plan B doesn't mean I want to use it.

The critical part comes now, passing the hut to get to the shuttle. At least this side is window-less, but the gaps in the side wall are still big enough they might see me passing. I hurry up. Almost past—

"I don't know, Bas. It's going to be tough."

That voice—

I stop dead in my tracks, heart skipping a beat. That voice…!

"Tom, you've got to stop fretting. It's going to be fine."

Oh, holy Sun and Stars—I know that voice too! Bas and Tom— Sebastian Grazer and Tom Thorburn! My future admiral and my dad!

"We're disobeying a direct order. And don't get me wrong, I'm not saying that it's not a risk worth taking, because it is, but we'll have to be real careful."

Slowly, I unfreeze. The pull to stay, to listen in, is unbelievably strong, but I can't. They're distracted, and I need that shuttle. I—

"So do we," a female voice chimes in. "You know how the Magellans think. Unions between our people aren't exactly encouraged."

"Kelia is right," my dad says. "We—"

Kelia.

My mom—my mom is in there!

There's no way I cannot take a look at the woman I've never met, never seen. It's my mom! One second is all I need, but I do need it. It's an opportunity I can't pass on.

My heart thumps so loudly they must hear it in there as I slowly turn to find a small gap between the wooden boards and peek through, angling my body so that as little of me as possible is visible to them.

"—have a plan for all of us, or else we're going to be in deep trouble," Dad continues. He's sitting on some kind of mattress on the floor, his back leaned against the wall to my right, his arms wrapped around the torso of a tall Magellan female nestled in between his legs.

That's my mom.

I swallow down the lump in my throat.

She looks so much more like me than I look like my dad. It's obvious. How nobody has ever asked me about my resemblance with Magellans is mind-blowing when I look at her. We're so much alike. So much. The hair, for starters, even though hers holds more of a shimmer, like Zio's and every Magellan's. But looking at her face is the real kicker: she could be my older sister, especially in this time, at her current age. It's such a striking resemblance, Dad must think of her every time he sees me.

Huh.

Maybe he had the double-whopper of shocks when Star Hopper had her one-on-one with him: A USEF-officer, who looks like his deceased wife, but turns out to be his time traveling daughter.

I kinda feel sorry for Dad for that one.

My mom gently caresses Dad's hands crossed in front of her stomach, a happy and content look on her face. So does Dad, by the way. Not only is he younger than I ever remember—duh, given that I went back in time—but also much more relaxed. At peace, even.

"I'm going to say it again. We're going to be fine." Grazer! My gaze jumps to the left to a young Admiral-then-Commander-Grazer! Like Dad he has made himself comfortable on a mattress, just opposite of Dad and... *Mom*, and like my parents Grazer is cuddling with a Magellan woman.

I never thought I'd use the words *Grazer, cuddling,* and *Magellan* in one sentence.

Grazer looks so happy; it puts the conversation we had during the conference with the Taro in a new light. He really lost big. Was it Mashaule's fault? Did he know? Blackmail, à la if you want to get promoted, this stops right now?

I make a mental note. There are a few conversations to be had once I return home-home.

My dad shakes his head. "I don't know, Bas. Easy for you to say. You know you're Mashey's favorite."

"Maybe, but I still don't plan on telling him. He finds out, my career is toast."

Ah. Well, that supports my theory for sure.

My mom squeezes Dad's hand. "We'll figure something out. For all of us." She gives my dad such a gooey-lovey look it should make any child embarrassed about their parents, but not me. It fills my heart and breaks it at the same time. They look so perfect together. And yet fate couldn't let a good thing be and killed her in childbirth.

Grazer sighs. "Yes, we will. We'll keep it secret, obviously, and I trust all of you. There's no reason why we shouldn't—"

A warm sensation, like a tingling down my spine, heightening my senses and quickening my pulse.

Steps to my left—

Barely in time, I flatten myself against the warm wood so *he* doesn't see me. As if my movement had caught his eye he stops, cocks his head to the side and… waits for a few seconds.

"Commander?" A young ensign has stopped a few steps behind *him*, waiting.

"Never mind, Winkler." *He* shrugs, dismissing whatever was going on, and continues to the door of this hut without another glance in my direction.

Whoa.

That was close.

He knocks and enters barely a second later. "Commander Graz—"

One of the women gasps, Grazer curses under his breath—

With a hasty move, Kieran closes the door again, pauses, then looks over his shoulder at the ensign. "Get the shuttle going, Winkler. I'm going to update the Commander."

"Aye, sir." The ensign gives one crisp nod, then strides toward the shuttle—the shuttle I need!

I creep deeper into the shadows, adrenaline spiking as a plan forms.

Kieran enters the hut, closing the door right behind him. Maybe three or four seconds have passed since he first knocked, but when I peek through the gap again everybody besides Kieran is still frozen in various stages of panic. *Busted.* Grazer looks nauseous. Dad is white as the wall, and my mom looks like she'd seen a ghost, eyes wide, mouth open, glancing from Dad to Kieran, an odd look on her face.

Kieran folds his hands behind his back, addressing Grazer. "Commander, I'll need the *Sunflare* to bring down some of the technical equipment. Ensign Winkler is starting her up as we speak." As if for emphasis the shuttle's engine's jump to life. "Also, your presence is required at the settlement for the evacuation process, sir."

Silence.

"Sir?" Kieran takes another step into the hut. Maybe that's what wakes Grazer from his surprise, but he jumps up, straightening out his uniform.

"You can't get that done alone, Wildason?"

"It's not about what I can or cannot get done, sir. As the captain said, this is an all-hands on deck operation, and the crew is struggling with limited guidance." He keeps his gaze glued to Grazer, ignoring both Magellans and my dad. Nothing to see here, people.

Grazer's Adam's apple moves with a swallow. "I'll be there soon, then. In the meantime, let the ensign take the shuttle and keep the show running, Commander."

"Will do, sir." Kieran turns swiftly, but before he can reach the door, Grazer calls his name.

"Wildason."

"Yes, sir?" He twists to face Grazer.

"Anything you'd like to comment on?"

For one moment the two men look each other in the eye, Grazer's jaw set tight, brows lowered, while Kieran is the epitome of cool professionalism. I know him well, and I can't read him. The moment's so thick with tension, I hold my breath.

"No, sir. Peaceful coexistence of any kind is the future of USEF, from my point of view."

Grazer's jaw relaxes the slightest bit. Something passes between them, something that makes Grazer nod once, and exhale heavily. "Thank you. 'Preciate it."

Kieran gives an acknowledging tilt of his head before he walks out and closes the door behind him.

"Sun and Stars," I hear my dad say. "That could've been—"

"He won't say anything. Wildason is a decent guy."

"Your lips to fate's ear—"

I've heard enough. Seen enough.

Pushing off the wall, I stay low and hidden behind a few bushes. Kieran walks straight over to the shuttle, its hatch open. "Ensign? You're good to go. I'd like you to leave right away, and please, we need the coil replacement, or else we're going to be in trouble."

The ensign replies something I can't make out, then Kieran taps the shuttle's hull twice. "See you in a bit." He turns and follows the little dirt road back to the main settlement. Once he's around the first corner, I dart out of my hiding spot over to the shuttle and then all but jump inside.

"Phew, made it!" I call out, tug on my uniform shirt and straighten my leisure cap. "Close call. Thanks for waiting. Closing the hatch!" I push the button. Let's get me out of view, people. The cap only does so much.

Up front in the cockpit, Winkler whirls around. He's a younger ensign for the time, early twenties. "Gee, you startled me! Wait, what— I thought I was supposed to—"

I make an annoyed disgruntled sound. "That's what I thought, too, but then Conolly said he needed the triple-magnetized spanner he doesn't trust anybody with, and here we are." I weave past the boxes and other items loaded into the shuttle to the cockpit. "At least it's a nice break, right?" Sitting in the co-pilot's seat, I give the other guy a smile. Come on, man, don't make this difficult. If he contacts Conolly or any superior officer to confirm, I'm toast. This version of him doesn't know me yet.

Winkler's frown is replaced by a sigh of relief. "Yes. There's only so much disassembling of cooling units I can do in a day." He enters the commands for liftoff, then grins at me, in a sly, mischievous way. "I don't think this shuttle flies very fast. What a bummer."

A laugh bursts free, powered by the joy of something going right for a change and the bonding that comes with the universal tendency to avoid manual labor. "By all means, don't push her too hard. We'll make it to the *Eclipse* eventually."

Winkler gives me a thumbs up, then engages the thrusters and lifts us off toward the *Eclipse*.

Here's hoping my lucky streak continues.

Chapter Sixteen –

ECLIPSE

USEF Eclipse, January 2ⁿᵈ, 2254, around noon

"Nah, that's fine, if I'm not back in ten minutes, you can go ahead, I'll come down with the next one. Thanks for the ride." I give Winkler a mock salute. Nice guy. Gotta look him up whenever I'm back home, want to see what became of him.

He grabs one of those boxes and carries it to a pile at the far end of the shuttle bay. "Don't make it too long, or it becomes suspicious. You can only play the system for so long when nobody's on board. I mean, even the chef's on the planet."

I know. "No worries, I won't sit out too long. A break's okay, but too much would feel unfair."

With one more nod to each other I leave him to do his work and walk out of the shuttle bay as if I belonged here. Wonder if Winkler will look me up as well and never find me. Probably not. Who cares about another ensign? Especially with the *Eclipse* soon getting a major staffing overhaul, when Kieran gets promoted to captain of the *Pioneer*, and Grazer doesn't.

And look at that, for that I do kind of feel sorry for Grazer.

Pulling my cap deeper into my face, I double-tap PADdy, and bull's eye: one human life sign, not far away from here, and a nice serving of Setayashi-radiation to top it off. There's Captain Mashaule in the engine room, and wherever he is, the communicator I need can't be far, or else I assume there wouldn't be any Setayashi-radiation.

Change of plans. Can't waltz into the engine room through the front doors, but I can sneak in from the side entrance. Admiral Conolly's schematics to the rescue. Maybe I do have to say thank you for those when I'm back.

Within a few turns I've made it to the engine room. The *Eclipse* is a nice ship, not as nice and new as the *Pioneer* will be, but still. It would be less spooky if it didn't feel so abandoned. It's too empty. Too silent.

The door to the jump-drive area opens automatically when I approach. I flinch with its hiss—either the *Eclipse's* doors are louder than what I'm used to, or it's the creepy silence emphasizing it.

Either way, I drop into a crouch on my way in and sneak to the right, behind the first consoles. Keeping my head low and angled to stay out of camera view, I check PADdy for the person who keeps eluding me. There he is, in the heart of the engine room, close to the jump reactor.

Crawling on all fours, I stay close to whatever I can find, which in engineering isn't tough. This area holds most of the engine's accessible parts, from pipes, access panels, connections, consoles, etc. It's busy and crowded with equipment, meaning, not hard to stay out of view.

My heart hammers like crazy as I sneak closer to where PADdy registered the human life. I glimpse around another corner and jerk back.

Mashaule, *Captain* Mashaule, is standing at the main engineering console, his back to me, an oval-shaped grey disk on the surface of the console next to where he's entering commands.

Yes! I knew it! With three taps, I initiate PADdy's scanning program. All I need is a frequency, please. Schematics would be nice, too, but overall just something, *anything*, I can use.

PADdy thinks and does his thing—

BOOM!

Uhh—the whole ship shakes and rattles, drowning out PADdy's vibration. *Firewall detected.* Ugh. That's annoy—

BOOM!

"What the—!" Mashaule grabs onto something to keep himself from falling. I'm luckier on all fours, but still bang my head against a pipe the diameter of my thigh.

BOOM!

"Shields up and holding at 54 percent. One ship in weapons' range," the *Eclipse*'s automatic voice sounds out.

The Quaneez! That must be the Quaneez, the attack where Kieran used the shuttle's shields to protect the crew on the planet! I still have a few minutes! As fast as I can, I enter the commands to hack the device's firewall and get me what I need. It's just a simple portable emitter, how hard can it be?

BOOM! BOOM!

Mashaule uses all ten fingers to hammer commands into the display. "*Eclipse*, reinforce shields, get me visual! Who the hell is firing on my ship?"

"That's none of your concern."

Holy Sun and Stars! I suck in a sharp breath. The disk lights up once in dark blue before a bright turquoise beam shoots out of its center, projecting the holo-image of a man standing next to Mashaule. And I mean, a *freakin' three-D-holo image* way beyond what I've seen before. It appears solid—I repeat, *solid*—and since that person faces Mashaule, I only see his back. Admiral Conolly would love this—the tech that must be behind it! Our holos project a two-D image, and it wouldn't matter if you looked at it from the front or behind, it would always be the same image, like a picture etched into glass, the same from either side. But not in this holo. Besides the blueish color, this one looks like a solid person. Gee, there's even a freakin' shadow from his projection! He's tall, but not very muscular. Still wide-shouldered. Short-cropped hair. Standing tall. Somebody used to giving orders.

I gawk at him, my mouth open. This kind of projection through space is one thing, but through space and time? Whom are we up against? I swallow hard. The level of detail is amazing. The man's dressed in some kind of uniform, and while I can't tell the color, because the whole image is blueish to a degree, I can make out every nook and cranny, every hook and button, heck, even wrinkles! I suck in my lower lip. If only I could see his front. There must be some kind of insignia, something that would tell me what organization we're talking about. Come on dude, turn around! I want to see your face! I want to know who the person is who wants Kieran dead.

My mouth is dry all of a sudden, because let's be real, this is the biggest step forward I've taken since I followed Mashaule into the past. It's progress. I'm making progress. And PADdy—

I check the screen and curse under my breath. Dang it! PADdy isn't getting through at all, there's some kind of block or interference. Crap, crap, crap. Not *now*, of all times! Letting go of a slow, deliberate breath—calm please, Thorburn, calm—I make a decision. Here's to plan B. If I can't have the data I need, at least I will take *something* from this encounter. I increase the output and enable recording for all spectral channels. Didn't come through time and space to be derailed by a stupid firewall, and for sure I'm not going to let this opportunity slide through my fingers! This is the man behind it all, the mastermind behind Kieran's murder, if I don't stop Mashaule.

Speaking of… Mashaule handles the other man's appearance really well. No gawking, like me, no surprise, no startling. I'd be surprised if he hadn't seen the man pop up solid before, or, maybe Mashaule has other priorities at the very moment, and I couldn't blame him. "None of my concern? There's a freakin' ship firing on mine—"

"They won't fire on you anymore. They'll target the colony."

Mashaule chokes. "The colony? I've got my crew down there, the Magellans! *Eclipse,* ready weapons—"

"Don't." The man holds out a hand, as if Mashaule were a dog and he told him to stay.

Mashaule freezes mid-word. "Excuse me? They're attacking—"

"They are. And for the greater good, some of the people on the ground must die. It is unfortunate, but necessary."

Hearing those words, spoken in that cold and uncaring tone… For once I'm with Mashaule. The captain's mouth opens and closes. "W-what did you do? That was you, wasn't it?"

"I did what was necessary to get their attention."

Something changes in Mashaule's expression, and he slams a fist onto the surface. "That's why you asked me to do the modifications from here and not the bridge! You didn't want me to hear the alert for the approaching ship! How dare you play me—"

"I dare because it's necessary." The disdain in the voice is palpable regardless of time and space separating its owner from us. *"This attack is one of many more to come, and it's part of the plan to improve the future."*

Improve the future? That guy is certifiable, for sure. How is the death of Mashaule's crew and the Magellans going to improve anything? And if he's only targeting Kieran, it seems quite the overkill, pun intended.

Mashaule hyperventilates, a vein popping in his temple as he takes in the readings on the display in front of him. "Who are those people? I've never seen a configuration even remotely close…" He shakes his head then clenches his jaw. "They're firing onto the colony! The Magellans have done nothing to those people!"

"That assessment lies in the eye of the beholder. Don't forget, you invaded their territory."

"Whose territory? There's nobody around for lightyears!" Mashaule makes a circling motion with his hand, and right he is. There still are no Quaneez colonies in this area of space. It's simply uninhabited and unexciting, besides a few nebulas and ion storms maybe.

The holographic projection of the man looks up to the ceiling with an exacerbated sigh. *"Ah, yes… The twenty-third century…!"*

"And either way, I've got to help them! *Eclipse*, bring us between—"

"Belay that." Sharpness is in those words, and it cuts Mashaule like a knife.

"I have to do something!"

"You have to adhere to our plan. I'll take care of the Eclipse's logs. Nobody will know you chose to not help. I'm sure you can find somebody to take the fall and distract from this situation." He pulls some kind of small, rectangular device from his pocket.

Ah, that must be what gave Zio his odd readings. How nice to get that cleared up.

The holo-man directs it at the same console Mashaule is working on, keeping his back toward me. *"Now move. Time is limited. You understand your orders?"*

"Yes." Mashaule grinds his teeth.

"Good." The man reaches out and *presses a button on the Eclipse's console!*

My sharp intake of air is drowned out by Mashaule's. "Your hologram can move matter?"

"Obviously."

OMG, I can't wait to show this to Admiral Conolly. He'll be out of his mind—a hologram moving matter! The technology behind such a task must be unbelievable! The energy it requires! I wonder how he's doing it. I glance at PADdy's display. Come on, get me something! Increasing the scanning output to two-hundred percent—

"There's interference." The holo-man lifts his device higher, adjusting something. *"What Setayashi-sources do you have on board?"*

Ice shoots through my veins, making my chest squeeze tight. Oh, crap! A Setayashi source? Me, that's me! I'm giving off Setayashi-radiation, and it's fair to say I'm trying to interfere with his device, since I'm trying to access it! Dabbing a finger at PADdy, I abort all actions and slowly scoot backward toward the door, throat tight. Time to get out of here, STAT. And oh, by the way, so much for that disk thingy being *just a simple portable emitter!* Lesson learned, time to retreat and get out of here. My heart hammers in my chest as I crawl back. Once I'm around the next console, I can stand up—

But I'm not fast enough.

Holo-man curses. *"There's somebody here! Lock the doors to engineering!"*

Mashaule stammers. "W-what?"

"Somebody is here! And overheard us, according to my proximity scan, so if you want your little non-involvement under wraps, you better lock engineering!"

I hear Mashaule gasp. Scrambling back, I get off my knees and into crouch once I'm behind the shield generator, scrambling forward on all fours. Almost—

"Doors locked and sealed!"

I hear a beeping signal from where Mashaule is working, and that beep, it makes my blood pressure drop. Doors locked. I can't get out.

My next breath comes in wheezy. I—

"Initiate a Level 10 containment field with subatomic stabilization! Do it! Now!"

Oh, crap, oh crap! No clue what the Level 10 field will do, but I bet he knows more than me, and I don't want to find out whether it traps me here or not. Not the way I wanted to leave, but there's no other way. I sneak one hand into my pocket and fumble for my SED.

Unfortunately for me, considering that Mashaule didn't seem to be the biggest fan of holo-man, he complies pretty fast this time around. Guess the difference is his own butt on the line. "*Eclipse*, set up a Level 10 containment field around all main engineering—"

Time to get out of here.

I press the button on my SED and focus on my next destination, the cave where my kidnappers held me. Must make that one work then.

PADdy vibrates, a bright flash of light—

Chapter Seventeen -
PAUSE

Somewhere, Somewhen

ime flies around me—no, swirls around me. Colors, scents, impressions, past and future surround me like a cocoon, brushing past me at a mind-boggling speed.

I catch glimpses of events I witnessed, gone too fast to quite register, replaced by other images and sensations. Focus on the cave, the kidnapping, come on. Cave, cave, cave—

Something tugs on my core, catching my attention—

And it's gone. The tugging sensation stays though.

I dig my heels in and throw my hands out.

The swirls of time, the tornado of events, slows down around me. Or, maybe I'm slowing down, who knows.

Kieran screams—

Shut it, subconscious. I slam both hands over my ears, but the bloodcurdling screams stay. Ignore it. Ignore it.

My heart beats like a drum on steroids, my breath comes out short. Distraction: Why am I breathing? Why is here, in this... realm, oxygen? Is there? Weird. I feel my body. And I feel good. I always feel whole in here, aside from those screams.

The time swirl picks it up, whisking me away from the screams, but also from the event that tugged on me.

Nu-uh. Focus. Maybe that's my First Sense. Maybe it's telling me something.

Again, I will myself to stop. To turn around. To look for the point in time that clearly wants me to stay. It's like I was learning to fly a shuttle. Everything's sluggish, but works.

There, like a beacon, an area of light glows brighter than the rest. Pulsates when I get closer, like it got all excited. It touches me on a molecular level and draws me in. I could resist, I could move on, but some inner sense tells me to not ignore it. I must heed its call.

Ignoring the swirl of colors and events around me, I reach out, focus on that bright spot in time—

—and slam into the ground in a crouch, the impact driving the air out of my lungs. "Ugh," I grunt. That hurt.

I blink a couple of times. It's pitch-black dark, the air smells of burned flesh and ash. The ground is cold, hard, and unforgiving. Cold be natural stone, or could be… pavement?

"What was that?" somebody asks.

That voice—

Somebody else sucks in a harsh breath through their teeth. Steps falter and stumble—

"Crap—are you okay? What's wrong?"

Really, that voice…! I blink, waiting for my eyes to adjust to the dark.

"N-nothing is wrong. Nothing. Actually, the opposite."

My heart roars to life and taps out a happy dance. I peer around the rubble I landed behind, a heap of bent out of shape metal, broken bricks, and splintered wood. The flickering of a fire somewhere throws enough light for me to make out the features of two men I'd recognize anywhere.

"Then why the heck are you stumbling and almost falling?" Chase doesn't sound happy.

"Because I feel… good. The pain is gone." Wonder swings in

Kieran's voice.

"Which pain? Oh— Oh. *That* pain. Why is it gone?"

Well, I guess the cat's out of the bag. Here's to hope the timeline had a reason to call me to this very moment.

I stand up and lift a hand. "That would be because of me, I'd say."

Like a whirlwind, Chase turns, weapon drawn, aimed at me. Its tactical light hits me straight in the face and I wince. "Geez, Chase!"

"Nonie?" He lowers the weapon. "You're… here?"

I wiggle jazz hands. "Surprise."

Thanks to Chase's light, I have an easier time making out Kieran's features. His eyes are wide, the same wonder shining in them I heard in his voice. The apple in his throat moves once. "Nonie." It's a mere whisper, but one loaded with emotion.

"Hi." I step past the rubble and debris. Only now do I notice this isn't the only pile. As far as I can see in the dark with the bit of their tactical flashlights illuminating our surroundings this place looks… destroyed. Must have been a town, but not much is left. Fires are burning in the distance, several, actually. It's unnaturally quiet as well. I swallow hard. "What happened—?"

Kieran darts forward and wraps me into his arms so tight, a little *ooomph*-sound breaks from my throat. "Nonie."

He snuggles his nose into my neck. His heart feels like it was about to jump out of his chest and into mine, that's how hard it hammers. And if I'd had any doubt that he'd missed me since whenever-he-saw-me-last, the way his fingers dig into my back would chase those doubts away. This hug, it speaks volumes.

"Kieran." I relax into his hold, let his scent wash over me, and his presence soothe my soul and strengthen our bond.

"Well, color me speechless." Chase shoves his weapon back into the holster, but keeps a flashlight shining at the ground. He scratches his temple. "And here I thought I'd have to wait forty years or something."

I stiffen in Kieran's arms. Forty years? When am I?

"So did I," Kieran whispers and brushes his lips across my cheek in the tiniest kiss. He loosens his hold on me. "I—"

A loud bang makes all three of us jump. In a flash Kieran whirls me around and brings me behind him, drawing his weapon and aiming it in the direction of the noise, and yes, I am a USEF lieutenant and yes, I can defend myself, but I do feel all lovey and gooey from his action. It's cute if a guy protects a girl, even if said girl can hold her own. Appreciate the sentiment.

For a few seconds we strain to hear, but no more noises break the unnatural, eerie silence.

Chase keeps his weapon drawn. "We should get out of here. I'm not convinced it's safe down here."

Sun and Stars! Not convinced it's safe? And they're *here*? Future-trained me shoots him a look from behind Kieran's back. "Maybe then don't bring the captain down here?" Because, in general, we're both interested in keeping Kieran alive. USEF's procedures and protocols haven't changed much over time, really. We're creatures of habit. One thing that has changed dramatically though is the emphasis on the captain staying on board the ship. The Quaneez Wars have taught us to keep the leaders safe as much as possible. Things tend to fall apart if we don't.

Rolling his eyes, Chase sighs. "Guess what I told him. But also, guess who pulled rank on me." He turns toward Kieran. "Told you it was fruitless coming here."

Kieran nods. "I needed to see it though."

"No, you didn't." Chase narrows his brows.

"Did," Kieran whispers, one hand reaching back to find mine. Louder he says, "We shouldn't demat into the demat room, Trip. I'm assuming we want to keep your arrival quiet?" He squeezes my hand twice.

I shrug, even though I doubt he sees it. "That would be appreciated."

The guys exchange a glance, and Kieran nods before Chase taps his Hablamate. "Conolly to *Pioneer*. Three to demat directly to sick bay. Notify Dr. Upinga to have a decon chamber running and drop us right in there when you're ready."

"Acknowledged," somebody's voice chimes through the Hablamate. Chocho, maybe?

I look from Chase to Kieran and back, but neither of them mentions Code Magenta. How early am I?

A prickling sensation engulfs my body—

—and the next moment I'm definitely not where I just was. The air in this small, windowless room smells clean, with a hint of sterility, the floor is clean and shiny, and the walls are held in a pristine white. If I hadn't known it, the medical bed and medical console make it quite obvious this is the medical bay on the *Pioneer,* and the man standing in front of us, in a full body decon-suit including hood and clear visor is no other than Zio Upinga, a medical PAD in his hands. As soon as his gaze falls on me, he raises an eyebrow. "Nonie. What an unexpected surprise."

"Technically, Zee, surprises are always unexpected." Chase flicks a finger against the other man's decon hood.

Zio ignores him with the patience of a saint. "I'm also happy to report that neither of you three are contaminated with anything worth mentioning, besides an incurable case of annoyance in Trip." He turns his PAD off and drops it onto a shelf to his right, then opens the seal on his decon hood and takes it off, electrostatic forces causing his dark black hair to stand up, giving him a faint halo. "Very much pleased to see you, Nonie." A smile comes with those words, and it feels real. Like home.

I throw myself around his neck. "Same here," I whisper. My mind is scrambled with the happenings of the last hours, days, decades, universes—I don't know. Everything, the pressure to protect Kieran, getting stabbed, my failure to apprehend Mashaule at the medal ceremony, that Quaneez kid attacked by the tiger-things, seeing my mom for the first time, the Upstream Holo Guy's unbelievable tech and my narrow escape—it all flows together into one big wave of events and breaks right over my head, threatening to pull me under.

In this very moment, I'm so, so tired.

Zio wraps his arms around me. "Hey there, Niece."

"Hey there, Uncle," I reply, burying my face in his decon outfit. Not the most glamorous way to say hi, but a good way. One that seals all the breaks in my armor and helps me stay upright. Zio has been and will be, depending on the point of view, one of my closest friends. And yes, even when he was an admiral and I was a simple, unsuspecting cadet and completely unaware of what lay ahead of me, he was a friend. So was and is Chase, but Zio is also my uncle. My mother's brother. By definition, our connection runs deeper.

Conolly coughs under his breath. "I'm not chopped liver."

I chuckle and let go of Zio. "Excuse me, I was of course saving the best for last," I say, and wrap Chase into a hug as intense as Zio's. It should feel odd to me, saying *hello* so often within such a short period of time and after I just left them, from my point of view. Yet, it doesn't. Coming back to the *Pioneer* and these guys always feels like coming home. Always feels right.

Chase squeezes me tight. "We were so worried about you, Nonie. We… we thought you died."

Those words, they suck that little bit of happiness right out of me and explain at least partially when I am: unless there are more situations where they thought I died I'm somewhen after the Battle of Balthar and before my visit when Kieran saved me from prosecution for t-shirt theft after my first jump back.

"I'm sorry," I whisper, deja vu striking hard, because I've done this before—or, I *will* do this, from their point of view, I guess. Doesn't make this apology less heartfelt.

Letting go of Chase, I back up and look at all three of them, Kieran and Chase in their tactical uniforms, Zio still in the decon suit. "Had I known there was a chance the Quaneez would trigger the Marmelite and send me back, I…" I shrug. What would I have done? *Not* repaired the *Pioneer*? But it needed to happen. Let's not kid ourselves. I would've still done what needed to be done, even if it meant never seeing Kieran again. Because the timeline needs to be preserved.

Bitterness rises up my throat, until I swallow it down.

Looking up, I meet Kieran's gaze. "I would've at least given you time to prepare yourself for the disruption of the Bond." If nothing else, I would've done that.

His eyes widen. "The Bond—you know?" Then, he looks over at Zio. "That means you were right."

Zio raises one eyebrow. "And you sound way too surprised with that statement. When did you find out?" He directs his attention to me.

Now, that's a tricky question, one I can't answer without giving away details. "Let's put it this way. Once I jumped, I had help figuring out the details of what happened. I had support." Once I jumped *back* from my time and got some help in the form of these three gentlemen standing in front of me. Look at that. Maybe another predestination paradox. I tell them now, they tell me later? Yes? No? Maybe? Honestly, I'm too exhausted to figure it out. My day has been going on forever. On the plus side, my First Sense doesn't give me any weird feelings, so I should be good with my disclosures.

Kieran blows out a puff of air through pursed lips and shoves and hand through his hair. "That's... good." He cringes and drops his gaze.

Ouch. I know. I know he hurt more than I did when I returned to my time. And if what I felt at the raspberry farm is any indication, the kind of pain trying to tear you apart, one molecule at a time, on and on, until nothing is left but the sensation of utter agony... Yeah. I remember, and I will never forget. Never have I felt worse than then, not with any jump.

Reaching out, I take Kieran's hand. "I'm sorry." Because I know what it feels like, even though I can't tell him.

He squeezes my hand and brushes his thumb over my fingers—

And stops, when he notices the ring.

His brows narrow as he lifts and turns his and my hand to inspect the ring—the ring he gave, or rather, will give me. The ring this Kieran, right now, clearly isn't happy about.

Oops.

I feel my cheeks warm. Change of topic, stat, please. "Uhh, when am I anyway?"

Chase sighs. "That's the colony on Tribega we dematted up from. Or rather, it was. It's gone. You saw all that's left of it."

No matter that's not what I asked, the information turns to lead in my stomach. "Gone?"

He nods. "Wiped out. The *Starlight*'s crew reported the attack and we were sent to look for survivors, but it seems the Quaneez were thorough."

Sun and Stars…! Intellectually I know all of this. I've read it. Studied it. We've added those casualties to our statistics, but up to now, that's what they were. Numbers in a statistic.

Now that I've smelled the fires, the burned flesh and structures, seen the destruction… It changes things. I lean forward, supporting my upper body with my hands on my knees. "How many?" It comes out as a croak.

"Fifteen K."

I close my eyes. I stood on the graves of fifteen thousand souls. Fifteen thousand. Wiped out by the Quaneez.

Kieran's voice sounds rough when he speaks. "They just transferred the colonists a few months earlier. Just finished terraforming. And now… All gone. The third terraformed colony within as many weeks."

"We should be happy they haven't attacked the natural planetary colonies in the same solar system." Zio drops his hood onto the med bed.

"Uh-huh." We all hear what Kieran doesn't say: *so far.*

Zio zips open his decon suit and steps out of it. "And we're sure it was them? The *Starlight* didn't give us the best readings."

"What we know so far? Yes. The pattern of destruction down there matches their usual attacks." I'd be lying if I said Kieran sounded unaffected. Every word he says is pushed out as if it cost him.

"Plus, the *Starlight* picked up on traces of their propulsion drive." Chase counts off his fingers. "And there is only one people I know using a drive barely functioning in space. If their engineering was only slightly worse, they'd blow themselves up on a regular basis. Would make our life easier."

"Trip, come on." Kieran rubs his eyes.

"What? You can't tell me you'd mind them gone."

"I'd be very happy with them leaving us in peace. I'd be very unhappy if us succeeding in doing what we're supposed to was the reason for them *being gone.*" Pressing his lips into a thin line, he stares at a spot on the wall across from him.

Chase sighs. "All right, all right, yes, I agree, but sorry, all this senseless killing, it gets to me."

The guys stay silent, mood somber, their pain a fourth entity in the room, large, looming, and palpable. If any admiral spent time on a ship like the *Pioneer*, trying to help the attacked colonies, seeing the devastation, feeling the same helplessness Kieran, Chase, and Zio are feeling—would we still have war? Or would we have invested more into establishing peace?

I take a slow breath in. Thoughts like that, they make me nauseous. "So, what date is today?"

"Tuesday. August eighteenth," Chase says.

I give him *the* look. "Thank you for letting me know it's Tuesday. The year would've been more beneficial though."

Chase blushes and mouths an *oops*, while Kieran and Zio both chuckle. Hey, at least it doesn't feel like a funeral for fifteen thousand people anymore.

"It's 2255," Kieran says, pulling me closer by the hand he hasn't let go since down on the planet.

Guess I was right. It's only three months after the Battle of Balthar, three months after I vanished for them. That would explain their reaction. Would be a fair bet to say to them I haven't been back yet, it seems.

"Okay, I totally messed that up. But let me make up for it, because I think this is funny and you might be interested in this news." Chase clears his throat for effect. "Today is actually the first day the newly appointed liaison to the Magellan people has started his duties."

Kieran whips his head over toward Chase. "It's through?"

"Through and official. Fleet Admiral Jones sent a communique earlier today." Chase nods.

"And you were planning on telling me that when, exactly, first officer?"

"When the time was right, pun intended, my captain. And now the time is perfect, after all, it was your suggestion to promote one Tom Thorburn for that position, who happens to be the father of one of the people present." He reaches for Kieran's shoulder and slaps it. "But all hints from the future aside, you got that man a tough job, Kieran."

A careful, proud grin steals over his face. "Naah, he'll be fine. I'd go out on a limb and say that Tom will be much more motivated to do right by the Magellan people than any other person I can think of."

"See? There are good people out there, and good news as well." Chase slaps Kieran's shoulder some more for good measure and slides off the medical beds. "What's next though? Nonie, your presence here, as much as I'm happy about that, brings several questions—"

"Which you know I can't answer." I add an apologetic shrug to my reply.

"Hm." Chase narrows his eyes at me. "Okay. Fair enough. I guess I appreciate you keeping the timeline on course, but what do you need?"

All three look at me, waiting.

What do I need? Besides the disk to finally figure out who's behind the Temporal War?

Good question.

I have no idea why I exited my jump exactly now, why I felt drawn to here, to now—if maybe Mashaule is about to kill Kieran at this very time. Maybe he is, maybe he isn't.

Anyway. "All I need for now is a place to crash and take a breath."

Chase cocks his head to the side, a look of surprised skepticism on his face. "And you have the means to leave this time? And excuse me if that's none of my business, but the last spike of Setayashi radiation that brought you home—"

Cringing as memory hits hard, I wave both hands. "Nope. No more blowing up planets. That's all I'm going to say about that." Luckily for me, I don't have to worry about a Setayashi source anymore.

Chase looks relieved. "That's good to hear. I hereby promise to keep my nose out of your business, now, and if or when you come back." He places one palm over his heart and raises the other.

Come to think about it, they didn't ask me the last time I was on the *Pioneer* how I planned to leave again, not that I noticed at the time. Huh. Filing that information for later, I look at the three men, my only constant within this chaos. "Thank you, Chase. And since we're at it, a fair disclaimer: I'm not going to stay long." Because I have places to be, get that stupid disk.

Even though he tries to hide it, Kieran's face falls. His reaction brings a weird twisting sensation to my stomach, like the butterflies were happy that he cares, but felt bad for him. What would that make them? Nosediving suicide butterflies?

I shake my head to bring myself back on track. "But it goes without saying, I really appreciate you guys taking me in. Again."

Kieran wraps one arm around my shoulders. "Any time. Literally." He grins and pulls me in tight. Funny how such a small gesture can sort of validate my decision to stop at this very time. Maybe it's a good pause to recover from that never-ending day I had. Recharge my batteries. Clear my mind. See why my First Sense led me here.

And while I'm at it might as well keep an eye on Kieran and keep him alive.

After all, he doesn't have much time left.

*USEF Pioneer, August 18*th*, 2255*

Kieran guides me through the hallways of the *Pioneer* like we were two school children sneaking off campus during school hours. At every corner he stops, peeks around, and, if he deems the area clear enough, leads me to the next.

I wonder what he'd do if somebody ran into us. Code Magenta was definitely more convenient. I tug on his hand. "Feels forbidden, you sneaking me around the *Pioneer*," I whisper.

Kieran wiggles an eyebrow, and it comes with a cute little grin. "One, doesn't that usually mean it's more fun anyway, and two, isn't everything about this"—he holds up our entwined hands—"forbidden? To a degree?"

Meh. "I feel like we've got the timeline's blessing." From everything I've learned, everything I've seen, Kieran and I are okay. In this time period, at least. Until he dies on June eight, fifty-seven. But at least I can be with him. We can live and share our lives for way too short, but share them in a more meaningful way than the other Nonie could. The way she looked at that older Kieran…

"And call me egoistic, but I like to keep you to myself." Stopping us a corner away from his quarters, he lifts our hands and places a kiss on mine—after covering my ring with his thumb.

The touch of his lips on my hands… I'll have to do the math of how long it has been since I last said goodbye to Kieran. How many hours. Half a day, maybe? Way less than Kieran had to wait for me, and yet it feels like I haven't seen him forever. Maybe that's the nature of our relationship, the volatility of time travel and keeping up with the regulations to not change anything. Maybe that's also the reason for the butterflies pulling off some serious aerial maneuvers in my belly.

He lowers my hand again, then leads me the last twenty steps to his quarters and palms them open. "And if I can keep you hidden and make your life easier… It's a bonus."

"Much appreciated, I was just wondering if there wasn't an easier way—"

Kieran enters his quarters and gives my hand a pull, yanking me into the room.

I squeak as I stumble in. "—an easier way to—"

He catches me by the waist and pushes me into the wall. Half a second later his body presses into mine, connecting all our important parts.

"—to hide my presence?" I breathe the last part softer than a whisper, because, *Kieran*. The heavenly weight of his body leaned into mine. His hands sliding over my shoulders, down my arms, lifting them and draping them around his neck. Kissing the inside of my wrist, he then turns his head and leans his forehead against mine.

His whisper caresses my face. "Are we still on the same page doing this?"

"Oh heck, yeah," I whisper back.

"Good. Then at this very moment I don't care about easier ways or whatever. Details." He lowers his head and brushes his lips across mine.

And honestly? I agree, who cares about details? Not me. Totally not me. Nu-uh. Details-shmetails. Unimportant. Kieran, on the other hand, is beyond important.

I lean in and connect our lips. Kieran sucks in a short breath he releases in a sigh. The sound of it does amazing things to those butterflies fluttering in my stomach holding *Kieran FTW*-signs.

He presses his mouth to mine for two or three quick pecks before he parts my lips with his tongue and we are *on*. We are *so* on. Who cares about time travel, Mashaule, or anything when you're kissing the coolest, most awesomest guy in the galaxy? Not me, that's for sure. All the chaos running through my mind is gone, replaced by the person who matters the most: Kieran.

Our tongues tangle, his lips moving fervently over mine, and my body gets this all-over-tingle with goosebumps all the way down my spine.

It feels natural to be in his arms. It fits. We fit. I arch into his touch, little tremors coursing through me, and Kieran isn't any less affected. A throaty groan leaves his throat as he slides one hand under my shirt, fingers skimming my skin as he tugs it over my head. Not wasting time, his follows STAT.

I glide my hands up his arms, circling the small starburst-like scar in his shoulder, the one that mirrors my own. My gaze drifts farther, getting hung up on his biceps, then the muscles on his chest and the scar I saw the reason for at the raspberry farm. Chills erupt over his skin, and he rolls his hips into mine.

"I would wait for you a lifetime, but Sun and Stars, Nonie, I can't wait right now." Desperation clouds his tone, the exasperated, good kind. He scoops me up in one big motion and carries me to the bed, laying me down gently and bringing our bodies flush together.

I wrap my legs around his waist and pull him in closer. Desire rushes through me like a tidal wave. I circle my hips against his, bringing friction to parts of me that have been demanding more of that for the last few minutes.

Kieran gasps, eyes wide. Mischief shines from his eyes. "I like the way you think. *Pioneer*, cut the lights."

Chapter Eighteen -
NIGHTMARES

I t's the middle of the night when I hear the scream.

My eyes snap open, breath stuck in my throat. Where am—?

Kieran screams again, panic breaking his voice. He twitches, thrashes, arms hitting the night stand, me—

Holy crap.

I jerk up to sitting, heart hammering. "*Pioneer*, lights!" Without delay, the computer initiates full illumination, and while hearing Kieran scream in panic is bad enough, as bad as during any of my jumps, seeing him like this breaks my heart. Like he was possessed, he defends against an enemy only he can see, arms flailing one second, then drawing them in to protect his face the next. But the worst part are his eyes: wide open, gaze darting around as if he was seeing something or looking for something, filled with stark horror.

I reach for his shoulder. "Kieran! Kieran! Hey, Kieran!" I give him a gentle shake, and when that doesn't suffice, a stronger one. One more. One—

He gulps in a desperate breath of air and freezes.

"Kieran," I repeat, quieter. My breath is coming out in little puffs. Nothing like being woken from deep sleep by screams. "Are you okay?"

He blinks once, twice, then releases the breath he held in one big exhale. The apple in his throat moves up and down. "Did I… did I scream?" He rubs a forearm across his eyes, then scoots himself up to sitting. Sweat stains the front of his shirt.

"Yeah, you did. Woke me up."

He grimaces. "Sorry, I—"

"No need to apologize." I pause. "I didn't know it was that bad." It wasn't when we last spoke about the nightmares. Or, when we *will* speak about them. Coming to think about it, he was quite embarrassed by them, not a difficult conclusion to make that he might've been not quite honest with me.

"Depends on the day. Overall, it's been getting worse." He shrugs. "There's nothing I can do about it, so I just live with it. Sorry I woke you."

"Again, no need to apologize. If there's anything I can do…?"

He drops his gaze and shakes his head. "No. Not really. I did make it longer than I normally do. Am attributing that to your calming presence." Trying out a small smile, he winks at me.

I raise one brow. "So, wait, usually you have more of this?"

"More for sure. Earlier nightmares, longer, more severe…" He notices the sweat stain on his shirt and grunts in annoyance before he yanks it over his head and tosses it aside. "But I got it covered."

"Sure." Nightly bad dreams, worse than what I witnessed. He's got that covered, obviously.

A real smile tugs on his lips. "Come on, help me calm down." Lying back down, he lifts his comforter up and motions for me to join him.

I cuddle into his side, my cheek on his bare shoulder, hand on his chest. Kieran pulls up the blanket to cover both of us, such a mundane yet caring gesture it close to tears me up.

For a moment, we lie still, enjoying each other's company. Silence is so unawkward when we're together. Eventually though I feel somebody needs to start talking about the elephant in the room.

I tap a finger onto his chest. "I'm sorry about those nightmares."

"They're not your fault."

"I still feel bad for you though." And yes, witnessing his nightmare in person, I'm pretty sure he was-slash-will be underselling it.

He squirms, then glides a finger over my back. "If you want to hear my layperson's option, I'm thinking I might be a bit more sensitive because of my PTSD. Got shot once, you know the story—"

Boy, do I ever…!

"—and then I can't really say being at the mercy of the Quaneez and experiencing their mind torture was fun in the original sense. Figured my mind just has a hard time coming to terms with it."

I splay my palm on his chest, the strong heartbeat the same rhythm as mine. "Could be." Yes, he's been saying that and it's a plausible explanation, but the way he screamed… It's exactly the way I hear him during the jumps. A chill erupts and travels down my spine, and this time, not the good kind.

I heard Kieran scream like this, in total panic, the first time today. How did my mind make up his sounds of utter terror so precisely, so real? A nagging feeling follows the path of the chills. What am I missing here?

He brings his hand up to mine on his chest and covers it. "See? Who needs a doctor? I got the whole diagnosing myself thing down like a pro."

"Zio might be out of a job if you keep it up, Captain. Good job coping." To a degree. When he's awake, at least.

"As a general rule, Lieutenant, nobody is coping better than the captain of a ship. As you can see."

"Of course, sir, I must have misinterpreted the situation."

We both chuckle, then fall into an easy silence.

Kieran twirls the ring on my finger. "You… you'd tell me if there was something I needed to know, right?" In this very moment he doesn't sound like a powerful USEF captain, but like a guy who's worried about his girlfriend. Insecure, worried, anxious maybe even.

"Kieran." I push myself up on one arm, using the other to tap the scar on his right shoulder, then to tap the same scar on my shoulder.

Heat colors his cheeks. "Well, I—"

"Nu-uh. What I meant is that you needn't worry. We're connected by the same scar," I touch his again, "and by a Bond," I lay my hand flat to cover his heart, "but even if neither of that had happened, there's nobody else but you." And I can't imagine that ever changing, which is crazy. I'm young. I hopefully have a long life ahead of me—even though history shows me that expectation doesn't always lead to the desired result—which will not include Kieran. I should enjoy my time with him, mentally prep for losing him and for eventually finding somebody else, but I can't. Even trying to think about a life without him makes me nauseous.

Relief shines in his eyes. "That's what I thought. And why I asked earlier if we were still on the same page."

Earlier. My heart skips a beat when the memory of *earlier* comes back. "Definitely on the same page."

As he gives the ring another twirl, a tugging sensation—no, more a touch of nausea flares up in my stomach, a feeling I've had many a time in my life, but one I'm still not quite accustomed to: My First Sense.

I chew on my cheek before I talk. It's not like I'm handing out state secrets, but I've grown so accustomed to not giving away details, it's hard to cater to a First Sense nobody gave me much of an intro on. "The ring… It was a gift from a person who means a lot to me. I cherish it a lot." The nausea eases, as if my First Sense was pleased with me, and maybe it is. Maybe Kieran needed to see the ring to buy it. After all, he could have bought something else in the store where I tried to steal that t-shirt. And if he had, I'd never gotten the ring and… what? Never realized Star Hopper was me? I would like to think I wasn't that slow. Huh. I crunch my brows together. The timeline is complicated.

Kieran stops playing with the ring and instead interlaces his fingers with mine. "You know, I… I didn't mean to be jealous."

A wide grin steals onto my face. "But you totally are."

He bursts out laughing. "Yes, I totally am." Pulling me closer he hugs me tightly until we've both calmed down. "Not that I'm telling you news, but time has a way of messing with your memories. The longer you were gone, the less convinced I was of what I remembered.

You know…" He sucks in his lower lips and regards me from under his lashes. "Can I tell you something cheesy?"

"Cheesy? Any time." I'm all ears.

"When you were gone, the pain from the broken Bond was so bad, it overshadowed many of the memories. But"—he holds up a finger before I can apologize for leaving him, then taps me onto my lips with it—"once I kissed you down there on the planet… Holy everything, all that pain, all the uncertainty if you'd ever be back, and what I'd do if not, bonded to a woman who may never return, all that faded away. Gone."

I guess I'm not the only one pondering the future without the other one.

Kieran pulls me closer and rolls us over, so that he's lying on top of me, connected in all the important places. "And when I'm close to you like this, when I can't tell if the heartbeat I'm feeling is yours or mine, then I'm thinking it was all worth it. And I'd do it again and again, if it means I get to see you again." Warmth shines from his eyes, lighting me up from the inside. "And I—"

"Bridge to Captain Wildason." The speakers integrated into the ceiling spring to life.

Kieran doesn't hesitate a single second. "Wildason here, go ahead."

"Sir, sorry to bother you in the middle of the night, but Admiral Rozell would like to talk to you."

"We talking audio or video?"

"Video, sir."

Kieran raises an eyebrow at me under him and rolls his hips down into mine, a mischievous uptick of his lips accompanying the movement. My eyes widen and I snap my lips closed.

"I'll need a second then. Put him through and I'll accept in a minute."

"Understood, sir." The com beeps once as a sign the channel is closed.

"Sorry." Kieran kisses the tip of my nose, then pushes himself up and off me.

"No worries. I'm sure being interrupted during private time is in the opening pages of *Being the Captain's Girlfriend: A Short Compendium.*"

Kieran chuckles as he slides into a fresh off-duty shirt. "Should be in the opening paragraph." He tip-toes over to his desk on bare feet and takes a seat, palm frozen in the air about two centimeters off the control panel. "It's a unidirectional call, so he won't see you."

I hear the non-verbal *but.* "I won't make a sound." Because Admiral Rozell doesn't need to know Kieran is accepting a confidential conversation in his quarters with somebody listening in. Even though, I would like to add in his and my defense, I'm an outside player. I don't count. I can probably read about the content of this conversation in Kieran's log, securely stored on my wrist pad.

Leaning back against the wall, I watch Kieran initiate the com. Besides his hair being a bit more disheveled than normally one could get the impression he'd been up and working for hours, and not been woken up by a nightmare and interrupted by an admiral during girlfriend time. Here's to professionalism.

The admiral is an older gentleman with a bald head and very expressive dark, thick eyebrows. Despite being seated at a desk and the background blurred out it doesn't look like a typical USEF office with the what I can make out as potted plants in the background and framed pictures on the wall. Just like with my dad, work doesn't stop because it's an inconvenient time.

The holo hovers at eye level for Kieran, every move of the admiral's facial muscles visible to him and as well to me. Definitely not as sophisticated as that 3-D solid hologram Mashaule spoke to on the *Eclipse*, but still good quality for the time. Said the time-traveller, who should know.

"Captain Wildason. Appreciate you taking my call. I know it's late—or rather, quite early—for you."

"No problem at all, Admiral. What's going on?" Straight to the point. The likelihood of this being a courtesy call in the middle of the night to chat about the weather is at minus a couple of million.

"Tribega, Wildason. Tribega is going on. I've read your report. You went to the surface. Any survivors?"

"None."

The admiral curses. "That's how many terraformed colonies in the last months?"

Kieran stays silent, as the admiral shakes his head, lifting a PAD from the desk.

"Fleet admiral Jones and I have spoken. We want the *Pioneer* to be more proactive."

Ouch. I remember how well that was received. Trip told me.

To his credit, Kieran stays calm. "Proactive in which regard, sir?"

"That's easy, Captain. We want you to actively seek the Quaneez out and prevent attacks on our property. On our people."

A short, heavy silence hovers.

"In other words, you want us to hunt them down and destroy them." No emotion colors Kieran's tone. If I didn't know how he felt about the order, I'd have no clue.

"It's about damn time we end this, Captain."

A muscle in Kieran's jaw pops. "I agree wholeheartedly, Admiral." He pauses. "May I speak freely, sir?"

Rozell waves a hand. "Of course. I appreciate candor in my officers."

"Sir, the Quaneez seem to value life differently than we do. They're awfully fast with their self-destruct, to a degree as if surviving didn't matter to them as it does to us. I don't feel attacking them first is going to make much of a difference. Instead, I would like us—the *Pioneer*—to find other means of winning the war. For example, collaborate more with the Magellans. Their scientific—"

"You think *science* is going to solve this war?" To say the admiral was flabbergasted would be an understatement.

"I think science might be the gateway into understanding each other and stopping the war, yes."

The admiral huffs. "You're quite alone with that opinion, son. The dominating opinion is one of shoot first, ask questions later." He harrumphs. "And I agree with it, which is why the *Pioneer*, our flagship, is going to start hunting the Quaneez."

"But—"

"Wildason, this is non-debatable! The Quaneez are merciless in attacking us first, and we're not going to stand for it anymore! You—"

"Daddy! Daddy!" A high-pitched whining voice interrupts the admiral a second before a small girl, maybe six years old, if that, throws herself around her father's neck. She sobs, her whole body shaking with every single one of them.

We all freeze. Kieran, with a look of anything-can-happen-at-any-time coolness on his face, me, with my lips forming a little *o*, and the admiral with shocked features as his arms circle around his daughter in slow motion. "Muffin—"

"M-mommy threw Po-pocky in the w-wash and now his stuffing is all w-weird, and—" Her shoulders rock, as her dad pats them, cringing.

"Muffin? Daddy is trying to work." He gently pries her off his chest. She sniffles and wipes her nose with the back of her hand, her red, shoulder-length hair sticking to her face.

"But he's like *this*!" She contorts herself into some twisted position. "And I can't cuddle with him like that, I—"

Rozell's face turns red. He's running out of patience. "We'll buy you a new stuffy. Now go—"

"New?" She shrieks, which turns into another sob. "B-but it's P-pocky, he—"

"Jazmine, I—"

Kieran leans forward. "Hey, Jazmine?" He waves toward the holo. Gone is the cool look, replaced by a warm, open smile.

The kid turns, her eyes popping wide when she realizes the holo was on. Despite her face being red from crying, she's a cute kiddo with differently colored eyes, one blue, one brown. She must've gotten her looks from her mom, not her dad. No offense, Admiral.

Snapping her mouth shut, she looks from Kieran to her dad, who gives her an exasperated *now-deal-with-it* gesture.

"Hi." She sucks in her lower lip. "I'm sorry—"

Kieran waves her off. "Don't be. The same thing happened to me once with my stuffed animal. You know how we fixed it? We put him into a jay-wave regenerator. It fluffed everything up, and all I had to do was massage his body." Kieran makes a kneading motion with his hands. "I'm sure that'll help with Pocky, too."

Hope lights up her face. "You think?"

"I'm pretty sure it'll work." He winks at her.

She bounces up and down twice. "I'll tell Mommy!" And off she runs, the slamming of a door announcing her exit.

For the shortest moment, Kieran allows his smile to linger before he straightens himself back up. The admiral clears his throat and pulls on his uniform top, as if straightening it could erase the last few moments.

He presses his lips together. "Appreciate that, Wildason." He pauses. "But it changes nothing about my orders."

Annnd… if that didn't drain whatever positivity was in the air, I don't know.

Judging by Kieran's blank impression I'm not the only one feeling that way. "I didn't think so, Admiral."

"Good. Because the *Pioneer* will be on the hunt for our enemies before they can strike. Am I making myself clear?"

Kieran opens his mouth and snaps it shut, muscles in his jaw working. "Yes, sir." His gaze burns, not sure if Admiral Rozell can pick up on that during the transmission, but if he can, hats off for ignoring the sting in it. I know what he's thinking: It's not true. The Quaneez are not merciless. They didn't attack Kieran on Alpha Rubrum, when he held still. They initially didn't attack during the Battle of Balthar. It seems to me that Kieran understands that on at least an intuitional level. And I know, I just know it, that if I look deeper into my theory, it will stand. It has to do with the hails. It must have.

Plus, if I'm honest with myself, there have been more unexplained coincidences when it comes to the Quaneez. Careful to not make any noise I shift my weight in the bed. Witnessing history unfold is like watching a train derail at slow speed. It's happening, and there's nothing I can do about it.

But is that true? Granted, I can't change anything in my past. But maybe I can change my future. I just need to make sense out of all these little peculiarities and oddities, because they seem to add up to more than that. The biggest difference between Kieran's situation and mine is that from my point of view, my future isn't written yet, while his is. I can do what fate denied him: find peace with the Quaneez.

I curl my fists, raking in the soft fabric of the sheets. It's possible. Can be done. Must be done.

The admiral gives Kieran a curt nod. "I'm looking forward to reading your battle statistics. Rozell out." He presses a button and the holo turns grey for a second, before Kieran's terminal ends the transmission. As if hypnotized, Kieran still stares at the space where, a second ago, the admiral's projection hovered, body coiled, tension radiating off him.

After a good twenty seconds he whispers so softly it wasn't meant for anybody but himself: "We'll see about that, sir. We'll see about that."

USEF Pioneer, August 19ᵗʰ, 2255

The ceiling in Kieran's quarters holds three hundred and twenty five bolts I can see from his couch. Fifty more if I turn my head a tad to the left. It's fair to say Kieran's ceiling is well secured. It's also fair to say since Kieran left for the bridge at 7:00 a.m., I've been doing my fair share of staring at said ceiling in an attempt to make sense of nothing less but life in general.

Kidding. If I could figure out the Temporal War and the Quaneez War, I'd be a happy camper. Hint: I haven't so far. Okay, not quite correct, because I feel like there's something to my theories.

Hypothesis number one: Quaneez don't want to kill us as a default. Proof: they're not shooting first, but from what I see, only after we hail, which leads me to hypothesis number two: Quaneez have an issue with hails, in whichever way, for whatever reason. Proof: they fire only once we hail.

So far, so good.

Still, there is this nagging I'm-overlooking-something feeling. I met actual live Quaneez three times. Once during First Contact. The second time when freeing Kieran from the mind torture, and a third time when I kept that Quaneez kid from becoming tiger-breakfast. All three times they smelled, for a lack of a better word. They stank, sorry, but they did during all occasions minus the adult Quaneez when I rescued the very much stinky kid.

Is that enough to conclude scent plays a role? For what? And how would it if they're stuck in those armored suits? Or, maybe they simply can't smell, and it means nothing besides they just don't pick up on their lack of body hygiene.

Either way, would knowing the Quaneez' olfactory system even matter if we're in freakin' space ships?

Still, I feel like I'm getting closer and closer with each day, no matter in which time it's spent, collecting bits and pieces of this galactic-sized puzzle.

But I'm not quite there.

The biggie, the missing link, the key to it all, is still missing.

I stick my tongue at the ceiling, not that it had anything to do with what's going on inside my head. Still makes me feel better.

Swinging my legs over the edge of the couch, I sit up.

The matter at hand though is protecting Kieran. My next jump needs to be spot on, and so far, that hasn't been my forte, even though I'm getting better. No pressure.

But I'll get it done, somehow. The cave where they held me during my abduction is the last location I know about where somebody had one of those disk-things. And while I'm not really looking forward to returning to that cold and frightening place, it's a lead I can't ignore.

These disks are hard to come by, it appears.

I rub both palms over my eyes. Question is, what do I do once I have it? Turn it on? See if it works better than Mashaule's did last time, without the flickering and sputtering? But what if activating that thing acts like a homing beacon, giving my location away? Or, more importantly, what if it alerts the Upstream Bad Guy that I'm onto him? A shudder runs down my back.

So, what about returning home, to my time, and using the FBTI's resources with that thingy? Find out who's behind it, find out how Mashaule is contacted through the disk, and track him down that way instead of a blind chase I'm no good at and I'm bound to lose. Maybe it was a mistake trying to follow Mashaule instead of thinking outside the box and tackling the problem from a different angle.

"*Pioneer*, any traces of Setayashi-radiation within scanner range?" Because, hello, I'm not leaving if Mashaule is about to execute another attempt on Kieran's life.

"*No Setayashi-radiation detected,*" *Pioneer* replies.

Okay then. I sigh. Maybe it's a sign. Go home, get the FBTI involved. Can't I hunt Mashaule from that time just as well as from when I am now? I have a Setayashi-emitter, I can jump whenever I want!

If Mashaule killed Kieran, my First Sense should pick up on a shift in the timeline, and I could then jump to right before his murder, fix it, and… *And* I'm the queen of hypothetical time warfare. No idea if that's how it works.

Absolutely none.

I groan and ball a fist, banging it against my forehead.

But then, maybe I'm not the one to solve those problems. The FBTI must have guidelines, know more. The Magellans are the experts when it comes to the time—

I jackknife up to sitting.

The Magellans.

I have my very own Magellan here, so to speak: Zio. He's my only resource, my best bet, and also needs to know when I'm leaving. Somebody's got to take care of Kieran when I pop out of his time.

Standing up, I raise my voice. "Thorburn to Upinga."

Pioneer's com system gets me Zio in no time. "Upinga here."

"Could I ask you for a favor? If you're not too busy, could you drop by for a minute? Please?" Since that's easier than me sneaking around the ship trying to avoid being spotted.

"Be there in two minutes. Upinga out."

To his credit, he means it. In less than two minutes, Kieran's doorbell rings right before Zio lets himself in. I love the trust the guys have with each other, their palm prints registered for their respective quarters.

His face lights up when he sees me. "Niece." Now that I've seen my mom in person, Zio looks so much like her when he smiles. Serious-Zio a little bit less, but once he smiles… the resemblance is uncanny.

And boy, if it didn't make me happy. A grin steals across my face. "Uncle."

He raises both palms to the ceiling. "See? When you call me that, I am completely fine with the name."

"Because it's accurate."

"Definitely is." He regards me with narrowed eyes, head tilted to the side, like trying to figure me out. "You need help, I take it?"

"Is it that obvious?" I flinch. "And yes. Help would be appreciated. Also, I'm leaving. And… I wanted to make sure you were ready for Kieran."

"The heads-up is appreciated. I would prefer for the captain to be primed against the effects of losing the Bond before it happens." His gaze softens. "And I sincerely hope that my counterpart took good care of you back in your time."

"Yeah, of course." I reply in a cringeworthy off-pitch voice, because thing is, he didn't. Coming to think about it, Zio seemed confused, like yes, he expected me to be in pain, which I was, but also he expected me to be more broken, which I wasn't. Only with one jump, I was close to non-functioning, and that wasn't even a jump, but at the raspberry fields, when young Kieran died in front of my very eyes. To be honest, it's been bothering me since I heard Kieran describe the effects on him when I first jumped back. I feel like I got away easy.

I chew on the inside of my cheek. "In your experience with the Bond, does it affect everybody the same? It's disruption, I mean?"

Zio pulls out the same chair he always sits on whenever we have dinner. "To a degree, yes. Some people handle it better than others, but an untreated loss of the Bond can take weeks to heal to the degree that the person is able to perform any activities of daily living on their own." He sits down and leans forward, both forearms on the table, hands folded. "Why are you asking?"

I shrug and sit down in my chair at the other side of the table. "Because I thought it felt different to me depending on—" *Oops.* Let's not give too much away. "Depending on."

Zio nods. "Depending on where you were. I would imagine if you reentered time and Kieran was far away from you it would influence the way you feel. Distance stretches the Bond, which can feel similar to its destruction, but milder, since the Bond is still there, only stretched. If you jumped to, say, Earth, and Kieran was on the *Pioneer* in a different sector what you're experiencing would make sense."

Me on Earth, Kieran on *Pioneer*. Wouldn't that be nice. What about the distance between life and death? In my time, he's dead, and the pain was bad. But still not as bad as at the raspberry fields, and not as bad as Kieran's seems to have been. Why? "Could it be it affects half-Magellans differently?"

"Of course. You're the only one I know, so my sample size is limited. On the other hand, I would like to point out that Kieran is affected just as severely as any Magellan, so I would assume your reaction to be quite similar to what we know. Remind me to check on that in the future. A study of two, in the making." He winks.

If only it was that easy. It still doesn't explain why my reaction is so different from his, but on the other hand, does it matter? Is my grief less real because my pain is less? No. Not at all. Grief isn't measured by one scale only. Grief is all encompassing.

When I stay silent, Zio leans back in his chair. "Was that what you wanted to talk to me about?"

I slide deeper into my chair and glide a hand over my hair. "No. I… I had questions about the timeline. About jumps." The universe, essence of life, you know, no biggies.

"I would actually refer to you as the expert in these things."

I slap my palm onto the table. "But I'm not, Zee! I'm not! I wish I were, but man, I got thrown into this with no prep and I'm flying by the seat of my pants!" I blink rapidly and refocus on my hands on the table. "I feel underprepared every minute of this, and—"

Zio holds up a hand. "Stop. I don't need too many details. You have questions, ask the questions and I'll do my very best to answer them, even though I hardly consider myself an expert in the topic."

But you're all I have. Out loud I say, "That's all I need. Thanks, Uncle."

"Any time, Niece."

We share a smile and quiet moment before I take a deep breath and release it in a heavy blow. "I really only have one question about the timeline. I was told," *by you and the Taro,* "the timeline tries to preserve its flow. Smaller changes in it don't lead to a change in its course, but bigger changes might. Correct?" I look up at him.

"Correct. That's the prevailing theory at the moment."

"So, to clarify, if something happened in the past, big enough to alter it, would I still feel it where I am, upstream from that event, and could I jump back and fix it?" Because what I have felt once in my life, when I was back at the FBTI-converted *Pioneer* in my time, was something that… trickled down, for a lack of a better term. I felt there was something or someone in the future connecting with Mashaule in the present, and that combo… it felt like it was going to reshape the past. But it hadn't happened yet. So, what do I know, it might work differently the other way around.

For a moment, Zio regards me with silent curiosity before he lowers his chin in a small nod. "Theoretically, yes to the first."

"The part where the past is changed and I would feel it."

"Correct. Your First Sense should alert you that something is happening. It would be a sense of urgency, and it comes with an idea of *when*, like a flavor to the feeling." He grimaces. "I know that's not the most scientific explanation, and I apologize. I'm trying to put my experience into words, and it's challenging."

I cock my head. "You experienced that?"

"Something similar. I experienced a shift in my present time during the mission at Alpha Rubrum."

My heart skips a beat. Mashaule—the Upstream Bad Guy! It must've been them! Keeping my poker face straight, I look at him. "But that shift, it didn't change the course of the timeline, I assume?"

"No, it didn't. Not from what my First Sense picked up on, mind you. Whatever the change to the original was, it didn't lead to a different outcome and the course of the timeline was preserved."

My mouth is dry. His description mirrors what I felt right before Mashaule escaped from USEF prison—what Zio and the Taro felt, too. A *flavor* to the feeling. That's reassuring, knowing my First Sense would at least be alerted. Back to the tough question though. "Okay, now let's assume the timeline gets altered in my past, I pick up on it—can I jump back from where I am to the point of alteration and fix it?"

Zio stays silent for so long I begin to wonder if he heard me. "I don't know," he finally says. "Time science theory predicts that with a downstream modification of the timeline, the upstream content changes according to what was altered in the past."

I grimace. "That gives me a headache, Zio."

"Understandably so, but here's an example. Take the two of us, as we sit here right now. Say, somebody was changing our past on a grand scale, for example, since I mentioned it, the attack on Alpha Rubrum. Let's hypothesize the attack had decimated the Magellan people and killed most of the *Pioneer*'s crew."

"Ouch." Too close to the truth of what was going on. Upstream Bad Guy didn't want survivors, the way it sounded.

"Yes, *ouch* indeed. Without being too presumptuous, *Pioneer* and its crew missing would change the timeline. No—or a different—first contact with the Quaneez. Maybe not even a Quaneez war, or if so, maybe it began later or earlier and progressed differently."

I sit up straighter. "Okay, here I am, feeling that change in my past through my First Sense. Then, I go back—"

"Who's saying that you'd know how to do that?"

"Because you think I'm not precise with my jumps?" Which I'm not, but thanks for the vote of confidence.

He shoots me a glance from under his lashes, the same one he will use on me during my academy training whenever I asked a question I should've known the answer to. "No, that's not what I'm thinking. I stand by what I said before. Whenever a Setayashi spike hits you, you should be able to control it. Your First Sense will guide you. Trust it."

Right. That really worked well for me so far, but at least he gave my ego a boost.

"But that was not what I was aiming for. Think about the scenario. The timeline has been changed. The Magellan people have been exterminated. No FBTI has been founded. If you even came into existence, maybe you never entered the Academy, you never accidentally got thrown into the past—surely not to the *Pioneer*, since it got destroyed at Alpha Rubrum in this theoretical scenario. What kind of person would you be?" He gives me a challenging look, one brow raised.

"I— Uhh, I don't know." Heat rises to my face. Zio is right. I wouldn't be the same me. I wouldn't know what I know now, because I hypothetically never experienced what I did. "So, you're saying the effect of the change would be immediate—even though I'd pick up on it."

"Exactly. And therein lies the problem with time travel and alterations to the timeline. The upstream effect is hardly predictable, but it is immediate. So far as the current theories claim."

That realization comes like a punch to the gut. It means that as long as I'm existing in the same time as Mashaule, I should be protected when it comes to changes, let's say, if he succeeded killing Kieran. I'd still be me, still know what I do now. But as soon as I'm upstream, the ripple effect would get me.

Translation: There's my answer. I can't just go home and regroup. The further I'm away from Mashaule's intervention, the slimmer the likelihood that I could fix it and the bigger the potential effect on the upstream timeline and myself if he ended up being successful.

Successful. I don't even want to use that word in context with Kieran's assassination. "There must be a way," I whisper. "There must."

Zio clears his throat. "You know, I'm not supposed to ask what's going on, but you are making me a bit nervous."

I wave both hands in front of my face, like chasing away mosquitos. "Oh! No, no, nothing has happened yet, I… I just want to be prepared in case it did. I can jump through time and space, there must be a way to fix what went wrong. In case it did, you know?" There must be other options besides the annihilation of a timeline—

My eyes pop open wide. That thought, it makes a lightbulb go off inside my mind. I whip my head up. "But Zio, if we stick to that example, what if the other timeline, ours right now, doesn't wither away? What if it splits off and now we have two timelines, one with the new events, one with the old?" Because I've seen it. I've been there: Other Nonie and Old Kieran. Definitely a different timeline. Universe.

Whatever. "Meaning, I will stay myself, because my timeline continues, so I could go back to the events at Alpha Rubrum and correct them, so that in that other timeline neither the Magellans nor the *Pioneer* get destroyed. Voila, timeline restored!" I beam at him.

My uncle ponders the idea for no more than a few seconds. "Good thinking, I see where you're coming from. You are suggesting a new timeline splitting off instead of the dominating one changing. From what science teaches us, we assume there are other timelines, but they aren't stable."

"Not stable? Like, they collapse?"

"Pretty much. There can only be one time continuum, as the flow of two different streams could upset the other and lead to complete destruction of the world as we know it. So yes, theoretically a split-off could happen, but we assume those branches won't survive. Again, sticking with the example: the new, dominant timeline would be one where the attack on Alpha Rubrum killed Magellans and the crew of the *Pioneer*. Us, here, now, would be the terminated branch. We wouldn't make it long."

I throw up my arms. "And do what? Stop existing?" That's just ridiculous! That other Nonie, the other Kieran—they're doomed? I can't believe that! It must've been years since whatever split their path from ours happened, and they're still there!

"That is, as I said, the prevailing theory."

I deflate. "It's all so confusing."

"I can't say it isn't." He pauses. "I still hope I could help you to a degree."

"You did, Zee. Thank you. I'm just frustrated with myself and fate in general." Because she's not making things easier for me. What if I'm already too far away from Mashaule, separated by literally too much time? All I can do is trust my First Sense and see where it leads me, and excuse me if I'm not the most confident about that.

My uncle inclines his head. "And you're leaving. Which won't be easy for either one of you. How long do I have?"

To prepare Kieran, of course. I lift my gaze to meet his. "I will be leaving within the hour."

"Okay then. I'll notify you when I'm ready."

"Thank you, Uncle."

He chuckles. "Anytime, Niece. And, Nonie?"

"Yes?"

"Trust in yourself like I trust in you." And with that he gets up, winks at me, and exits Kieran's quarters. But even after the doors have closed behind him, the uplifting effect of his words still lingers.

Trust in myself.

Maybe it's about time I do that again.

Chapter Nineteen -

PAYBACK

Somewhere, Somewhen

This time it's even clearer, like my mind was getting used to the craziness of a time-jump.

Still cold and hot at the same time.

Still a whirlwind of colors, events, things and people rushing past me, engulfing me and swallowing me, only to spit me out again. Bright specks whizz past me once in a while, leaving with streaks in the center of my vision.

But this time, I can think even more. Be me more. Feel more of what's going on. First Sense and self-confidence to the rescue. Still, it's the most unsettling sensation, like I was in the center of a hurricane, inside the eye of the storm: Chaos whirls around me, but where I am...

It's peaceful, somewhat.

Can't focus on anything specific, but I feel time rushing by. Feel places, much better than before. Also feel nothing at all.

The cloud-band of something light and colorful weaves around me, never touching, but close, so close, I can feel its pull. It wants me to touch it.

Is it the same I bumped into before? It feels peaceful though.

I reach out, drawn in by its beauty and something stronger, a longing—
Voices, a language I don't understand.
Yelling, panic—
SCREAMS.
QuaneezwarbattledeathdyingQuaneezscreamsscreamspainQuaneezKI
ERANSCREAMS—
Too much, too much, too much, stop that, stop it—
I pull back, begin to wobble, to lose my balance inside the eye of the
storm—
Dates, times, locations rush at me, assault me, trying to pull me off
course into the normal realm—
No, no, no, no! Not again! Focus, Nonie! First Sense, trust it, trust it—
Focus on the cavethecavethecaveTHECAVE—

I land in a crouched position on a cold, uneven surface, one hand stabilizing my fall on the ground, the other in the air for balance, superhero-style. Nicely don— Ow.

Ow, ow, ow. Chest.

Suppressing a grunt, I bend over. Each heartbeat stings and cramps, pumping a flood of barb-wired blood cells through my body. It feels like the first time the Bond was disrupted, after I arrived back in my time, and it felt like this times ten when I witnessed him getting shot in the raspberry fields.

Feeling this pain, it means I landed in the correct time, or at least… at least in a time where Kieran is dead.

A wave of absolute sadness crushes over me, worse than the pain, worse than anything, and yet it reminds me I'm here on purpose: to prevent Kieran from dying before his time. To *give* him time.

I force myself up to standing, my body protesting the movement by sending another ripple of pain through every single nerve fiber of my body. It's bad, but not nearly as bad as it was at the raspberry farm, when young Kieran's heart stopped in front of my very eyes. Yes, everything hurts, but I can function.

For a moment, guilt sets in, but I brush it off.

Throwing a look around, I can't believe my luck—or maybe my

skills. Thank you, Zio, for the pep talk. I'm exactly where I wanted to be, for a change! Maybe I'm getting the hang of things after all. Still, memory brings a chill to my spine. The cave is like I remember. Dark, cool, humid, reeking of old water and mold. A few battery-powered lights are haphazardly attached to the walls. I made it to the right location, let's hope it's also the right time. Chances are better than they've ever been, since I could focus more during the jump, despite those bloodcurdling screams.

A rough wheeze breaks from my throat, courtesy of the memory and the pain in my chest. But hey, I made it. I'm through. I'm out. Another wheeze. Another one. That. Was. Scary. Maybe the scariest jump of them all. Like being assaulted by Kieran's nightmares. A shudder runs down my back. Staying on track, not getting thrown out like when I landed with the young Quaneez—

Somebody screams. A child.

A girl.

I whirl to the right as fast as I can, considering my heart feels like it's being crushed by an ice berg, hand reaching for my weapon.

Another scream, this one loaded with pain.

I ball my hands into fists as acid rises up my throat.

This kid needs saving, too, and I won't let her down.

"PADdy, landing scan." I don't recall the exact layout. The last time I was here, my mind was caught in a fog of fear.

PADdy displays an outline of the caverns I jumped to, and *POP*, a sudden bright flash of Setayashi-radiation. "What—?"

"Just me," a female voice whispers from somewhere behind me.

Ignoring the sting in my heart and throbbing pain in my body, I spin around, the bit of artificial light shining right onto… "Hi, Me." I blink. That sounded wrong.

The other me grins. "Hi. And man, that sounded weird, didn't it?" Au contraire to me, she isn't hunched over by the loss of the Bond, but standing tall, like Nonie, Super-Hero Version.

"Totally." I stare at her. At *me*. Dressed in the black uniform of the FBTI, the rainbow patch on her—my—shoulder, Kieran's ring sparkling on her finger and her hair tied up in a ponytail, like I usually do. She looks good. *I* look good.

And speaking of—she looks so much like me, like young-me even, that I can't understand why nine-year-old Nonie never picked up on the similarities. Dad saw it—after he probably thought my mom resurrected from the dead—that much is clear.

This time, seeing myself triggers the newsflash that came quite delayed with our other encounter at the raspberry farm. This time, I can do the math. "It's good to see you. Means the timeline is staying on its path." Super-Hero Nonie to the rescue of Little Nonie and making sure everything comes as it should. I give her two thumbs up, for twice the luck. Plus, Future-Nonie serves as a visual reminder I will get my mission completed. I will make it home. Talk about a pick-me-upper after all those failures with Mashaule.

The other me cringes. "We-ll…" She stretches the word over four syllables, and it brings goosebumps to rise on my neck as alarms sound in my head.

Suddenly I'm not so sure anymore seeing her is good. "*Well*, what?"

She takes a fast breath in and cuts it off by snapping her mouth shut. Giving me an apologetic glance from underneath her lashes, she lifts and drops her shoulders. "You know, the funny thing is—"

Another scream pierces the silence, this one followed by pitiful yelps of pain.

Both of us older Nonie's turn a shade paler.

Star Hopper-Nonie takes three long strides until she's next to me. "Priorities. You'll be fine."

O-kaay.

That's reassuring at least.

She glances at her PADdy, which looks like mine. "We're just in time. You, the other cavern, where they keep the food. Me, I'll be taking care of little Nonie." She cracks her knuckles, then holds out a fist for me. "It's about time, isn't it?"

I know what she means. "It's about time." I bump her fist. "Take care in there."

For a moment, a small smile crosses her face. "You know I will. And so will you." She cracks her knuckles again, then her neck, and walks past me to the room that holds both our nightmares, straight and unafraid.

Power surges through me, the kind that numbs the constant ache and pain and makes me feel unstoppable. I'm not a born fighter. I'm good at it out of a need to never feel helpless again, but all fight I ever had stayed in the cave Star Hopper is going to right now—until this very moment. It feels like I've come full circle. For the first time since I was nine years old, I want to punch somebody. Hard.

And lucky me, because I think that can be arranged, because I do need that communicator. This is my last chance. If I fail, I have no clue what to do next.

But here's the thing: I won't fail. I'm going to make it back and make things right, and if that isn't an ego boost, I don't know.

I don't bother sneaking through the cavern. I've been here, and I've lived in fear for the days they held me.

I'm not that person anymore.

Like Star Hopper, I do my best to walk straight, with a purpose. Unafraid, my gun at the ready, pointing at the ground in front of me.

The cave is narrow around here, but opens up to a larger area once I'm around a little bend. It's still not very big, maybe five by six meters or so, but quite high, at least six or seven meters. They put up more lights here than anywhere else, because this is their quote-unquote room: two mattresses at the far end. Food in boxes on the floor to the left. A table and two chairs smack in the middle—and in one of the chairs facing me, Bad Guy #1.

He's focusing on the PAD on the table in front of him and doesn't even look up, even though he must've picked up on my steps. I'm waiting for the surge of panic I had every time this guy came close to me.

It's not there.

He's not the monster my mind made him to be—actually, he is, but from an ethical point of view. In reality, he's nothing more than a man who made the wrong choices in his life.

Abducting me was one of them.

They held me in this cave until I was too broken and afraid to fight back, to move, or even to breathe. They beat me, didn't feed me, made me feel like at any point they were going to snuff out my life.

Anger rises, and it comes with a boost of aggression very unlike me. But boy, does it fuel me up.

I lost a piece of myself in these caverns. It's time I take it back.

Shoving my weapon back into the holster, I ready myself. For this, I won't need a gun. I don't *want* a gun.

Maybe the lack of steps triggered the man's awareness, because he lifts his gaze from the book. "You done with your disgusting—" His eyes pop wide. "Who are you?"

"Hello. It's me, your future nightmare." I smirk, wink—and burst forward.

The guy's about to push himself off the table and get up, but I'm faster. *SMACK!* My right round kick connects with his temple, knocking him off the chair and onto the cold, wet cave ground. Try it out. I was tied to that for days.

Recoiling my leg over the table, I drop into my fighting stance and move to the side. Bad Guy is on all fours, pressing a hand against the left side of his mouth. Some blood trickles out from between his fingers. He groans. "What the—?"

Time to set my agenda. "You know, I'm looking for something." *BOOM!* This kick lands right in his flank, its force throwing him onto his side.

A suffocated grunt breaks from his throat as he curls up in pain.

Welcome to how life with you was for me. As it is my chest spasms with each breath, but the pain I suffered in this cave when I was nine years old was so much greater than what I'm feeling now, robbed of Kieran's Bond. I'll be fine.

One more kick, for good measure, and to help him remember. "It's oval, grey, and somebody who's on my bad list gave it to you." I stomp onto his exposed side, and while yes, it feels great to give payback to the monster fueling my nightmares, he isn't getting up, isn't fighting.

What am I missing?

Lightning fast, I dart forward and drop my knee on his belly to keep him in place. Grabbing him by the shirt I cock my left fist back. "What's wrong with you? Fight!"

I feel him trying to catch a breath under my knee. "Don't want to fight," he rasps, each word cut short from my weight focused on one single spot in his abdomen and the courtesy of eating four prior kicks.

"Well, too bad, then you shouldn't have kidnapped—" Me. "—the girl in there."

"Agreed." His breath comes out short. "Left pocket. The disk."

Hope and wariness shoot through me, competing for first place. "You're just going to give it to me?" I increase pressure on his stomach, and while it's not fun to be on the receiving end of this, if he had any training, he'd tolerate it. The way he's not contracting his abs, not regulating his breathing—this man isn't a fighter.

But that doesn't mean he can't be dangerous to me. Buzzwords *Mashaule, raspberry farm.*

I grab his arm and roll him onto his stomach, then lock his arm into a police hold. He yelps out when I stretch his shoulder to the max, but again, it's not *that* bad. "Left pocket?"

"Uh-huh." He gives a weak nod.

Keeping my hold on him, I slide my hand into the pocket, which is borderline creepy and disgusting. The things we do for the timeline…! I feel around—and there we go! Wrapping my fingers around the small disk I pull my hand out and check my bounty.

Score! It's the communicator-thingy!

Keeping the pressure on his shoulder, I stuff the device into my pocket. "Does your friend have another one?" Can't believe I'm making sure they have a means to leave this time, like they're *supposed* to. Grr.

"Yes." A wheeze follows his word. "We each got one."

"Who gave it to you?"

"I dunno."

I move his elbow higher and he yelps out. "I don't know! I don't! I swear!"

And for some reason, I believe him. Both, getting the communicator and this fight—they didn't go as I imagined it. Not at all. For one, I was afraid coming here would wake up old demons, but turns out I have enough new ones to make the old ones look less scary.

For another, I thought I would have to fight tooth and nail to take the device from Bad Guy #1, but in the end, he wasn't a worthy opponent for Lieutenant Nonie Thorburn. All he ever was was a nightmare to young Nonie.

But what really bugs me the most is the feeling that I'm missing something, and I have no clue what, or even in which direction it's going. Like I knew the answer to a riddle before the riddle was even said. It's there, at the outskirts of my mind, just out of reach, teasing and taunting me.

Why did the other Nonie react so weird just now? Why did this guy here not fight? And most of all, why the heck does the blue future holo-man want Kieran dead, even though he's going to die soon anyway?

What am I missing?

What. Am. I. Missing?

The guy on the floor groans, and it brings me back to the fight in front of me.

I bend lower to whisper into his ear. "If I were you, I'd stay down here. I've got a gun trained at you. One move, and *bang*. You got me?"

A frantic nod tells me the answer before he says it out loud. "Y-yes."

Letting go of his arm I stand back up and move out of his reach. Playing possum won't fool me twice. Thank you for that lesson, former admiral.

And now that I have the disc, and possibly a means to get ahead of Mashaule, I have to find a safe place to sort things out. Away from critical moments in time. Just me and my disc, somewhere, somewhen. Finding a way to the future guy's mind, or at least his plans. It's time I stay a step ahead of him, not vice-versa.

I throw one more glance at the man who helped kidnap me. His breath comes out ragged, the only body part moving being his chest. That's how afraid he is. Of me.

I hope I gave him the same nightmares he gave me.

"Sweet dreams," I whisper, then press the button on my SED.

The piercing bright white light flares up—

Chapter Twenty -
HISTORY

Somewhere, Somewhen

Like the last time, I stay awake during the jump.

Time swirls around me, a chaotic maelstrom of events, flavored with love, loss, hate, aggression—

The one colorful, different cloudy strand is there, calling out to me, but I'm not touching it this time. No need for more screams and fuel for nightmares.

Instead, I try to open up my First Sense and focus on Mashaule. Must try to find him. Or, find a safe spot in time—

I do my best to relax, to welcome any sensations, to not overlook the slightest twinge of my First Sense. Like a dying storm, the Maelstrom calms down, little, by little, the chaotic waves losing velocity and strength, passing me by at a much slower pace—

There! Mashaule! Mashaule, I'm sure! I saw him, felt him, whatever! Like a blip—

I throw my arms out and dig my heels in, like I was a desperate snowboarder on a fast run trying to slow down, and focus on the glimpse of

174

Mashaule I saw and felt.

The maelstrom stops, reverts, picks up speed— There! I was right, I was so right! I feel him, right there, Mashaule, the old admiral, not the younger one!

Elation runs high. Must land there. Must land—

My toes touch carpeted floors, then my heels, as I land in a soft stance in… the back of a shuttle? I blink. A shuttle. Older model, similar to the *Odysseus.* Why a shuttle?

"Weapons loaded and ready," the shuttle's computer voice announces.

"Acknowledged. *Yosemite*, keep sensors open—"

Mashaule! A mix of giddiness and determination floods me. I felt him—I landed in the right time and the right location! For the second time in a row! Who's rocking the whole time-jumping thing? Me! And who's going to keep Mashaule from killing Kieran?

Also me.

"—and fire on any launching shuttle." He confirms the order with the push of a button.

"Confirmed. Parameters set and locked."

Fire on any launching shuttle…! Oh heck, not with me here to prevent just that! There's no shooting on anybody nor anything in this time, whenever I may be.

Dropping low, I sneak forward into the cockpit, fast, but taking care to make not any hasty movements that he could pick up on. My biggest enemy besides Mashaule is the large, wide front window and the potential for my reflection popping up in there.

I needn't worry. Mashaule, seated on the left seat of the two seats in the cockpit, is focused on the readouts the shuttle is providing for him. I sneak a peek out the windows, and my heart all but stops. *Pioneer* hangs in space to our right, across a beautiful nebula.

I don't care who's going to be in that shuttle, even though I can make an educated guess.

No time to lose. With a growl, I charge forward.

Mashaule jerks from the unexpected sound coming from behind him, but before he can react, I have one arm wrapped around his neck, pinning him against the seat in a headlock from behind.

He gurgles and scrambles to pull down my forearm blocking his airway, frantically pushing up with his feet to take pressure off his strangulated throat.

I'm not letting go. With all the willpower I have, I hold on to my forearms, pulling with all my might, but it's not enough. Mashaule uses both hands to pluck on the weakest part of my hold, at my thumbs, buying himself enough space to not get choked out. Strength against strength he overpowers me, no questions asked, I'm the first one to admit that, and right now he's using his one advantage against me. Mashaule moves his lower body to the side while I still have his torso pinned to the seat by his neck, and what was an advantage a few seconds ago—the backrest of the seat as a barrier for me to choke him against—has now turned into a disadvantage for me. Mashaule reaches into a side pocket and draws a knife. The absurdity of the situation isn't lost on me, because from where I'm standing, all I see is a body below the belly button, a hand, a knife in it.

It looks surreal and freaky, but is no less dangerous than if I didn't have him by the neck.

Mashaule growls—and blindly stabs the knife forward to where he assumes I'm standing.

With a yelp, I barely evade the blade, but my grip on his neck slips. Mashaule pulls his head out of my hold and bounces up to standing, a tad wobbly, hair in total disarray from escaping my hold.

I don't give him time to process what he's seeing. Whom he's seeing. The last time Mashaule, me, and a knife met, it didn't go well for me, and I have no desire for a repeat performance. That weapon needs to go.

Before he can find his bearings and stab again, I kick him right in the groin. His eyes pop wide. With a chocked-off *oomph*, he doubles over—

I dart forward, grabbing his wrist holding the knife and bend it over, so he loses his tight grip on the hilt and I can peel the weapon out of his hand—

Mashaule drives his shoulder into my midsection and tackles me against the shuttle's lateral console. "You again." He sneers, and rams his knee upward into my stomach.

I barely get one arm forward to block some of the impact—no room to avoid it completely with me flush against the console. The knee lands with a thud, drawing a pained groan from my throat. Mashaule has his full weight pushing forward into me, keeping me pinned and leaving me no room to defend myself.

He recoils his leg for another knee—

I act more on instinct than anything else, part of me realizing this is my only valid defense, no matter if I want to or not. Blocking his knee as much as I can with one forearm, I stab Mashaule in the other leg with his knife.

He howls out, curses—

But doesn't crumble, doesn't lose his grip on me.

Quite the opposite. Anger flares in his eyes, paired with rage and a touch of madness. "You're going to pay for that," he hisses at me, spittle flying. Like me stabbing him had popped a bubble of restraint, Mashaule turns wild. He elbows my face, knees, grabs, yanks, head butts—all at the same time.

I cry out and defend, defend, *defend*, miss several attacks, get hit, defend more—I'm slicing him with the knife during my attempts to keep myself in one piece, but it has no effect at all.

An elbow hits me smack in the temple, bringing a wave of dizziness and disorientation, but also clarity. I'm fighting a mad man. I've stabbed him, sliced him, and yet he barges on, like the pain didn't even register.

Icy fear shoots through my veins. Mashaule has turned himself into the most dangerous opponent one could fight: a man who's either lost it or has nothing left to lose, a man who doesn't care about his own life, willing to sacrifice it for the greater good.

Not. Going. To. Happen.

With the strength of absolute desperation, I shove Mashaule off me, creating the slightest bit of distance. Change of plans. I ram my palm onto the reader on the console to my left. "*Yosemite*, abort locked and loaded parameters! Power down weapons—" I squeak when Mashaule kicks to my midsection and redirect the kick with my forearm in the nick of time.

"Unable to comply. Admiral's override needed."

What the absolute—

My blood pressure drops. Even if I defeat Mashaule, the shuttle's going to fire. That bastard!

I deflect a haymaker punch, counter with a cross to Mashaule's face, and get rewarded with a crunching sound. Blood pours from his nose, but he doesn't seem to care.

"No way out, Thorburn. I'm killing Wildason, and you're going to be watching every second of it." His lips spread into a mad grin, showing dark red teeth, courtesy of the blood running down his face. "I'll kill him! Kill him! *Kill him!*" he screeches as spittle flies with every word.

Holy Sun and Stars, he's mad. He's gone mad for reals, there's no other explanation for his behavior.

All tiny hairs on my body rise in response, as if they could protect me from the evil oozing off the man in front of me.

He charges—

I jump to the side and behind the seat, keeping it between myself and Mashaule. Change of plans, again. Can't win this alone unless I kill Mashaule, and that's not very high on my to-do-list. *"Yosemite,* open emergency channel to *USEF Pioneer!"*

"Channel opened."

I can only hope we're in a time where Kieran and the others know me, or else this might backfire spectacularly: *"Pioneer,* this is Nonie. Hold all shuttle traffic! Code Magenta, emergency demat, two people!"

Mashaule's eyes widen as realization strikes. "No!" He throws himself at me, over the seat, frantically reaching for me, getting me by the shirt—

"Acknowledged, Yosemite. Stand by." Chase!

Mashaule roars out in frustration, rams his fist into my face, while I grab him by the shirt, raise my knife—

Warmth, tingling, everything turning dark—

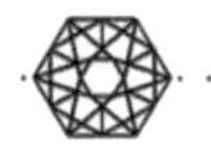

USEF Pioneer, Demat room, Somewhen

—and we materialize in a heap of tangled extremities smack in the middle of the *Pioneer*'s demat room. Thank the Universe!

Somebody gasps in surprise, and I jump into action. With one quick turn and shift of weight, I take all support from Mashaule. He staggers forward, and before he can reveal himself to the crew of the *Pioneer,* I bring him down with a kick to the back of his knees. He crumbles to the ground, and I throw myself onto his back, taking him into another headlock and pressing the blade against his neck. "One move and I'll slice you. Bye-bye, carotid."

Mashaule freezes, his heavy panting ending in a grunt. But he doesn't fight.

"Holy Sun and Stars," somebody whispers behind me. Alyssa? Sounded like her, but I'm not taking my eyes off Mashaule.

"I need a prison hood and two guards plus a cell in the brig. You might want to throw in medical as well." I want to bring him back to our time alive and in one piece. No matter what information he has, we need every little bit. "And let the bridge know to *really* hold *all* shuttle launches, I'll explain in a minute."

Here's to the senior officers having seen me before, because all Alyssa says is, "Got it." Then, she gets to work. Not even twenty seconds later, a security team storms into the demat room, heavy boots clattering on the floors with every hasty step.

I hold up a hand. "Take position behind us, ready your weapons. I need the hood first." Even though I'd love to ruin Mashaule's reputation for the next decades to come, it wouldn't help to keep the timeline on its natural path. Hence, the hood.

Ever so carefully I release the non-armed hand from around Mashaule's neck. He's got several weapons aimed at him, but if he's truly so crazy that he has nothing to lose, he might consider dying fast by the hand of a security officer the best option. "Shoot only to disable. No killing the prisoner." He misbehaves, he pays for it.

But he doesn't.

Somebody places a thin fabric item into my outstretched hands.

Good. Can't say I'm a big fan of prison hoods, but they get the job done. Sound proof in both directions. Light proof. O2-permeable. Vital sign supervision. Nothing better to deprive a prisoner of their senses and to keep them safe and their identity hidden. Wouldn't call it pleasant for the person wearing it, but given that my tolerance for Mashaule has expired times ten, I couldn't possibly care less for him.

I press the knife harder against Mashaule's neck. He rewards me with a stiffening of his body and a sharp inhale. "I'll remove the knife. You twitch, do anything, they shoot you and I promise it will hurt. Understood?"

He nods.

For a gal who hates fighting, I've come a long way.

I shove the knife into the shaft of my boots, then pull the hood above his head and activate it. Once it has tightened to fit his head, the control light blinks green: maximum permeability for oxygen and deprivation features activated.

I wave to the guards. "Take him to the brig."

The security officers rush forward and grab Mashaule by the arms, yanking him up to standing and helping him limp toward the door. He leaves smeared blood stains on the previously spotless floors.

If I was expecting a fight, I'm not getting one. Like a good prisoner, Mashaule complies—

Ugh. I mentally facepalm myself. "Wait!" Almost enabled him. I'm sure he would've had a chance to sneak a hand into his pocket. I pat him down, which is way more physical contact I ever want with this man again. There—in his right front pocket. I reach in and take the communicator. Mashaule's shoulders slump forward when I take the device from him. Guess that was his plan. Sorry-not-sorry.

Too funny. First, I couldn't find Mashaule or one of those things, now I have two disks and one admiral.

I like it.

"Carry on. Keep him within a Level 10 containment field with subatomic stabilization. No access besides by Commander Upinga or myself." Look at that, me learning from the future, or rather, past. But hey, if it adds another layer of safety, I'm fine with that.

And now we've got to take care of that shuttle.

I dart to the console Alyssa is standing at and hit the com button. "Demat room to bridge."

"Conolly here. Good to hear your voice, traveller."

A smile spreads across my face. "Likewise. About holding of those launches: we have an issue with the shuttle hidden inside that nebula."

There's a short pause before he answers. *"We found it after your hail. Was hidden from our sensors pretty well. What kind of problem? Because we're about to launch a shuttle with the captain on board."* I hear the implied question: does it endanger him?

"Can you delay until I'm there?" I'm already jogging to the doors.

"Yes, we ca—"

I run through the blissfully empty hallways. Could be my imagination, but they seem a little less new, a little less sparkly. When am I? Late enough for them to know Code Magenta and not be surprised by me showing up again and out of nowhere, but that doesn't really narrow it down much.

The doors to the bridge open automatically when they sense me, and I slow down. Straightening my black shirt I enter the bridge. Chocho looks up from his work, skin waxy and dark circles under his eyes, like he wasn't feeling well. He gives me a curt nod that I return.

Chase gets out of the captain's chair, his probing gaze scanning over me. A frown crosses his face, then turns into a worried expression. He points to his jawbone and temple, giving me a pointed look. "Should I get Zio—?"

"I'm fine." I lift one hand to where Chase pointed. Swollen. Bruised. But a small price to pay considering it got me Mashaule. Didn't even feel it thanks to the adrenaline high. I drop my hand, a grin pulling on the corners of my mouth. "Hey, I didn't get stabbed." A comment innocent enough if my bloody reappearance on the *Pioneer* hasn't happened yet for him, but a nice nod to the improvement of my situation if it did.

"And despite the bruises, you seem to be in good spirits." He winks.

Given that I just fulfilled my job description, an appropriate assessment. I shrug, then blow on my cuticles and rub them over my shirt. "I may not look like it, but so far things went well." Don't want to jinx it. Speaking of. Dropping my hand, I cut a look at Chase. "As long as we're holding all shuttles."

Within a second, Chase is all business. "We are. Give me the rundown."

I lower my voice. "The shuttle is programmed to shoot at any shuttle the *Pioneer* is launching."

He grimaces. "Override?"

"Admiral level only." And really, whenever I return to my time, can we just give me some kind of super-FBTI-agent override status? Being powerless doesn't make my work any easier.

"That's a problem." He points at the view screen and the purple-blueish tendrils of a nebula displayed on it.

I agree. "Since the Captain was about to take a shuttle out there."

"Correct."

Well, it might be a problem, but not one we couldn't solve. I shrug. "The only way to keep him safe then is to destroy that shuttle." Which would play right into me. Less evidence left in this time of whatever Mashaule planned.

Chase nods. "Agreed." He turns to his left. "Manazari, target practice. You destroy that shuttle with one hit, you get yourself an early start into the weekend. Think you can do it?"

Manazari cracks his knuckles. "Sir, please." He adjusts something, and *ZING*, the *Pioneer* fires, its weapons hitting the shuttle dead center.

BOOM!

A fireball of explosion lights up the screen.

"I'll take my early weekend then, sir."

Chase chuckles. "At 1500 hours, freedom is yours." He taps his Hablamate. "Bridge to Wildason."

"Wildason here."

"You'd be good to go, Captain, but we just switched to Code Magenta, but I think you were probably ahead of us on that one." Hint-hint, since the revival of the Bond would have been hard to not notice.

"By a mile, Commander. Already out of the shuttle." He pauses. *"Lieutenant? You know where to find me."*

My tummy flops in anticipation. "Of course, sir." Mashaule can sit in the brig for another few days if it's up to me. I'll take any opportunity to see Kieran.

He sounds businesslike, appropriate over the general com. *"See you soon then. Wildason out."*

Chase sits back down, leaning forward. "All right, everybody. I want the sensors on full sensitivity. Anything happens in that nebula, I want to know about it. Just because the captain has a hunch doesn't mean it's all unicorns and rainbows from here."

I tilt my head. "What kind of hunch?" That doesn't sound like Kieran. He's not the man to act on hunches without data or facts. Guess that's what being friends with Zio teaches you.

Chase curves a finger at me to come closer, then lowers his voice. "He's been talking about a theory that there's life in those L-class nebulas. Zio hasn't found anything, neither has Hayes, but both agreed that the captain might be able to gather more conclusive data from inside that nebula, even though it's one of the nasty ones." He shrugs. "If you ask me, he's been having a hard time with the war and the nightmares. He needs something good to happen. A discovery of life, whatever type or form it may be, would be just the thing."

Pressure builds in my chest together with a ball of unease forming in my stomach. Why don't I like the sound of that? Kieran, a nebula… It rings a bell I'd rather not hear making a sound at all. "Chase, what's the date today?"

"Today? June 8th, 2257." He focuses on his PAD, a saving grace for me, because there's no way he'd have missed my reaction otherwise.

No.

No, no, no.

Absolute horror wraps around my heart and squeezes until no blood is left to pump, leaving me dizzy and lightheaded.

June 8th, 2257.

Today is the day Kieran is going to die.

He's not going to come out of that nebula again. They won't find much left—

Trip looks up from his PAD. "Me personally, I'd prefer to not stay too long in this region of space. The nebula is quite rough to fly, which is why the *Pioneer* won't go in. Plus, too much Quaneez activity. Actually, I'd have preferred not being here at all, but Captain's orders. Anyway, my point is, go." He winks at me. "I'd like a short briefing later, because your presence usually comes with an extra serving of surprises, but for now I'd be happy if we didn't delay Kieran's expedition for too long." He winks again, and I get the hint: speed it up.

Only speeding it up is the last thing I want to do.

I want to drag it out.

Drag it out until eternity.

Delay him.

Convince him to stay.

I want to change the freakin' flow of time.

And I know I can't.

"Nonie?" Chase waves a hand in front of my eyes. "You okay?"

"Y-yeah. Sure. S-sorry," I mumble, fixing the fakest of fake smiles on my face. "Just had a weird jump getting here, you know?" I back up. "I'll… I'll go and see the captain now."

Conolly nods slowly, one eye brow cocked up. "You do that, you little weirdo," he adds with a soft chuckle, and waves me off. "This nebula gives me the creeps. I want to get out of here before something jumps us."

The last bit of blood drains from my face.

He doesn't even know how right he is. Only, it's not going to jump the *Pioneer*.

No, the only casualty is going to be Kieran.

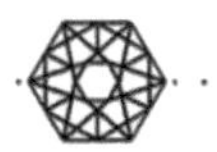

USEF Pioneer, Captain's Quarters, June 8th, 2257

Never have I been more thankful for Code Magenta. If anybody saw me racing through the *Pioneer*'s hallways like it was a matter of life or death I'd have a hard time explaining that it's exactly that: a matter of life or death.

Of death, actually.

Logically, I know Kieran is safe for now. He will die in that nebula, not here on the *Pioneer*, but I can't shake the feeling that if I delayed his departure for too long, the timeline might find another way to kill him right in front of me to stay intact.

Because the timeline is bitchy and mean like that.

Bitterness rises, adding to the overwhelming sense of nausea. How unfair, sarcastic, and sadistic to lead me to this very day. I save Kieran from Mashaule—why? To grant him another hour or two? I'll happily do that, but it feels like fate just laughed in my face and showed me the middle finger. *Nice try, Nonie, he'll still die.*

No, Mashaule didn't kill Kieran—but everything about this whole spiel feels wrong. Mashaule gets his instructions from the future, so why would they make him kill Kieran *minutes* before his death? The person calling the shots upstream must know he dies in this nebula, it's common knowledge at my time, why shouldn't it be in his? Mashaule knows for sure, he was on active duty during that time, so he lived this part of history. Did he completely lose his mind? He seemed quite unhinged when we fought in the shuttle, that's for sure, but is that all there is, or am I missing something? Is whatever the upstream power wants to prevent happening in the next few minutes, before his departure into the nebula? But there's nothing logged at all, nothing! Enter the shuttle, fly into the nebula, get killed.

I stop dead in my tracks and kick the wall to my right with all I have, a frustrated, animalistic grunt breaking from my throat. Screw you, fate! Screw you, timeline! Kieran doesn't deserve to die this young, and neither do I to lose him! I kick the wall once more, leaving marks, then bend over and support my weight with my hands on my knees. Every breath comes out wheezy and harsh, while my heart hammers away as if it was trying out if it could beat for Kieran's and keep it alive.

Only that's not going to happen.

It's not going to happen.

I know that.

Swallowing down the rising bile, I straighten up and press the heel of my palm against my eyes. I want to see Kieran once more before... before he dies. I just saw him about an hour ago, but that doesn't count. Jumping through time, blinking in and out of existence for him, it makes me appreciate every second we have even more, because even though I can go back, it wouldn't be the same if I did.

It can't be.

I drag myself the last few meters until I'm in front of his quarters. Deep breath, Nonie. Deep breath.

Focusing on the deep inhale, I lay my hand on the palm reader and the door opens a second later.

Kieran looks up from the desk he's standing in front of. "Nonie." He closes the little secret chocolate drawer with the push of his palm. I can't put my finger on it, but he sounds off somehow.

Stepping inside, the doors hiss shut behind me. Since the lights are quite dimmed, it takes me a while to see Kieran clearly when he walks around the desk and toward me, and when I do, I almost wish I hadn't. He looks horrible. The contrast of quote-unquote *just* having seen him a short while ago for me, but at the beginning of this war for him, versus now, is hard to overlook: hollowed cheeks, dark circles under his eyes, pale skin. He smiles at me, but only with an uptick to his lips. Not his eyes. They look... dull. Haunted.

It hurts me to the core to see him like this. "Kieran." I whisper and meet him half way. "What—?"

He wraps his arms around me in such a tender, gentle way it tugs on a heart string. This isn't the overjoyed reunion we've had the other times we met. This is different. Slow. Controlled. Careful. Like the brakes were on.

Leaning his forehead against mine, he whispers, "Hey, stranger. You look like you had a rough day."

So do you.

I swallow hard. "It's nothing. And I'm... happy to be here." With you. To have the privilege of... saying goodbye. An ache opens up in my chest, deep as a chasm.

Kieran glides one careful finger over my swollen cheek bone. "I was thinking quite a bit about you for the last two days. I didn't think I was going to see you for a while. I—" He snaps his mouth shut, then releases a soft breath.

He what?

I swallow all the sadness, all the grief down and focus on this very moment, cupping his face with both my palms. "Stupid. You're always supposed to think about me. Girlfriend. Remember?" I tap the nail of my thumb against the ring on my fourth finger.

Recognizing the sound Kieran breathes out a soft chuckle. "You're still wearing it."

"I'll never take it off." The words are spoken before my brain had even time to think them through, but it doesn't matter. They're true.

"Good."

If he wasn't right in front of me, I'd have a hard time hearing him. Compared to the Kieran I left an hour ago, this Kieran is a different person. Subdued and quiet, like somebody had pressed the mute button. I suck in my lower lip. "What's wrong?"

His fingers dig into my shirt on my back. "Everything."

"That's a lot." I kiss the tip of his nose, and he smiles the faintest of all smiles.

"I know. But I'll be fine." His resigned tone isn't matching the words at all.

Seeing him like this is beyond hard. I chew on my lower lip when Kieran doesn't elaborate. "Are you?" I know he won't, but right now I don't think even he believes what he says.

He stays silent, the muscles in his jaw working overtime under my palms. Eventually, he swallows hard. "Chocho's wife died last month. Suzie died."

My thumbs still their tender brushing across his cheeks. "Suzie died?"

"We were fighting two Quaneez battleships. Had a hull breach. Only one casualty. Her."

"Shit," I whisper. Chocho's wife. They just got married. And now… she's gone, he a widower. My throat feels dry and rough. No wonder he looked off when I saw him on the bridge a few minutes ago.

"Yeah," he whispers back. "And you're probably thinking we've lost hundreds of thousands of people, if not millions already. Why is he making such a big deal about one person?"

"Kieran—"

"I can't tell you why. It just hit me on a different level. Another life gone. Another family destroyed. Another person's future ruined by an unnecessary war."

"It wears on you." No surprise. Chocho is part of his bridge crew. He officiated their wedding. That's gotta make you feel closer to somebody. Plus, Kieran was against this war from the very beginning. Had they let him handle it his way, who knows, history might have turned out differently. Seeing the effect of the war, its destruction, it changes people.

He moves his head up and down in the smallest of all nods. "And that's why… That nebula… Don't tell Chase, but I'm about ninety percent sure there are Quaneez in there."

The breath I was about to take gets stuck in my throat. "Come again?" I squeak.

"You heard me right. It might sound crazy, but I feel like they're there."

"You *feel* like they're there." As in, he knew he was going into Quaneez territory before they killed him? He freakin' *knew*? And he still went in—and he still got killed!

"Every time I close my eyes."

I cock my head. "Your nightmares." Unease stirs in my stomach.

"Not just nightmares, Nonie. They're too real. Like *they* were there with me. I hear them scream, Nonie. Every. Single. Night." His chest heaves with erratic breaths, and boy, can I relate. Hearing Kieran scream when I jump through time, seeing images of Quaneez… If I had to hear that every night, I'd be teetering on the edge of sanity.

"And I know it's not logical or based on any data at all, but they're there. They must be. I know their drive is fast and they pop up out of nowhere, but it isn't *that* great." He huffs out a dry laugh. "Ask Trip about it. But my point is, they must be hiding somewhere. Why not a nebula our sensors are having a hard time with? And if we want peace, we've got to take risks. We can't keep on killing each other. There must be a way to start the dialog, and I want to find it."

"Kieran—"

"You're not going to change my mind about it, Nonie."

I snap my mouth shut, and Kieran continues. "I need to give it all I got. I couldn't live with myself if I didn't." His voice drops, barely audible. "I'm having a hard time with myself the way it is." He flattens his palms against my back, but keeps his forehead pressed into mine. "And I know you don't like me to go on away missions, but this one I have to do."

My heart goes out to him. In this very moment I'm more than tempted to ignore what I've been taught and tell him he's not going to find any peace in that nebula aside from final eternal peace. Why shouldn't I tell him? What's in it for me to keep him in the dark?

Absolutely nothing.

Isn't it typical human arrogance to assume we have to preserve the timeline? Maybe it needed to change! Why do we think we have the right to say what should or shouldn't happen? Just because it did happen once before it must happen again? Isn't that just self-protection of the people upstream, in the future? *Oh, let's not change the past because it might alter what we have now.* And what if it did? I don't see how that could be considered bad from the get-go! Nobody should be playing God, but aren't we doing exactly that by trying to keep things from changing? Maybe change is necessary—I'm really starting to think that maybe if Kieran hadn't died, the war would've gone differently.

The image of Old Kieran and Other Nonie pops back into my mind. I should've asked her. Should've found out what was different in their universe, so that I had a case to bring up to the FBTI and Taro Magona. On the other hand—who cares? How about I tell Kieran all I know, and maybe then he won't fly into that nebula. Maybe he'll live on and turn a hundred and twenty. But if I'm to believe the Taro and what I've been taught, they—I—might not exist if the past changed. Which is why we preserve the oh-so-holy timeline.

Anger rises. No idea what brought my change in attitude, but the last few jumps have changed *something*, because I feel cheated, cheated by a timeline I have to protect, but that in return is taking from me what

I desire most.

All I want is more of Kieran.

More life. More love. More us. More *everything*.

And there just isn't enough time.

I wish I was more daring. More egoistic. Then I could tell the timeline to go screw itself and warn Kieran, keep him alive.

But, I'm not.

Like Kieran couldn't live with himself if he didn't try to make peace, I couldn't live with myself knowing I sacrificed the future of generations for my own purpose. I'm an obedient little soldier.

Which leaves only one option.

I let go of his face and lean back to get a better look at him. The next words will tear my soul in two, no doubt about it, but they have to be spoken to preserve the stupid, idiotic timeline.

"Kieran?" I whisper.

"Hm?" He keeps his eyes closed, and I'm thankful for it.

Drawing in a deep breath and holding it for a moment I pull together all the maturity I have, all the strength, all the professionalism. "I know you have to do this mission. Go and check out that nebula. Chase is getting nervous."

I smooth my thumb over his cheeks, committing the feel of his stubble under my hands to memory, the outline of his face, the scent of his skin... everything that makes Kieran Kieran. Even though I could go back and see him again, it won't be the same. This is final.

He opens his eyes and locks his gaze with mine. "Okay." A small smile pulls on the corners of his lips. "Do me a favor?"

"Anything."

"Keep an eye on things from the bridge, will you? I feel better with you around. Always."

From the bridge—

Front row seats to Kieran's death.

I swallow hard. Suck it up, Thorburn. It's a price I need to be able to pay. I *chose* to comply with fate and not warn him. I *chose* to let him die. In the grand scheme of things, it feels right that I should bear witness to what I know will happen. "Of course." I lean forward and connect my lips to his for a kiss that only lasts a moment, but one I will remember for the rest of my life.

My next words have to be said. I'd never forgive myself if I didn't. Pulling back, I look at the man I felt connected to ever since I learned about him, the man I fell in love with the moment I met him, the man whose presence will be with me for the rest of my life. I wish I could save him, or if not that, then at least take some of that weight off his shoulders for the last minutes of his life. I can do neither, but I can make sure he knows what I feel for him. Maybe it's going to give his soul something to cling to.

Emotion clogs my throat. "I love you, Kieran. Through time and space, and no matter what."

I feel a little shock going through his system, like he touched a live wire. His eyes flicker shut, long lashes fanning his cheeks, and when he opens them, he looks me straight in the eye. He stares at me for an eternal second with a breathtaking intensity I can feel all the way down to my toes, and when he answers me, his voice carries the emotion to match his words. "I love you too, Nonie. I love you so much I can't even tell you, because I don't want to scare you away."

"You'll never scare me away," I whisper.

"That's good to know, because I kind of have to rely on you visiting me. I'm limited like that." He winks, for the first time in this visit some of Kieran's mischievousness shining through. "And just for the record, I was yours since you saved my butt on that godforsaken planet, and cheesy as it is, I will love you for the rest of my life." The apple in his throat moves up and down and his smile falters the slightest.

The words of his letter he left for me, the letter I found back in my present, return with a vengeance: *We never did have time on our side, did we?*

Like a dark cloud, his short future washes over me.

He was right.

We never had enough time.

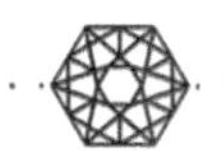

USEF Pioneer, Bridge, June 8ᵗʰ, 2257

"Sir, the *Adventurer* has left the hangar bay." Manazari changes the front view screen to a forward overview.

Chase gives him a curt nod. "Acknowledged. Keep her on screen and the sensors open, like I said."

"Aye, sir."

Everybody on the bridge is doing their job like it was any ordinary day. Only I know that in less than five minutes their captain, their friend, will be gone, and their lives forever changed, just like mine. The repetition of history in front of my very eyes twists my stomach into a Gordian knot and suffocates my lungs.

Kieran.

The urge to speak up, to say *something*, to come up with any excuse to keep him on the *Pioneer* is beyond imperative.

And yet I don't move.

Don't speak up.

Don't do anything besides watching Kieran's shuttle on the view screen in the front of the bridge.

The biggest pity is that history will never know the role his early death played. That it saved billions of people. I refuse to believe the nonsense Mashaule spouted before he jumped from USEF jail. In the depth of my heart, I know it would be the other way around. If Kieran had survived, the war would have been shorter.

Technically speaking, I succeeded in my mission to keep Kieran alive until now. Still, unease stirs in the pit of my stomach and adds another layer to the misery washing over me. Mashaule is crazy. Truly crazy, judging by the way he behaved in the shuttle, but... But what if he isn't?

Something beeps at Hayes' workstation. "Commander, I'm picking up on quite a few spots of Tau radiation."

"Tau? You telling me there's a terraformed colony in there we don't know about?" Chase sits up straight and turns to look at his science officer as my heart skips a beat. Tau radiation... It's always that Tau-radiation. I spent all my Academy training without ever hearing about it, but out in the field, it's everywhere.

Correction. It's everywhere the Quaneez pop up.

Heat rushes through my body. Sun and Stars, could that be—

Hayes shakes his head. "No, sir, no terraformed planet or anything I can get a reading on."

Chase exhales. "Good. At least I don't have to worry about a population of unknowns in there."

"No, you don't. And sir, the *Adventurer* is entering the nebula."

Breathing through the sharp rise of nausea, I dig my nails into my palms, or else I might jump forward and open a channel to the shuttle. Might tell Kieran to abort. Might tell him to screw the timeline and save himself.

"Whoa—Commander, a Quaneez ship! Hold on, I—" Manazari dances his fingers over his station at lightning speed.

Chase bolts out of the chair. "Where the hell are they coming from? Everybody, red alert, battle stations, shields up! Call the captain back, *now*!"

Sweat breaks out and runs down my spine. Tau-ration. Quaneez popping up. One and one equals—

"Sir, the shuttle's not responding!" Nerves let Hayes' voice tremble.

"What do you mean isn't responding?" With three large steps Chase has crossed the bridge to Hayes' station. "Call on all frequencies—"

Manazari interrupts with a wave of his hand. "I'm getting a high-energy spike, sir! Right where the shuttle is—"

"On screen!"

A sudden hot, slicing pain shoots through my body at the same time as a flash lights up the screen, uber-bright, the internal sensors lagging behind darkening the display. Everybody else grunts and covers their eyes or turns away to avoid the blinding light, but not me.

I take the pain, the soul-tearing agony standing up straight. I owe it to him to keep on witnessing what I knew all my life would happen, yet never truly understood until today.

Kieran is gone.

Gone.

Utter despair wrecks my body, wrapping itself around my organs until I'm not sure how they're still functioning. I lean over with my hands on my knees, gaze glued to the view screen, fighting for my next breath, to not let the agony overwhelm me, but it's close to impossible. I'm being torn apart from the inside. Somebody must've taken a blowtorch to my heart and set it aflame together with the Bond.

Kieran is gone.

Only nobody else knows it yet.

As the blinding light fizzles out, Chase is the first to recover. "What the hell was that? Report! And get me the captain!"

"Commander, the Quaneez ship is gone! I'm scanning on all frequencies, but—"

"That's great news, but I need that shuttle and the captain!"

Manazari sucks in a choked breath. "Sir—"

There's the slightest delay before Chase responds. As if he'd feel what Manazari was about to say. As if he picked up on what's so obvious to me. "What is it?"

Manazari swivels in his chair to face his commander. "I— It's— The sensors—" He closes his eyes, then swallows and tries again. "The *Adventurer* is gone, sir."

Silence.

Chase stills. "Gone?"

"There's nothing in that nebula with a USEF signature. I read no artificial metals—"

"Did the Quaneez fire?

"I don't know, Commander! The nebula is hard to penetrate for our sensors—"

"How can you be sure the shuttle is gone then? I need definite answers, dammit!" He rams a fist onto the nearest console.

Manazari pales. "I quadruple-checked, sir. There's nothing there, no debris, no nothing—maybe the Tau radiation has picked up, but that's within normal natural fluctuation. There's..." He swallows. "There's nothing left. The shuttle's gone. *He's* gone."

Heavy silence hovers after his last words.

Peripherally, I take note of the increase in Tau radiation, but I don't care. Can't care.

Chase turns around in slow-motion, his gaze falling onto me, bent over from losing the Bond, every breath wheezy and short.

In that very moment, he understands.

"Oh, Lords," he whispers, his voice hoarse. He reaches for the backrest of the captain's chair to support himself as he leans over, chest heaving with heavy inhales.

Somebody sobs.

Nobody says a single word.

A mind-numbing, soul crushing collective agony hovers like a living being on the bridge, heavy, dark, suffocating. It wraps itself around my heart and squeezes until it breaks into so many pieces, I wonder how nobody can hear the crack.

Kieran is gone.

There is no more tomorrow for him.

No more new memories.

This. Is. It.

Even if I went back and we made new memories, everything we have, everything he is, every memory, gets cut off in this very moment.

I force myself upright and to look at the view screen. A pang of longing slices through me. It's crazy, because I'm imagining I can still feel him. Like phantom pain, I'm having phantom sensations of him.

The protection of a mind close to losing it.

Misery lodges in my throat as a strangled choke breaks from Chase. "Kieran."

One word, loaded with a myriad of emotions. Grief, sadness, anguish, pain.

Thaler bursts out crying.

Manazari leans forward, hands folded behind his head between his knees.

Chocho's mouth opens and closes with silent words. He's whiter than the wall. He lost his wife and now his captain within a matter of a few weeks. Too much death. Too much loss.

Their collective sorrow is choking the last bit of remaining air out of me. It grinds on the pieces of my heart still left functioning.

I can't stay here anymore. I just can't.
Without anybody noticing, I turn on my heel and walk to the door.
Goodbye, *Pioneer*.
Goodbye, Kieran.

Chapter Twenty-One -
HOPE

Breathing hurts, like fire rushing down my windpipe, singeing me from the inside, just like every heartbeat tears through me with the force of a sonic bomb, destroying my cells one by one instead of powering them up.

Kieran is gone. Dead.

Walking down the hallway of his ship feels like walking over his grave.

The few meters between the bridge and his quarters are the worst. With every heavy step of mine the nausea and dread in my stomach get worse, and—

I come to a dead stop in front of his quarters. Bits and pieces of thoughts, images, ideas float through my mind, all flavored by a *feeling*. My First Sense?

Maybe it's my First Sense, maybe something else, but I palm the door to Kieran's quarters open and walk inside.

The trace of his scent assaults me, bringing butterflies with razor-sharp wings to lift off in my stomach and wreak havoc.

I don't stop.

I don't look around.

I don't allow myself to think or feel.

I only cater to the whims of this sensation, palm Kieran's secret chocolate drawer open, and drop the second disk, the one I took from Mashaule, in the very far corner. Last time I saw it in action, it looked like was on its last legs anyway, and—

As I retract my hand, my fingers brush against the letter he left me. That small touch, it shatters the last bit of clear thinking I have and sends me into a loop of thoughts and feelings, like a never-ending loop of misery.

Trance. That's the best word describing the way I feel.

I'm in a trance walking out of Kieran's quarters and while making my way down the hallways of the *Pioneer* toward the brig.

In a trance as I order Mashaule's release.

In a trance when I handcuff him to me.

In a trance when I press the button on my own trusted SED.

The bright flash of light—

So similar to the one Kieran died in.

Time whirls past us.

Mashaule tugs on the handcuffs, his outcries muted by our travels.

I want to go home.

Home.

As if that made it better.

My First Sense takes over as years blast past us, events take shape and fall apart around us, everything's chaos, yet orderly, too much to be completely understood, yet easy enough to follow if one trusts her senses.

I know which way to go, and it leads me further and further away from Kieran, from a time where he was still alive.

Thinking his name brings another wave of pain. Knowing about somebody's death and witnessing it are two completely different things.

The colorful cloud-band wafts closer to me and rubs against my hand, like it wanted my attention—

Screamsyellspainscreams KIERANSCREAMS—

Quaneez—I hear them, see them, feel them, Kieran SCREAMS—

I yank my hand back, press my fingers into my ears, still hear the echo of his screams. Like I was hearing him die.

Can't take it. Don't want to hear that. Not now, not ever.

Must get out of the jump.

Almost there—

Like before, something tugs on me, like time had gotten a hold of my sleeve.

By now my body is sensitive. Listens. I follow the tug, Mashaule in tow.

We pass the time I came from, my now.

Continue on—

Until the tug stops.

Finally, I can let go.

I grab on to Mashaule with both hands and focus on reality.

With a slight stumble both of us land on soft, carpeted floor.

In a large room.

With stars in front of the window.

An oval table with several chairs in the middle of the room.

And three people I didn't know I needed in this very moment until I saw them. Seeing them breaks through the pain encasing my heart and soul, reviving the parts of me that can still be resuscitated.

"Dad," I whisper through the soul-scorching agony Kieran's loss is causing me. "Chase. Zio."

Shocked, they all turn around in unison, Zio raising one eyebrow at my intrusion. Chase breaks into a wide grin, and Dad—

Dad doesn't rush forward to wrap me in the biggest embrace known to mankind, but taps his Hablamate. "Code Magenta. Security team to conference room one." He steps away from the head of the table. "Nonie."

If I wasn't handcuffed to Mashaule, *I'd* be throwing my arms around him. I need my dad, now more than ever. To be honest, I'm considering hugging him despite the cuffs, which would make for a weird threesome-embrace, so that's a no.

Plus, Chase has caught on. He's on his feet, weapon trained on Mashaule. "And you brought us a present. Given that we're still here, I assume that's Mashaule under the prison hood, meaning, you succeeded."

Zio shakes his head. "Technically speaking, we wouldn't know if the past had been changed. To us it would always be our past, no matter which version it is." He aims his medical PAD at me.

Chase cocks his head, never letting Mashaule out of his line of sight. "But your… special talent should feel something, right?"

"Correct." He pauses. "And I'm not feeling any major changes."

I, on the other hand, am feeling all kinds of messed up, but I have the loss of a Bond to blame for that.

The loss of the man I loved.

Chase motions for me to release the cuff on my arm, then closes it around Mashaule's other hand. "Ergo, I was right. Nicely done, Nonie. Let me take this criminal from you. I've got to say I'd pay to have a look at his face, now that his game is over."

I pull myself together and ignore the stinging of tears behind my eyes. "I looked at him way enough, and he hasn't gotten any prettier," I say. "You've missed nothing. Oh, and I slashed him up real good. He might need somebody to look at that."

Chase chuckles at the same time as a security team storms into the conference room. He keeps his weapon trained on the former admiral. "Detain this man as a high-security prisoner until further notice. Hood stays on. No access besides the three of us." He nods to my dad and Upinga.

The security officer securing Mashaule with a heavy-duty version of the same cuffs I used looks over at my dad. "Sir?"

"Confirmed, Jenkins. Keep him under constant supervision."

I hold up a hand. "Oh, and add a level 10 containment field with subatomic stabilization." I sneak my other hand into my pocket to make sure I still have the disk I took from my abductor in the cave.

Zio cuts me a glance. "That's new."

I shrug. "Fool me once…"

The security team leads Mashaule out of the conference room, hands cuffed, feet shackled, several weapons aimed at him. As soon as the doors close, Dad wraps me in the tightest embrace ever. "Nonie."

"Dad." I let myself be held and rocked left to right. It doesn't help against the physical pain, but it's soothing. Soul-soothing. Very much needed after what I just witnessed.

Dad sighs deep next to my ear, then pulls away, concern etched into his features. "Are you okay? What happened to your—?"

"My face? Mashaule. He needed convincing to come with me. I'm fine, don't worry." My face is the least of my problems. It doesn't even register compared to the disruption of the Bond. To the agony of a heart split in two.

The color drains from Dad's face. "I guess we have a lot to talk about, don't we?"

Understatement of the year. I pat PADdy. "I have a list, Dad. Hope you're free for the next day or so."

He chuckles. "Fair enough. But at the moment we're in the middle of something. Have a seat. I want your report asap, but our mission is quite sensitive." He taps the back of a chair for me and walks back to his *at the head of the table.*

Huh. Now, wait a second. "Odd question. Why did they confirm Admiral Conolly's order with you, and why are you…?" I point at his spot at the table.

"Why I am in charge?"

I nod. Last time I checked, Conolly and Upinga outranked Dad in seniority. Plus, security is also Chase's area of expertise, not Dad's. I wouldn't have expected the officers to check in with Dad to confirm Chase's order. Or for Dad to lead this mission, whatever it is about.

A shadow crosses his face, together with a slight reddening in his cheeks. "Well, it's complicated, but you're looking at the new interim president of the USEF." He adds a bow at the end, then sits down.

Holy Sun and Stars! "You won? You were elected president?" I shake my head, as if that would do anything to clear it or clarify what I just heard.

Dad's scratching his neck, the redness intensifying. "Well, no. Yes. To a degree."

"What your father wanted to say is that people have lost their minds in the past few months." Chase wears a scowl any first-year cadet would run from.

I look from one to the other, not a trace of the smile they wore a second ago left on their faces. "Why don't I like what I'm hearing?" Why does it make the tearing sensation inside my heart even worse?

Chase cuts me an eye. "Because democracy as you know it is on the brink of extinction."

"What?" The word leaves my throat as a yelp, and it comes with the sinking feeling that I might *need* a break, but might not *get* one. I pull out a chair and hold on to its back. "What happened?"

Chase shrugs, his arms folded in front of his chest. "Oh, the regular chaos. Mashaule vanishes into the past—which of course is *not* public knowledge—and his supporters, a.k.a everybody from Humanity First, speak of fraud, deception. They think we kidnapped him and kept him from the election. Which still was held, by the way."

"And which your father won, in a landslide. Mashaule still came up second with thirty percent in absentia, while a solid five percent were distributed between the other two candidates." Zio taps on something on his PAD.

Okay, I'm not getting it. "So, Dad won. Why is that an issue?"

"Because thirty percent of the population don't want to accept the result. Travis Roodt has been spewing the same lies since the election, claiming we kidnapped Mashaule to cheat the result, that Mashaule was telling them to fight for him and their values, you name it. It's quite the mess." Chase rakes one hand through his hair, tousling it up. Together with the dark circles under his eyes, it makes him look quite tired.

"Holy Sun and Stars," I whisper. "That's... I don't know. Apocalyptic?"

"Well phrased." Chase huffs out a dry laugh. "We never thought something like this could happen, but there are thirty percent of USEF who won't follow orders. Who are working on separating from us and chasing their own goals. People were attacked for their opinion if it differed from theirs, and nothing has helped. Nothing. We even let people into USEF jail to understand we don't hold Mashaule captive. It only convinced them we're keeping him somewhere else."

"We better not let them check now," Zio quips, and Chase sighs.

"No, we better not. It would undermine the last bit of credibility those thirty percent still give us. We barely got the vaccine mandate supported—"

"Vaccine mandate?" I tilt my head. "For—"

"—the Reptilian Flu, which is officially now endemic, and not pandemic, thanks to you. And treatable. Also thanks to you." Zio wiggles the PAD in his hand.

"Wait, what?" Holy everything, that's right, neither of them is wearing a mask! I mean, neither am I, but I couldn't really conjure one up out of thin air.

Zio nods. "It is under control, thanks to the fastest vaccine roll-out ever. Ninety-six percent of all humanity is vaccinated and safe from the virus. The plants you retrieved held exactly the components we needed. No more Reptilian Flu." He checks the readout on his PAD. "And you'll be happy to hear that one, your facial injuries will heal, and two, more importantly, that you're not contaminated."

Warmth rises, melting the outer layer of ice witnessing Kieran's death and hearing the latest news has put around my heart. "It worked?" There still was a ginormous chance it could have been a setup. I mean, that's what I assumed to a degree. Mashaule finding a somewhat convincing excuse to get rid of me, and therefore Dad. But that it really worked…

"Yes, it worked." Dad has the proud father look on his face. "Zio will get you vaccinated today. We've had no more deaths by that virus for the last three months."

"Not that anybody was thanking us for that," Chase mumbles under his breath.

I'm hung up on the bigger picture though. "No deaths in the last three months…!" That's amazing, wonderful, fantastic! But also: three months? "Thanks for mentioning it: When am I?" I look at Zio again.

"September 14th, 2295. We saw you last at USEF jail when Mashaule jumped back in time and you followed. Judging by your facial expression that's a surprise?"

I snap my gaping mouth shut. I'm several months later than when I left. "N-no. No. I just…" I shrug and sit down, letting my weight lean against the chair's back rest. I'm just so emotionally exhausted.

Taking a seat, Zio lays the PAD down in front of him. "Your neurotransmitters are off the charts. Heart rate elevated. All readings show symptoms similar to what Kieran went through whenever you left." He gives me a worried look. "I would suggest trying out the cocktail. It worked well for him." He reaches for his med pack attached to his belt.

"What cocktail?" Dad's brows narrow as he looks from Zio to me. "Worked for what?"

Right. Dad is the only person in the room unaware of Kieran's and my… affiliation.

"Nonie?" Zio opens his med pack.

"What's wrong with her neurotransmitters?" A mix of worry and… I dunno, suspicion, maybe, swings in Dad's voice, and I… I just can't talk about it right now. The crack in my chest is barely held together by my memories of Kieran, but if I have to talk about him now… I'm going to lose it.

"Dad, nothing is wrong, calm down. And Zio, no, thank you." Lifting one palm up, I shake my head. "Really, thank you. But it's… it's not necessary."

"It's not?" The look Zio gives me calls me a liar, and he's right. It's necessary. I feel like crap. The cocktail would lessen the symptoms, but I don't want that. I couldn't accept it.

Dulling what I feel now, after seeing Kieran die… It would feel like a betrayal to him. Like I chose the easy way out, when for him there was only the hard way. Only one way.

I already feel like a cheater. Kieran is dead, but the pain is not too bad all in all, when it should be devastating and destructive, but no. I can function much better than at the raspberry fields.

Dad lets go of a deep, resigned sigh as Zio closes his med pack.

"Very well," Zio says slowly. "But if you change your mind…"

I nod, the lump in my throat too thick to talk around. Being here, with three men who all were friends with Kieran, but who all know he has been dead for decades—as did I—it brings something close to shame rise to the surface. Do I even have the right to grieve since history was quite clear about how short Kieran's life would be?

But the act of losing him, of *being there*, it changed things for me.

Tears sting, so I rub a quick palm across my eyes, faking a yawn. Nobody needs to see me tear up over a fact I've known all my life. I clear my throat. "Uhh, piggybacking off what you said, Chase, no, not surprised I'm not when I left you. I tried to jump back to the time at USEF jail, but something about today pulled me forward."

Zio tilts his head. "Pulled you forward?"

Well, I don't exactly have a manual with time-travel friendly terms in it. "It's hard to explain. I jumped and felt the need to keep on going to this point in time." I shrug. Nobody explained time-jumps one-oh-one to me, so excuse me if I'm not super precise with my description. "It's happened before, also no idea why, but I figured the timeline gets what the timeline wants." We wouldn't want it to throw tantrums.

The three men exchange a glance.

"Well, we hope that today is indeed going to be a significant date. Maybe we're on to something." Dad lets go of another one of his signature sighs, and I'm not sure how to interpret that.

"Okay, so... what? Is it classified? Can I know? Because you three here in one room on a mission with enough impact it literally pulled me here is a tad scary after what you just told me and after the day I've had." Especially after the last traumatizing hour.

Dad grimaces. "I don't like the sound of that. I know I've had a while to come to terms with you traveling through time—"

"Since you met *Star Hopper* after my abduction?" I put *Star Hopper* in verbal quotation marks, because at this point, we all know she's me. Even I know it, having been late to the party.

Dad blows out air through pursed lips. "Yes. That was... Let's just say I've never been as close to a heart attack as I was when she—you— walked through the door." He shudders. "You made it very clear to me what was supposed to happen. That you were supposed to join the academy. That I was supposed to talk to nobody, until Admiral Conolly and Upinga approached me."

"That was a fun conversation," Chase cuts in.

Dad huffs. "Took us a while until both parties figured out the other one knew you were going to travel back. Still remains the only work meeting I ever needed a Scotch after."

I narrow my eyes at him. "And still you tried to keep me out of the academy." A problem Other Nonie didn't have. Must've been nice.

"Can you blame a father for trying to protect his daughter?"

"Bridge to President Thorburn." Dad's Hablamate lights up.

"Thorburn here."

"Mr. President, we're within sensor reach of the Kanouse nebula."

"Acknowledged. Hold position and get ready to execute our plan." He silences the Hablamate with another tap on it, his business demeanor taking over. "Gentlemen, we need to get ready."

Zio and Chase nod, while I… I look from one to the other. "Okay, now would be a good time to give me the short version of what we're doing here, given that it pulled me off course."

Dad turns a bit, so he can look out the floor-to-ceiling windows behind him. "We're trying to right decades of wrong. It's our last-ditch effort to build peace." I get a smile, but it's half-hearted and doesn't quite look convincing, given how pale he is.

"O-kay," I stretch. "That sounds good, so why the pessimism?"

"Not pessimism. More desperation. Those thirty percent we mentioned, Humanity First?"

I nod, and Dad carries on. "Humanity First is gung-ho on finishing what Mashaule started. It's obvious Travis Roodt and his followers want the war to continue. They won't accept any other end to it other than the Quaneez' absolute extinction." He presses his lips together into a tight line, emphasizing the wrinkles around his mouth. "As we speak, a counter movement is going strong, and if we don't succeed… I fear we won't be able to stop them from reinitiating the war." He lifts his gaze and brings it up to mine. "I don't think I'm overreaching if I say that if we fail here, it's not the Quaneez who will be extinct. It's going to be humanity."

USEF Hope, Main Conference Room, September 14ᵗʰ, 2295

It's going to be humanity.

Dad's words echo through my mind, burying themselves deeper into my brain until they and Chase's earlier explanation make sense. "Are you saying we've lost control over those thirty percent, and they might go against orders?" Against common sense? Who wants war instead of peace!

"Correct." Zio aligns his PAD parallel to the edge of the table. "We cannot afford war within the USEF. The Reptilian Influenza has diminished our troop sizes, and despite designing a treatment and vaccine we're nowhere as strong as we need should the war restart. Fighting amongst ourselves is going to lead to defeat. We must make peace, now more than ever."

I wholeheartedly support making peace, for any reason. It's just that we've been trying to do exactly that for the last four decades, so excuse me if I'm a wee bit skeptical. "Agreed, and now I'm curious. What's your plan?"

Dad speaks up. "The same we have been using to hold armistice for the last months. We'll enter an area of known Quaneez activity, tilt our ship to the same angle that has proven to not have them fire on us, power down our systems to show we mean no harm."

I narrow my eyes. "So far, so good, but what then? How are you planning to discuss peace with them?"

The three men exchange a three-way glance, which is no easy feat to pull off. "We developed a new communication protocol spanning more frequencies, up into the ultrasonic and beyond." Chase taps onto his PAD, and the schematic of a wave form appears, hovering in the middle of the table for all to see.

"A new communication protocol." I sit up straighter and lean forward, ignoring the flare of pain shooting through my body. I'm the one who's alive. I have no reason to complain.

Chase points at two areas of the waveform. "We improved the bandwidth, to simplify it. It did really well with all known species we tested it with and ran it by. It should work."

Only problem is, if my working theory is correct, it won't. I swallow dry. And that could be why I felt the pull to come here, to keep the war from flaring up again by our own fault.

Now's the time to speak up, quite literally. Would've liked to verify my theory, but, alas, there's no time. I look from Zio to Chase, and lastly to Dad. "I'm afraid I have bad news. I'm very sure it's not going to work. You execute that plan, and you're most likely going to get everybody on board killed."

Like a bomb hit, all three jerk back.

"What?" Dad's brows slam down into a V. "What—"

I shake my head. Here goes nothing. "Listen—actually, think! Have the Quaneez ever talked to us? No. Why not? We assumed because they didn't want to, but..." I suck in my lower lip and chew on it. "From what I've been seeing over the last days, weeks, months, decades, whatever you want to call it, is that they never attack first—"

"But they do," Chase says. "Always have. The *Pioneer* never was the first to open fire on them. We always hailed—"

I hold up one finger. "Ah, there you go. You *hailed* them. Think back, look at bridge protocols if you don't believe me, but the Quaneez never fired if we didn't hail first." I hope I'm not putting too much weight on my observations. I saw how many Quaneez encounters out of the thousands we've had? Enough to extract significant data? Probably not. But enough to come up with a hypothesis. One I need to sell to these three Admirals, or I doubt we're going to come out of this mission alive.

And then, neither is humanity.

Zio's typing into his PAD.

Pauses.

Types some more.

Pauses.

Pauses.

"Zee, come on." Chase pats his palm onto the table twice. "Pattern?"

Zio looks up, and for the first time since I've met him, no matter in which time, he's pale. "Nonie is correct. From a quick data scan, I can confirm her theory."

"Sun and Stars. They always started it," Chase whispers hoarsely, "only they didn't."

"No, I don't think they did." I fold my hands on top of the table and sit straighter. "I have a theory. What if the Quaneez have different senses than we do? We see no openings for ears on their helmets. What if they can't hear? Or, what if they hear at frequencies we're not even thinking of, or feel it with a different organ than ears? Every time we hail, they fire at us. What if they perceive that as an attack? What if our hails hurt them?"

All color drains from Dad's face. "Then we have been inadvertently fueling this war for the last forty years."

"Until we accidentally held still and didn't hail, because we couldn't." Chase blows out air through pursed lips.

I give him a thumbs up. "And Kieran did the same, on Alpha Rubrum, remember?"

The two admirals exchange another glance. "Yes," Zio says. "We should've seen it."

"I think you did, in the beginning. Remember, Kieran didn't want to hail them. He was only following orders from Command. I think he knew, on some level." Talking about him in past tense… I try to swallow, but my throat's too dry. "During the initial encounters, before the Battle of Balthar, that's when I noticed the difference from what I was taught to what I was seeing. Plus, Chase, Zio, remember how they used Kieran's updates to the *Pioneer* when he was captured by them? How you saw they pieced his calls together and how it made no sense? They had no clue what they were doing. I don't think they understand verbal communication as a concept. Maybe they considered the audio waves an attack and were throwing it back up against the *Pioneer*, and that's why some of it didn't make any sense."

Right? It's a good theory, if I may say so. It sounds way out there, but of you give it enough time to actually think about it… we've seen crazier things. *Cough, cough, time-travel.*

Chase pours himself a glass of Lubbeck's from the bottle on a tray off to the side. "But they must communicate somehow. How can we not know how they transmit messages? How they talk?" He throws his head back and downs the soda in one big gulp.

Now, here comes my second theory. "I have an idea. Granted, this one is wobbly, but better than nothing."

Dad closes his eyes, like he was in pain. "Please, go ahead and enlighten us, child. We've only been working on cracking the Quaneez' communication for forty years."

I grimace. "Sorry, Dad, but to be honest, you didn't stand a chance."

"Why? Because we didn't travel through time?"

"No. Because you didn't meet them in person."

His eyes widen. "And you did?"

I cringe. "Well, *meeting* is overstating it, but I was in contact with them, several times." I count off my fingers. "One, when I got Kieran out of the mind torture, and two, when I accidentally jumped to the wrong time and place." I might or might not blush the slightest bit with that last sentence.

Dad stares at me, wide-eyed. "I'm not sure I want to hear any details about any of this."

I cringe again, harder this time. Not my finest moment. "Yeah, I get it. But what I noticed is, that scent seems to play a role."

"Scent?" Chase lifts and drops his shoulders. "Why do you think that?"

"Because when I dematted into their bunker, it smelled like flowers. Nauseatingly so. Oh!" I facepalm myself. "I remember from history class that the one survivor they interviewed reported that too. *Smelled like heaven*, or something. And then, later, like hell, or sulfur, when the Quaneez were there. The same happened to me. I *think* the Quaneez don't smell bad, until they get angry—well, I assume they get angry. What I wanted to say is they smell different, when I fought them. Like decay, old socks… And it smells different than fear." That was the kid I pulled out of the hole and saved from those saber tooth tiger-thingies. It reeked, but differently than in the bunker. The adult Quaneez coming for that kid on the other hand… had more of a soapy flowery scent. And they weren't attacking me, so yeah, from my sample size of two encounters I'd say angry Quaneez stink, quite literally, and non-angry Quaneez smell sweeter.

Zio lays the PAD on the table and addresses Dad. "It would align with a theory Captain Wildason proposed at the very beginning of the Quaneez wars."

"And we didn't follow that theory for what reason, exactly?" Dad's voice is tight.

"After First Contact, Captain Wildason was questioning whether the Quaneez could have tracked him and the security officers by scent, if I recall correctly. He had covered himself in mud on T-12 and wasn't discovered as quickly as his team. When we rendezvoused with the M-3 we discussed and dismissed that theory. Prematurely so, apparently." I get an approving nod with the last statement, which feels good, yet undeserved, because if I'm not mistaken, we dismissed the theory also partially because I was lying about my duration on the planet. Surviving several days without being found? Then they didn't track by scent. Ahem.

Chase pours himself another glass of Lubbeck's and holds on to it. "As always, Kieran was a step ahead of us. The last forty years… what a nightmare."

Yeah. A nightmare for humanity living generations of war. A nightmare for Kieran, living it during the day and being tortured by it at night, hearing the Quaneez, seeing them—

Click.

As if drawn together by magnets, the puzzle pieces align to from a picture that… that… "Oh, Sun and Stars." I lean forward until my forehead rests on the cool table top. Can't get oxygen into my lung, no matter how fast I breathe, and I'm breathing really fast. Getting lightheaded. Nightmares… The one connecting factor.

Kieran *heard* them, every night, worse and worse as time progressed. The way he screamed from his nightmares—the exact way I've been hearing him scream when I jump, when I touch that colorful band, and all I see is war, pain, suffering, and Quaneez. When all I hear is them and him screaming.

Kieran *felt* them, even to the degree that he thought they were hidden in the nebula, but… what if it's not in the way we think? What if there's a different factor connecting the dots?

What if…

What if when I jump through time I'm seeing and hearing what he heard at night? And that would beg the question why. *Why* I would see and hear the Quaneez when jumping through time, when I get too close to this colorful cloud-thingy? Why would I hear Kieran?

That's a good question, one that needs an open mind. We thought time travel was impossible. It isn't. What if the Quaneez are truly different than we thought? Not only the way they communicate, but *everything* about them?

Anxiety, the good kind, lets my heart beat at rabbit-speed. I'm onto something, I can feel it.

Where do they come from so fast? Like the kiddo on the planet with the tiger-thingy. Or the adult Quaneez looking for him. One second PADdy presents me a clear scan, the next the kid is there, and then a whole bunch of adult Quaneez.

Or, what about the Quaneez attack I witnessed on the *Eclipse*? Even the young Captain Mashaule was surprised where their ship came from without them noticing. Now let's add on the comments of two of my favorite people in the world: Kieran was right, we know their ships are fast—but Trip is also right, their drives, or what we understand of them, even forty years later, are also crap. Nobody knows where they're getting that kind of speed from.

What if it's not speed?

What if it's a matter of *location*?

And what if the impossible was possible and Kieran—

And Kieran was in *there*.

Wherever that is, but *there*. Wherever the Quaneez are. What if he was with *them*? Had been, since June 8th, 2257.

It would explain so much, like why I'm less affected by the loss of the Bond compared to Kieran. Because for me, in my time, he's still alive. Just very, very far away. Why I feel whole when I jump. Because he is *there* somewhere, closer. Why I see those Quaneez when I jump, why I hear his screams, *Kieran's screams*—because he's *there*. They're *there.*

And considering that theory, it would make so much sense for Mashaule to want to kill him mere hours before his flight into that nebula—to end him for real.

If there's anything to my theory, it would mean there's hope—hope not only to end the war, but also that Kieran might—

My stomach cramps, and so does my heart. Or maybe it's my First Sense, telling me I'm on the right path. I can't afford to hope, but I crave it with every fiber of my being. I *must* be right. So many oddities, but taken together they make sense, and… and I could even throw Tau-radiation into that mix! I mean, why not, since I'm going all out with wild ideas already? It—

"Nonie?" Dad leans forward and squeezes my shoulder. "What's going on?"

I force my lungs to calm their breathing, then lift my head. It weighs a ton, by the way. "I have a theory I need to prove." Several, actually, but the most important one to me I'm keeping to myself for now. If I'm wrong… Well, it's enough for one person to live though losing hope all over again. I don't need to put that on Chase and Zio.

I look at my dad and my two friends, willing them to understand what hangs in the balance. What could be possible. What could be prevented. "And to prove that theory, I need you to trust me. If I'm right, it could end this war forever."

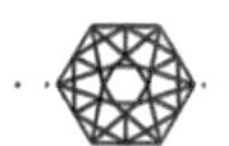

USEF Hope, September 14ᵗʰ, 2295, Shuttle Bay

"I still don't like it." Dad grumbles, and I get it. He came here with a mission planned, and then I pop up with a theory more shaky than not, throwing everything into chaos—limited chaos, since we're at least off Code Magenta. This is my time, after all. Just skipped a few months ahead.

Zio comes to my rescue. "But, Tom, you've got to say, Nonie's idea makes sense. Tau-radiation could be the connecting factor."

Dad harrumphs. "I agree it makes sense. It's a pattern hard to overlook once you see it." Disbelief swings in his voice, not for my theory, but our failure to pick up on it over the last decades.

I brush my palms off on my thighs. "It's a pattern hard to *see*, Dad, period. Keep in mind, my exposure was different than everybody else's, so eventually it just struck me as odd." I count off my fingers. "Here I am, on an empty planet, some Tau-radiation present, and *boom*, there's a Quaneez kid out of nowhere. Then, they pop up mostly around our terraformed worlds—and Tau-radiation is a byproduct of terraforming." I leave out the part where there was some of it in the nebula before Kieran went in, and more after the Quaneez popped up, because… I'm not ready for a discussion—or failure—of that specific theory. "Something connected to Tau-radiation draws them in. I only ever heard the word Tau-radiation in context with the Quaneez, so…" I shrug. "It made me think there might be a connection."

Zio opens the door to my shuttle and disappears inside. "I agree," he calls out after entering. "Looking at the preliminary data, I'd be surprised if you were wrong."

I hear him opening an instrument panel as Dad gives the *Reliant*'s hull a melancholic pat, like an old friend's back. "Tau-radiation opening or announcing a passage to the Quaneez space—their *realm*…" He lets the sentence hang. "This could truly mean a turn-around for the war, no matter if you can communicate with them or not."

Because if nothing else, we could scan for Tau-radiation as an indicator for Quaneez activity and at least be prepared before they pop up.

I wrap my arms around his neck in a much-needed daughter-father-hug. "I'll do my very best, Dad. And thank you for letting me do this." I loosen one arm and pat the little bag attached to my hip, filled with tiny vials with different scents: color-coded from white to black, and ranging from light and flowery to sweeter and all the way to bitter and completely disgusting.

I really hope I'm not going to say something impolite.

Dad returns the embrace. He smells like Dad, like home. No need to color-code that. "I'm a hundred percent behind you, Nonie, don't get me wrong. You just gotta give an old man some time to readjust his view of the world. The Quaneez may be living in a different realm… What an idea…" He shakes his head and releases me from the hug.

I know the idea is quite out there, but then, it's not really that far out there. Chase himself brought me onto it, actually. The way he was constantly offended by the Quaneez' impractical drive, how it was perfect for interrupting the fabric of space—what if it was made for exactly that, and not space flight as we know and understand it? What if Tau radiation indicated their travel from their realm to ours, and that's why their ships didn't need to function well in our space?

And what did the Upstream Evil Guy say when I listened in on him and Mashaule on the *Eclipse*? *Don't forget, you invaded their territory.* Neither Mashaule nor I understood it, because there was nobody around for lightyears—unless the Quaneez' quote-unquote space exists on a different plane than our reality. Wouldn't that make sense? They pop up out of nowhere. I felt them during my time-jumps, which are definitely a different plane of reality. Heard Kieran there.

My heart stumbles and catches itself.

I still don't dare to hold on to hope, but I can't help that tiny spark of want, of *what if* flaring to life.

What if I'm right?

What if Kieran's screams are real? Have been real for the last thirty-five years?

I swallow down a lump in my throat. First things first. The more I think about it, the more convinced I am there's something to my theory. Why else would we not have found their home world? They must come from somewhere. And why wear the full-body armor if not to protect yourself from something? And that something doesn't have to be an attack—what about the environment? What if the Quaneez weren't made for our plane of the universe? I mean, even the kids I saw wore the armor. The armor, that could be a protective suit.

It would make so much sense.

Zio exits from the shuttle and wipes his arm across his forehead. "I set the parameters for the Tau-radiation to a gradual increase. Whenever the shuttle detects a rift—if there is going to be such a thing—it will hold that level of output, therefore keeping the connection to the Quaneez realm open. I assume."

"Zio, you're not helping me send my daughter in there." Dad groans. Still too funny they're finally on a first-name basis. Only took them about four decades. "That's what they mean when they say command and family don't mix."

"Relax, Dad. I'll be fine." I pat his shoulder as he glances at me from the side with my last word, as if he could see how much my body is missing the connection with Kieran. How much it's hurting for him, on a physical and emotional level.

"That's what you say, but all I can think of is you traveling through time into potentially some other realm where our enemies are. Excuse me if I'm not exactly thrilled to send you off."

His words kindle my sparking hope to a flame, a flame I need to squash before it becomes so big, it consumes me.

The doors to the shuttle bay open for Chase. "Bad news, everybody. I hope you're ready and your plan works, Nonie." He hands Dad a PAD. "Roodt and his stupid party have officially taken over part of USEF."

"What?" The outcry comes from all three of us together, Dad's the loudest.

"Are you kidding me? Details please, stat!" He takes the PAD and activates it, scanning over the information.

"It means that I just got alerted to the fact that several of our battle ships aren't responding to hails. And no, they're not destroyed. Just choosing to forego communication. Two of them have dropped off the grid, but Gerard and Chen never were the smartest captains, so we're able to still track them. If you don't want your mass to give you away, maybe stay away from anything that could be attracted to you." He rocks back on his heels, hands folded behind his back. "That's part one of the bad news. Part two is that we picked up some scattered chatter we could piece together."

Dad sucks in a gasp of air, then lets the PAD sink down slowly. "They're about to distribute to all major battle ground locations, wait for the Quaneez, and… fire." All color has drained from his face. "In the next few hours, once everybody is in position. The war… Under no circumstances can we allow that."

Nausea rises. Because we all know what it would mean. For both our species.

Dad pulls his shoulders back and straightens his uniform. "I don't think diplomacy is going to work with these people. We tried that for years, and all it did was give them the ground to stand on. Now's the time to make a strong stance. Raise the fleet to condition yellow. I want it clear that anybody going against my orders to hold fire against the Quaneez will be seen and prosecuted as a traitor. Deploy ships to the same locations they're planning to jump to. They may have thirty percent of USEF, but we still have seventy."

The words *I hope* swing in his tone, even if he doesn't say them.

"Consider it done." Chase nods curtly. "And since time seems to be more of a problem now, I know, very funny, we need to speed it up. Nonie, if your plan works, we need it to work now."

Good thing we're adding absolutely no pressure to my mission. That bout of nausea flares up, but I swallow it down. Not the time for it. "Got it."

"Good. The team's updated. We'll hold our position and wait. If we're getting company—"

Dad looks at me, steely resolve in his eyes. "We'll have your back and keep them away from the *Reliant* and the nebula. But if they're Quaneez—"

If they're Quaneez, there's absolutely no change to our plan. "Then you do exactly as you planned to, minus the hailing." Right?

Dad clenches and unclenches his hands twice. "Yes. But please, if there's anything not going to plan, come back out of that realm ASAP. We need peace, but the situation is too volatile to add another layer of war to it."

What he knows just as well as I do but doesn't say is that it took us forty years to even have an idea how to find the Quaneez. If I fail, if I'm wrong, we're nowhere closer to a solution.

Still, I nod. "I'll be safe, Dad." I pop up on my tippy-toes and give his cheek a kiss. "I'll be back in no time, quite literally."

"Your word to Fate's ear." He gives me another fatherly look, then switches to his command voice. "Go make contact, Lieutenant. Make us proud. Help us end this war."

"I will, Dad." Heart fluttering, I step into the *Reliant* and look back at the three men who mean everything to me. My Dad, the current USEF President. Chase, and Zio, my mentors and friends, no matter in which time period.

Three men.

It should be four.

And maybe, if my theory holds, it will be again.

Chapter Twenty-Two –

REALM

USEF Shuttle Reliant, September 14th, 2295, Kanouse Nebula

The moment I set the shuttle to hold the position within the nebula, nerves get to me.

It's one thing talking about my theory and contacting the Quaneez, a completely different one to actually do it.

Once I get into their realm—*if* my theory holds and I get into their realm—who's to say I'll know what to do? How to use those scents effectively to communicate with them? And what if they perceive me as a threat? After all, I'm entering their home. Uninvited, and without knocking, so to speak, potentially quote-unquote saying all the wrong things.

I shake out my arms and crack my neck. It's a risk I'll have to take. We're already at war, and while yes, it could be worse if the Quaneez decided to attack us without our provocation, I doubt they will. They had forty years to do that, yet if I'm right, they acted to defend themselves.

I doubt me entering their home will tip the scale for the worse.

I hope.

"*Reliant*, initiate protocol Upinga Beta."

"*Initiating protocol. Tau-beam set to pre-programmed parameters.*"

Here goes nothing. I shove my hand into my pocket and fumble for the SED. Don't want to accidentally activate the disk and get the Upstream Bad Guy to find me. I press the button on my SED.

A bright flash of light—

Time swirls around me, like during my jumps, only slower, maybe because I'm not trying to go to a new point in time, but a different location. It wafts and waves, billows up and folds into itself, and there—

The same cloud I've tried to ignore. Maybe I shouldn't have.

It grows by the second, getting thicker, wider, taking over my complete vision, shimmering as if all colors of the rainbow were doused in glitter, and it's calling to me.

Like before, I feel a pull toward it, a connection. It wants me to touch it.

It swirls closer to me, closer, closer—

And swallows me up.

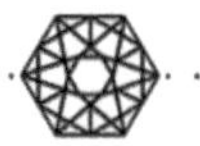

Somewhere, Probably the Realm, Somewhen, Probably Now

Dark.

Warm.

I blink hard. Where am I? Am I in? Can't tell whether I'm standing on something or floating. Gravity seems off, somehow. A bit of light breaks up the darkness, like a glowworm was hovering at arm's length from me.

Two glowworms.

Three.

Four, five, six—

The tiny dots of light fuse into a warm ball of light, the balls of light into a sphere, until it becomes so bright and hot, I have to squeeze my eyes shut and cover them with my arm.

The moment I do, I feel the intensity of the light go down, until I can open my eyes. Problem is, just because they're open doesn't mean I can trust them. I'm on the bridge of the *Pioneer*—the empty *Pioneer*, but that's not what makes this freaky. It's that there are no walls: The bridge seamlessly morphs into a field of flowers. To my right in the far distance, I spot a tree—upside down. To my left, a river flows up a little hill, through a hut not unlike the one I saw on Alpha Rubrum. The sky is blue in parts, but red-orange or light-blue in others, as if the sun was going down in some areas and coming up in others. Clouds hang low and float up and down. The whole scenery looks like somebody high on something had patched reality together.

I step forward, but instead of feeling the solid surface of the bridge under my foot, I sink in to my ankle. "Whoa." *Whoa—oooaa—ooaa— oaa—aa—a...*

Okay. And there's an echo. Looking down I check on my foot. I'm hovering a good twenty centimeters above the ground.

Holy Sun and Stars. Either this is the Quaneez realm and it's way different from ours, or Tau-radiation is not good for my head. Swallowing hard, I take another step. It comes with the same sensation of sinking into quicksand, only I can walk without problems. It's slightly creepy. Everything, I mean. Nature keeps changing around me. The river changes its color. The tree rotates, and not around its axis, but jumps from roots up to roots down and back, undecided which position to favor. Wind picks up and tugs on my clothing, yet I don't feel any resistance when walking off the bridge and into the field of flowers.

I also don't feel much of my body, come to think about it.

But what I do feel is… good. The pain from the loss of the Bond, the soul-tearing and splitting agony, it's gone. In fact, I feel fully charged. Like when the medic revived him at the raspberry fields.

My heart stammers, then resumes beating.

Turning to check my left and right side, a wave of dizziness sweeps over me. Ugh, never mind being fully charged. Moving fast feels weird, like my internal sensors were lagging behind. And weirdest of all, I hear no sounds at all. The river is quiet, the jumping tree is soundless, and my steps make no noise either.

I take a big breath of air, if it's even air I'm breathing. "Hello?" *Ellooo—ooo—oo—o...*

The air shimmers and wafts in front of me, and two seconds later, I'm looking at an adult Quaneez in their armor.

Holy Sun and Stars. I swallow dry. No pressure, Lieutenant.

The Quaneez stands so still I'm not sure whether he's a figment of my imagination or not.

But I'm here to make contact, right?

Slowly, I inch one hand to the pouch with my scents, while raising the other one. "Hi." *Iiii—iii—ii...*

The Quaneez tilts his head, the universal sign for 'Huh?', but lifts his hand like I did.

Elation shoots through me. Progress! Maybe I should've learned sign language—

A hissing sound shoots through my head, accompanied by a sharp spike of pain. I flinch and throw both hands up, pressing them against my temple. The hissing increases, then changes, until—

"Sssssssorry. Can you hear me better now?"

Holy Sun and Stars, that voice— That voice is directly inside my head. I let my hands sink down from my temples. "I... I can hear you." *Eeeeaaar-uuu—ear-uu—ee-uu.... I* can't believe it—we're talking!

The Quaneez makes a gesture with his hand, as if he was gliding it over an invisible ball hovering in front of him before I hear him right inside my head again. "It isss fortunate you understand usss."

Wait— "You heard what I thought?" I ask.

"Yess."

Whoa. My head is like a giant speaker. "You can hear me like that?" This time, I don't say, but think it, focusing on every word, mentally screaming it out.

"I can. Jusst like you can hear me."

Mind blown. Okay, I'm in a different realm, so maybe I should expect our laws of nature not applying here, but still. In my defense, it's the first foreign realm I'm visiting. There wasn't exactly a manual to read before. "And we speak the same language." The Quaneez sounds a bit like he was talking with his mouth full, but that's it. Clear, good ol' English otherwise. He sounds like a male in my head, deep voice and all.

"All thoughts are universal," he says. *Thinks.* Whatever.

A small laugh bubbles out of me and echoes through the air. "That is… unbelievable. In a good way." And that means, finally introductions are in order. And apologies. "My name is Nonie Thorburn. My species calls itself human. I was sent to talk to you." Maybe that's a bit of an exaggeration, but we've gotta work with what we've got.

"I am called Lorr. I am one of the leaders. We are Essken."

One of their leaders. Responsibility makes me stand straighter. Also: he didn't call himself Quaneez.

"No. But we are aware you call us that."

I blush. Gotta be careful what I think. "I apologize. We tried to communicate with you, but obviously, it didn't work."

"We tried to communicate with you, too. You never answer us either." Lorr taps his head. "Your realm works differently than ours."

No kidding! I concentrate really hard on what I'm going to think-say next. It's imperative they understand we didn't mean harm by that. "In our realm we use our mouth and vocal cords in our throat to communicate. We make sounds. Communicating via thought is something we can't do in our universe. I've never done *this*," I tap my temple with one finger, "before. It's not in our nature."

Lorr tilts his head. "That explains our problems. We have tried to help you understand, tried again and again to make contact, but nobody responded. Nobody but one."

I don't get it. There was never an attempt for communication. "What do you mean?"

Lorr lifts his right hand, and out of nowhere a Quanee—an *Essken* torture chamber appears on the field off to the right, like the *Pioneer*'s bridge without walls. My jaw drops. "How did that— How did you make it appear?"

"Appear?"

"It wasn't here before."

Lorr pauses. "Before."

"When I arrived."

"But it was in your thoughts."

"Yes, but…" Never mind. Memory hits, and with it a pang of sadness. That's a chamber like the one I rescued Kieran from.

Lorr points at the chair. "We tried to talk to him, to make him understand, but then he didn't."

Holy— "You used that to try to communicate with us?" The Quaneez torture chamber, a communication device? I didn't see that coming. At all.

"It didn't work, no matter what we tried. None of them understood. You were there, you saw that. You sent several of us home."

Okay, now I'm completely confused. "I—we—sent whom back where? Kieran? He was going to die—"

"Die?"

I nod. "What you did to him was about to kill him."

"He would have returned home."

Now, that's a euphemism for death if I ever heard one. "He would have stopped functioning. He would've been—" gone. Which is also not a good description. I sigh. "His *existence* would have ended."

Lorr stays silent for a good ten seconds. "Ended. You do not transfer?"

Transfer? What kind of—

Realization strikes, and it feels like somebody pulled the rug from under my feet. I thought it a minute ago, but didn't take my own advice to heart: our laws of nature don't count here. Transfer. If it means what I think it does… "Lorr, when something destroys your body in our universe, what happens to you?"

"We come back here." He motions to the area around us.

"And you're still alive?"

"We continue on. Here, we heal. Correct."

My heart skips a few beats, keeping my thoughts in order is nearly impossible with the magnitude of what's happening. "We shot at you. We destroyed your ships and everybody on board. Did you stop functioning?"

He points to his chest, then the ground. "Losing the armor hurts.

Destruction of our ships hurts. We need to heal, so we come back here when your realm stops us from functioning."

I wheeze as realization strikes, wonderful and painful at the same time. "You don't die."

"We continue on. This is our home. It is good to us."

The image of an adult Essken doing something to the kid I pulled out of the pit until he *poof*ed out of existence pops up in my mind.

Lorr looks to the right—where *the exact scene is playing out*, like somebody pressed review on my memory, just a tad more fuzzy and foggy. This realm is truly something. "He came to your world through a rift. By accident," he says.

And now I understand. They didn't kill him. "You helped him. You brought him back here."

"Yes. But first, *you* helped him." I feel like there's surprise swinging in his tone.

"I was worried the mammal was going to kill him. To make him stop functioning." I guess clarifications are important.

The Essken cocks his head. "And we returned him here to heal. You did not like that."

"I didn't know he was coming home. I thought you ended his existence. We didn't know you don't die." Had we known... I don't know what would've changed. We would've probably looked for other ways to keep them from coming back. And while we apparently didn't kill any Quaneez-slash-Essken during the war, they still killed billions of humans.

Lorr looks back to me, the upcoming sun reflecting on his armor. "We... killed."

I give a small nod. "Yes. When our bodies are injured too gravely, we stop functioning. Forever."

Silence.

"We did not know that. We did not want to cause this kind of harm. We only needed the interruptions to stop."

The responsibility for the world falls off my shoulders like a boulder. They didn't want to kill. We're talking, explaining—working on making the war stop. Hope has never been as strong as it is in this very moment, but something in his words makes me tense. "Tell me about the interruptions." It sounds like—

"Your realm interferes with ours. Your worlds. Burns holes, destroys it. Makes it unlivable and hurts us. We asked you to stop, but you didn't listen. We had to keep our home intact. We had to defend ourselves."

Goosebumps rise, leaving unease in their wake. "We didn't—"

"You use *this*. On some of your worlds." Lorr makes some kind of swiping gesture with his hand, and the light around us dims and shifts into the maroonish. "This happens from your side." All around us bright light trails pop up, like somebody shot a bullet into the air and its path was illuminated. To stick with that analogy, if there were bullets, I'd be toast. The whole area is filled with these things. It looks like a sieve, especially the area where I think I came from.

Click.

Where I came from: where my Tau-generator is shooting Tau-radiation into this realm.

You use this on some of your worlds. Every terraformed colony ever designed had Tau-radiation as a byproduct.

Guilt rises as realization dawns. I twist and nod my chin in the direction my shuttle should be. "The tau radiation? The same I'm using now?"

"Yes. It weakens our home."

Pressure builds in my chest. "We harmed your world," I whisper, falling back into vocalizing from the magnitude of the realization. "We didn't mean to, we didn't know. I'm so sorry we didn't realize it." It was *us* doing the damaging—it was us *continuing* to do the damaging. That thought alone is scary enough, but its translation even worse. The war, the reason for it, was all *us*. Not the Essken attacking out of nowhere, but us attacking them. All they did was defend their home. Blood drains from my face.

Lorr brings the light back to normal, or rather, to as crazy as it was before, and the light paths vanish. "And we had to learn that you didn't understand, but still had to defend ourselves. The radiation you use weakens the barrier between our two worlds, then breaks it. Once it is gone, we can't live there anymore."

I swallow hard. And here I am, blasting their home with more Tau-radiation. That's not what I intended. I thought I needed the Tau-radiation to cross into their realm—

"You don't. We've seen you pass." Lorr, having picked up on my thoughts

"You've seen me pass?" I've never been here—

"You pass through to travel. No others do. You are different."

The jumps! He must mean the jumps. "Yes. I can travel through time."

Lorr pauses. "Time."

Something in his voice, maybe the lack of understanding, brings cold goosebumps to my spine. "Do you… do you know what time is?" I hold my breath. Such a basic question, so impossible to imagine any other response but *yes*, and yet I'm not sure that's what he's going to say. Call it a gut feeling.

It takes him a good five seconds to respond. "I think I understand. You said you can stop existing. It suggests you exist at one point."

Those cold goosebumps get company by chills. Oh heck, it's not always cool to be right. I swallow hard. "I think so?" Even inside my head, my voice trails up at the end, but it seems to be the right answer for Lorr.

"That confirms our theory. You are linear." He uses a finger and draws an imaginary line between the two of us. "That's very interesting."

"Linear." *Linear time.* There's only one way to interpret what he's saying, and its implication is mind blowing. Like him, I use my finger to draw a line, emphasizing each station I'm listing. "You mean we start to exist, live our lives, and then we die—stop functioning. And that's not the same for you?"

"That is correct. We exist. We are not limited compared to you. We can choose our… place."

Holy everything—do I understand correctly what he's talking about? "Time works different for you. Not linear." I can't quite explain it, but in the depth of my gut I feel it's right. Maybe because of my Magellan genes, but the Essken Realm feels different to me.

"We are where we choose to exist."

The scenery changes around us. What was a field of grass and flowers is now a barren planet with a dark sky and the oh-so-typical doors to Essken bunkers around us. I feel wind, smell something tangy, but how can we be there? "Wait, is this a projection, or the real place?" Because I can still see that field of flowers in the distance, and maybe if I squint enough, the *Pioneer*'s bridge.

"We are here." Lorr stomps his foot onto the ground, bringing up dust. "We can be anywhere."

Something flashes up in the sky. "Ships firing," I murmur, even though I don't have to say it out loud. If I'm not mistaken, I see several V-shaped ships and one… One USEF vessel. The USEF vessel fires—and *BOOM*, one of the Essken ships blows up into a ginormous fireball.

Ouch. I flinch. "I'm sorry we destroyed your ship—"

Movement catches my attention. One of the ships is diving toward the atmosphere, coming closer and closer, the USEF ship hot on its heels, then reversing course—

Click! I know where we are. When we are.

I whirl toward Lorr. "The Battle of Balthar—that's now! That ship's going to kill everybody on this planet—"

"No. Close the connection to our home. Bring everybody back. We cannot hold shape on your ships."

"Hold shape?"

"The armor. Without it, we can't stay in your Realm."

"Why are you still wearing it right now if we're in your home?"

The ship's diving into the atmosphere, its outer hull glowing in bright red-orange. It can't be much longer than another ten seconds until impact—I've seen it, only from a different perspective.

I really, really don't want to experience it from this.

"Uhh, Lorr, never mind, just—"

He makes no movement at all, but in the blink of an eye, we're back in the field of flowers. Relief washes over me. That was way too realistic for my taste.

Lorr regards me like a specimen in the zoo, or whatever equivalent the Essken have. "You were afraid. I could smell that."

Now, with a human I might've been offended, but not with an

Essken. After all, I've been suspecting it for a while and I came prepared to put said theory to use. "Because you use scent to communicate?"

"Of course. All emotions are conveyed via scent. You?"

I guess we've reached the stage where we automatically assume it's different for the other one. "Facial expressions. The way we act. How our voice changes." I look at him, in his armor, the glaring proof of how unlike each other we are. "We're quite different people."

Lorr nods. "But you understand our home. You see us. You hear us. Nobody ever has this clearly."

"Maybe because I'm not a hundred percent human? My mom was Magellan." Now, let's give this a try… I focus really hard on the image of my mom in front of my inner eye, the way she looked when I saw her with Dad in that hut on Alpha Rubrum. Young, carefree, optimistic.

And, to my very surprise, the image I imagine pops up on the flower field. Not as realistic as Lorr's, but it's there.

"Oh," Lorr's voice sounds surprised inside my head. "We have met them. They smell better than humans. We thought it meant they were less aggressive, but now I know their smell, or yours, didn't mean anything. We have tried communicating with them, too, but they didn't understand either. The only one we could reach with basic images was *him*. He is different. He understands a little."

There it is again, the use of *he*, fueling my hope.

I'm not sure I want to go down that route. There's a reason I didn't mention any of my theory to Zio or Chase. Or Dad, for that matter. It's out there. *Way* out there. Maybe generated by a desperate mind. But then…

Anxiety makes my stomach cramp to the point of nausea when I ask the one-million-dollar question, knowing its answer will shape the rest of my life. "Who is *he*?"

"The one who came on his own. He understands some, but not like you." Lorr steps aside for me to see—and my heart stumbles.

About ten meters from us, right next to the topsy-turvy tree the shape of a shuttle takes form. "*Adventurer,*" I read out in a whisper.

Adventurer.

Kieran's shuttle, the one he die—

I whip my gaze over to Lorr. I take it back: *This* is the one-million-dollar question. "Is it real?"

"Real?"

"Is the shuttle here, like I am, or is he like the *Pioneer*, or the chair?" I jab my finger at my chest, then in the direction of the two locations.

Lorr pauses. "This vessel is here. So is he. He—"

I don't hear him out. Sprinting like a madwoman, I pump my legs over the short distance, all but crashing into the shuttle. "Kieran! Kieran?" The *Adventurer*'s hatch is open. I stretch one careful hand out and touch the outer hull. Solid. *Real.* A tingling sensation runs down my neck and my heart pitter-patters, overwhelmed with hope I don't dare to cling to.

But I can't help it.

Lorr pops up next to me. "He came here by accident. We didn't know how to bring him back to you without harming him. He is not Essken. He functions differently."

He.

No air. No air in my lungs.

I take one careful, tentative step into the shuttle. The lights are on—in fact, all instrument panels are running on full output, like the shuttle was in mid-flight. "Kieran?"

No response. I hold my breath and take a second step in. "Kieran?" To the left, the Demat pad and sleep area are empty. I swivel my head to the right—

Dark, tousled hair, a limp arm hanging down from behind the pilot's chair—

My breath comes back in a painful heave. "Kieran!" With the fastest four steps of my life, I'm next to the chair, turn it around—

Like he'd fallen asleep on the job, Kieran is leaned back into the chair, eyes closed, head leaned to the left, a peaceful expression on his face, mouth slightly agape, not moving a muscle. All air flees my lungs. Is he—

My gaze drops to the exposed side of his neck: *Dub. Dub. Dub. Dub.*

Slow, but regular, a pulse beats in his carotid artery.

Dizziness crashes over me as I sink to my knees next to the chair. Next to Kieran.

He is here. He is *really* here.

My biggest hope, my grandest theory, my wildest dream: Come true.

Kieran is alive.

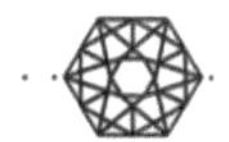

Quaneez Realm, Now

For one tiny moment I allow relief to wash over me. Kieran is here, in the Realm—the reason why I felt whole whenever I jumped. So obvious, when you think about it, yet so impossible.

But here he is.

Reaching one shaking hand out, I cup his cheek. Warm. Soft, with a bit of stubble. He looks at peace, not tortured like I heard him scream. "You're alive," I whisper, wonder swinging in my voice. With my other hand I give his shoulder a little wiggle. "Wake up, sleepy head."

He doesn't budge.

I wiggle his shoulder harder. "Kieran? Wake up."

Nothing.

Panic rises. Why isn't he responding? "Kieran? Kieran!" I pat his cheek, shake his shoulder. "Wake up! Kieran!" What's wrong with him? Hope crashes to the ground, writhing in pain. I'm so stupid. So, so stupid. Just because he's alive doesn't mean he's okay. He's pale, has stubble on his face, and his eyes are sunken deeper than I ever remember. And—

And Sun and Stars, he looks like he did forty years ago.

I suck in a sharp breath. He hasn't aged. Not that I can tell. This is a young man, not somebody in his sixties. Conolly still looks young, so does Upinga, but they have aged.

Kieran hasn't. The air in my lungs dies.

What happened to him, or rather, what didn't? "Kieran—?"

Lorr's voice sounds in my head. "Adjustment is hard for him."

I turn toward the Quaneez standing a few feet behind the pilot's chair. "Adjustment? To what?"

"Our world. We try to shape it according to what you might understand. What you know."

I shoot a quick glance out the window to the tree with its roots up in the air. Apparently, that shaping-thing isn't going so well.

And it's unimportant.

"He looks the same," I whisper. "He didn't age."

"Age?"

"Change. Grow. Like, children grow up. Get old."

"Old." He pauses. "I think I understand."

"So, why is he like that?" Because he should look old, and… I don't know. I don't know! I only know that him looking like the day he left and like he's sleeping, or… or in a coma or something isn't okay!

Lorr motions to our surroundings. "The laws of nature differ from yours. His mind entered a protective state. He can't comprehend our world, but in this state, we can communicate. Like when he was asleep."

Asleep—so Kieran was right, they've been trying to communicate with him when he slept! Everything makes sense now. "The nightmares. The dreams… the things he saw at night, when he was sleeping. That was you."

"Yes. We had to try to reach you. He was the only one who understood a little. We showed him how much you were hurting us, and tried to understand him. Tried to make sense of what we learned. Now we're able to communicate even more, not like with you, but better than before."

I perk up. "Communicate?" Communication means he's okay, even though he doesn't look it. "So, he's okay?"

"His body is functioning within normal parameters, for what we know."

I allow myself a short moment of relief. I can work with that. I—we—can fix this, even if I can't explain it.

Lorr carries on. "None of the others were this receptive to us. He helped us understand."

"Understand what?" I brush my palm across Kieran's cheek again, like an addict getting her fix.

"That some of you didn't mean to hurt us."

My heart skips a beat. "He told you that?" Even in this… coma, he fought for peace?

"We saw his concern for us. We didn't understand his grief, but knowing what we know now, it makes sense."

Emotion clogs my throat. Kieran's biggest regret. The war and its casualties. "He never wanted to kill any of you."

"And he didn't. We returned home."

And, as devastating as the losses were on our side, that's still good to know.

Lorr moves closer. "Because of him, we never sought to remove as many of you as we could. We removed others who harmed our world before you. But because of him, we only defended where we needed to. We planned on getting him back to you, he could have relayed our message. But we couldn't get him to cross over."

I still my hand on Kieran's cheek. "Do you think I can take him? The same way I came here?" The whole speaking with your mind thing is going pretty well at this point, surprisingly. Like my mind was more focused on what needed to be said, not so much on other details.

Laying a hand on the top of Kieran's head, Lorr looks like he's blessing him. "I would assume so. You are different. You passed us several times. You entered on your own. You communicate with us. Yet you crossed here in a different way from ours. Maybe that is the reason we can't get him back. Maybe you can."

A steely resolve takes root in me. I took Mashaule through time with me. Taking Kieran shouldn't be much different, I hope. Travel back, get Kieran into the shuttle, fly him home, done.

Home.

Lorr nods. "Yes. You are also welcome to return. Please convey our sincerest apologies to your people. The Essken will stop attacking your worlds and ships. We did not understand we ended your existence instead of sending you home, that you are linear. We only ask that you discontinue using this radiation." He points toward the fake bridge of the *Pioneer*. "It is our hope that you and him act as ambassadors between our people. Tell them of us and our world. We feel the universe is big enough for all of us, without destroying each others' homes."

Truer words never have been spoken. "I will bring them your message. I'm very happy we got to talk today, Lorr."

"So am I, Nonie Thorburn. I'm looking forward to the next time."

And with that, he makes a rotating gesture with his hand—

And he's gone.

I force down a dry swallow as I reach for Kieran's hand and take it. It's limp in mine, but I don't need him to hold on. I've got enough strength for the two of us.

Okay. Here goes nothing. I hope the way out of here is as smooth as the way into this realm. Shoving a hand into my pocket I press the button on my SED—

A blinding flash of light—

There we go.

Time swirls, billows, and wafts around me—around us. Kieran weighs nothing as he floats with me like my own personal kite. I tighten my fingers around his like a bench vise.

The colorful cloud-thing retreats, leaving me to sort out time and location. My destination. Our destination.

I open myself to my First Sense and focus. Shuttle. Reliant. Go back to the Reliant. Reliant. Reliant—

With an *oomph*, I land in the pilot's seat, hitting my knee against the forward console. I move both my hands to rub the throbbing spot—

Both my hands— Where's Kieran? I whirl around—

And the weight of the world, no, the universe, falls off my shoulders.

Kieran is in the seat next to me, as out of it as he was in the *Adventurer*.

But he's here, with me.

Alive.

Chapter Twenty-Three –
OLD AND NEW TIMES

With wobbly knees I work myself out of the pilot's seat and reach one hand out toward Kieran. First things first though. "*Reliant*, cut Tau-radiation." We've done enough damage with that.

"*Radiation discontinued.*"

I take his hand in mine and kneel next to his seat. "Thank you, *Reliant*. Give me our position, date and time." I brush one hand over Kieran's hair.

"*It is eighteen-oh-eight hours on September 14th, 2295. Location—Kanouse nebula, sector—*"

A groan leaves Kieran's throat, and I swear, never in my life have I heard a more beautiful sound. Elation crashes through me, together with a myriad of emotions, all bringing a high unlike any I could ever have imagined. "Kieran!"

Kieran… Kieran opens his eyes, blinks, lifts one slow and sluggish hand toward his face—

And I jump up and crash into him, wrapping my arms around his neck, pressing myself against him. "Kieran!" He feels wonderful and real and warm and alive and like he did before he left to enter this nebula.

He jerks from my assault, his arms moving up in slow motion to circle around me— "No-nie?" It comes out slurred, but nobody has ever said my name in a more beautiful way.

I pull away and cup his face with both hands, unbridled joy coursing through me. "Yes, it's me. I've got you, Kieran. I've got you."

He blinks two, three more times before awareness lights up in his eyes. "Where—where am I? Everything's... off." He tries to push himself up some more, but fails.

"Shh, easy." He tries to stand up again, like a newborn foal, staggering, unsteady, so I grab him by the arm and help him up. Leaning forward, he supports his weight on the forward console. Shakes his head. Blows out several big puffs of air. Rubs a hand across his eyes.

Then, he stills.

Looks to the side, at me.

"Nonie." He stares at me like he was seeing me for real for the first time. "You're here." He sways some more, slurring his speech. "I'm... out." He reaches for my arm, missing several times, like he was drunk. He gets a hold on to my hand and glides his fingers in-between, every move slow, like through quicksand, or on time delay. "I'm out." His voice breaks with the last word as tears fill his eyes.

Tears.

Raising one shaking hand he cups my cheek. He leans forward and rests his forehead against mine. "They spoke to me," he whispers. "I think they understand. I think I understand."

My Hablamate beeps. *"Hope to Lieutenant Thorburn."*

I tap it to reply. "Thorburn here."

"You cut the beam. What's your condition?" Chase sounds tense—but not as tense as Kieran gets when he hears his friend's voice. He stiffens, going rigid like a rod, with a little sway to him.

"The mission was successful, sir. I would prefer to update you face to face and not via the comm. I request all admirals to the shuttle bay, and Code Magenta to be initiated." I can all but hear the confusion in the ensuing silence. "And I'll need a minute before I come back."

Here's to Chase's experience with anything weird and unexpected. He doesn't question me, but trusts me. *"Acknowledged. Hope out."* The channel beeps once as a sign that the *Hope* has disconnected the call.

Kieran's chest heaves up and down fast. He sucks in one more breath and holds it. "That was Trip," he says. "He sounds off."

Not off. Older. I wrap both arms around his waist again and I splay my palms on his back. "He's a bit stressed with this mission."

"And he's calling from a ship named *Hope*."

I hear what he doesn't say: Not the *Pioneer*.

"Correct." I know I have to come clean, but... How do you tell somebody he's been gone for thirty-five years? That thirty-five years of his life have passed without him? Friends have aged, family died? I'll have to break the news gently.

He swallows loudly. "And he called you *lieutenant*. On an *official* channel."

I cringe. Oops. "That he did," I whisper, my heart going out to him, because I know the math he's doing right now. I know how it adds up.

Kieran exhales in an unsteady rush. "How long?" he croaks. "How long was I gone?"

There's no easy way to say it. I pull him tighter, as if that could give hold to his soul when I tear the rug from under his feet. "Thirty-five years," I whisper. "Thirty-five years."

A soft, inhuman sound tears from Kieran's throat as his knees buckle and he sinks to the ground. "Thirty-five..." His mouth opens and closes, no words coming out.

I kneel and catch him just before he falls forward. "Kieran!"

He doesn't brace himself, doesn't try to break his fall. If I hadn't caught him, he'd fallen face first onto the floor. Hands shaking, he reaches out for me, pulling me closer, like a drowning man. "Thirty-five years... Thirty-five years in there..."

I kneel, so that he can hold on to me and bury his head into my shirt. His shoulders begin to shake as I brush one hand over his hair, and pull him tighter with the other one.

Then, I let him cry.

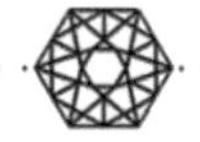

USEF Shuttle Reliant, September 14th, 2295, Kanouse Nebula

For the next several minutes I hold and gently rock Kieran. Soothe him. Try to give him the hold my revelation has taken from him.

Over time, his crying calms down, and his breathing turns regular again. Still I'm caressing his hair, holding him tight. He's balled his fingers into fists, crumbling my shirt between them.

Eventually, he takes one long stuttering inhale and relaxes his hands. "Chase is still alive."

"Yes."

"Zio?"

"Alive. They're still the same bickering couple they've always been."

A small chuckle moves Kieran's shoulders. "That's good to know." Then, he stills. "My dad?"

I swallow dry. "Gone. He died about ten years ago." And from what I heard, he never gave up on Kieran. Knowing what I do now, his actions and convictions seem rather like premonitions than a father's refusal to accept his only son's death.

Kieran rolls into me some more and presses his face into my shirt. For a good thirty seconds, he stays coiled tight, doesn't breathe, doesn't move. After a while, I feel him release the breath he held, the puff of air warming my stomach. He relaxes his hold on me and rolls on his back, head in my lap. His eyes are red and shine with tears. "That's rough," he whispers. "He lost Mom, then me. He knew USEF was a risk, of course he did, we all do, but I still…" He shakes his head. "I still wish he didn't have to go through that." Grief radiates from him in waves.

I stroke a wave of hair out of his face. "I know. I never met your dad, but mine did a long time ago, during—" I blush.

"During what?"

Well, this is awkward. "During the grand opening of the Kieran Wildason USEF Academy in Toronto."

Kieran jackknifes up to sitting and turns to face me, disbelief written all over his face. "They named an academy after me?"

"That they did. I don't know how much you want to know right now, but I can tell you I don't think we have time to go through everything that's dedicated to you. Or all the chapters in the history books."

"I'm in history books?" Surprise flickers across his face. "What the hell happened or didn't happen that *I* made it into the history books?"

"I'm not sure I can summarize that in one sentence."

"Give me two?" His lips tug into a half-smile close to reaching his eyes, so much like him it stills my heart.

I reach and take his hand into my lap, sliding my fingers in-between his. "You might not like the answer."

The smile fades. "Then I'll have to deal with it."

Drawing a pattern onto the back of his hand, I keep a close eye on his reaction. "Well, you're in the history books because you've been the most successful captain in fighting the—" *Essken...* "—Quaneez up to this day." Grazer is close, but only in second or third place. None of the others who came after survived long enough to reach the numbers of the captains active in the first years of the war.

His throat works on a slow swallow. "Not what I wanted to be remembered for."

I know. Which is why I give his hand a squeeze. "That was only the first of the two sentences you requested." I wink, and tension falls off his shoulders. "You're also in the history books because of your ongoing pursuit of peace through other means than war. And here's a third sentence, for free: People still quote what you said during your medal ceremony. Your thoughts still hold power over others."

Kieran lets out a shaky, soft laugh. "You gave me four sentences, and I still feel it's undeserved. History books..." He shakes his head, then cocks it to the side, figuring something out. "Wait a minute... The way you phrased it. The war is still ongoing? Today? Thirty-five years—"

"Yes. But that being said, we've had several months of a cease fire—"

Kieran stares down at our entwined hands. For the longest time, he doesn't move, doesn't even blink, like he was frozen in time. A myriad of emotions skates across his face, none of them happy ones.

I bring his hand to my mouth and kiss his knuckles. "Kieran?"

He exhales roughly. "I spend thirty-five years with them, and out here…"

"Nothing has changed," I say softly. Something that Lorr said comes back to me. "The Quaneez—"

"Essken," he corrects me.

Oh. "The *Essken* I spoke to in their realm, Lorr, said he communicated with you—"

His eyes widen. "You understood him?"

"Clear as day. What… what about you?" He knows they're Essken. They got that across. Even though he looked like he was unconscious, the communication between them must've been quite something.

Drawing in a deep, shuddering breath, blood drains from Kieran's face. "It wasn't like that for me," he whispers. "When I was… when I was in there, I felt them. I heard them. We communicated to a degree, more in images, bits and pieces, emotions, maybe. It wasn't like you and I are talking. Most of the time it was like a nightmare, a never-ending, continuous nightmare."

A dart of horror shoots through my veins. "What do you mean?"

He lifts his gaze to mine, the pain shining in it causing my heart to misfire. "All I saw was *them*. Their worlds exploding from our attacks. Their home being destroyed by our colonies. A never-ending nightmare of pain and suffering."

A never-ending nightmare. A nightmare I didn't understand he had, when I should have. "I heard you scream." It comes out in a rough whisper. "When I jumped and came close to the Essken realm, I heard you scream." Knowing his screams were real rips my chest right open. I heard the horror in them, felt the despair.

And it took me way too long to realize they weren't a figment of imagination.

Way too long.

I can't get close to fathom the horror of somebody screaming like this for decades. Can't even get close to imagine what he went through.

The apple in his throat moves up and down. "I lost all sense of time.

Before you told me how long I'd been in there… could have been a year, could have been ten. Time lost all meaning. Didn't exist, I don't know. All I know is it felt never-ending, like all I'd ever done in my life was be in that realm and watch them get hurt and tortured over and over again. Hear their screams, feel their pain. I think…" His voice shakes. "I think for a while I lost myself."

Tears prick my eyes from the raw quality to his words. "You must've felt—"

"Alone," he says matter-of-factly. "Completely and utterly alone."

Alone.

For thirty-five years.

Alone.

I swallow all the tears down, push the sorrow, the hurt for him as far away as I can. Kieran needs an anchor, not somebody to pull him under. "And yet you managed what nobody else achieved before. You spoke to them."

He lowers his chin in a slow nod. "That's giving me too much credit. Like I said, I understood them through what they were showing me. I can't explain it, but it changed over time. Or maybe I changed, but I understood they were Essken. I understood I was in their world. I understood they wanted peace. I tried to… I tried to *think* who we were, how we saw the war, for a lack of a better term, and it felt like they understood me. On a certain level, we did communicate. I feel like I know them. But it doesn't change that I was completely helpless. Helpless and hopeless." He gives a dry chuckle. "Not the guy you'd put in history books."

"Oh, stop it." I play-slap the side of his head and it breaks the somber mood. "You—"

"Hope to Lieutenant Thorburn."

Within a split-second Kieran's expression changes. Gone is the vulnerability and hurt, replaced by alertness and awareness. We both hear the urgency in the call. It's all it takes to switch Kieran into captain mode, thirty-five years in the Essken realm or not. He gives me a small nod, and I take one hand off Kieran's and tap my Hablamate. "Thorburn here."

My dad's voice sounds strained through the speaker. "*We're getting reports on troop movement. I'd be more comfortable with you back here.*"

"Acknowledged. I'll be there as soon as I can. Thorburn out."

After another moment, Kieran points at the Hablamate. "Was that—"

"My dad."

Something lights up in his eyes. "He got his own command?"

I stand up and pull on his hand in mine, glad to have a different topic on hand than Kieran's suffering in the realm. "A big one, actually. Apparently, he is the new interim USEF President."

Kieran works himself up to standing with my help. "What?" A small astonished chuckle breaks free. "Man, the world has changed."

"You have no idea," I mumble. "You have no idea."

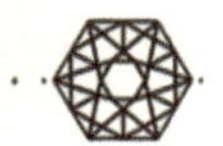

**USEF Shuttle Reliant, September 14th, 2295,
right outside the Kanouse Nebula**

I set the *Reliant* on autopilot for the landing in the *Hope*'s shuttle bay. Since I programmed a course out of the nebula and back to the ship Kieran has been quiet. Has been checking out the console, but not commented on the innovations of the last thirty-five years. Has been looking at the *Hope* as it grew bigger and bigger in the view screen, but not commented on its appearance. In short, he's been trying to digest what fate threw at him.

Hi, fate. Thanks again for all that you did. Although, I kind of mean it this time, because Kieran is alive.

Alive.

Whenever I think it, a jolt of happiness shoots through me, from my head to my toes. *Kieran is alive.* And while it looks like he'll have a lot to work through, it also looks like if anybody can overcome the damage done by thirty-five years of solitary detention in a foreign realm, it's him.

When the Hope is so close its landing port takes up the complete view screen I swivel in my chair toward Kieran. "Ready?"

He chews on the inside of his cheek, then looks me in the eye. "Ready to see everybody again? Yes. Ready to see them as… old men? Not really." He sighs. "But at least I'm seeing them again, so there's that."

"And they're not really that old. They aged well." A smile crosses my face. "Remember when you guys first picked me up—"

"You mean, when you saved my butt? First contact? How could I forget that? Of course."

"Well, imagine the shock when I saw young Chase and young Zio. Those two were my mentors at the academy, by the way. So, waking up and seeing them wrinkle-free and not recognizing me was quite the shock. I think I considered every option from stroke over concussion to straight up illusions." Well, I considered every option besides time travel. That took me a bit to come to terms with.

Kieran turns his head toward me. "And then you saw me."

There'd be a million different options how to reply to that. Humorous, flirty, matter-of-factly, but it's not what Kieran needs. Honesty is. "I saw you and couldn't believe my eyes."

"Because in your time, I was long gone." He manages to keep his voice close to even, although it rises a tad too much for somebody unaffected. "You always knew I was going into that nebula, didn't you?" It's more than a rhetorical question. An emotional one. For the first time since Kieran found out about my time-traveling he might understand what it actually meant. Understand the burden accompanying it.

I hold his gaze. He needs to know that I was aware of his early death, and that it weighed me down every day since I met him in person. "From the very moment I first heard about you in school."

Kieran closes his eyes and gives a short, small nod when he reopens them. "I think I've underestimated the amount of secret-keeping required by you." He faces the view screen again, the guiding lights of the *Hope*'s hangar bay bathing his face in light green. "I can't process all of that right now, but at one point we'll have to sit down and talk about all the times when you knew more than we did. It must be—" Cocking his head, he shoots a questioning glance over to me again. "We can talk about it, right? You're not in the past? *This* is your present?"

I stand up from my chair. We're going to touch down in less than twenty seconds. "This is my native time." That's the term Other Nonie used, and I feel it fits. "Whatever is happening now is new to both of us. And not that I could complain, I like the way life is going right now." Minus Humanity First's idiocy to continue the war, but I guess one can't have everything.

Stepping out from behind the chair and console, I hold out my hand. "Let's do this. Shall we?"

Kieran takes my hand and lets me lead him toward the hatch. The *Reliant* shakes ever so slightly when she touches down. *"Atmosphere in landing bubble restored in ten seconds,"* the shuttle's computer voice announces. Dad, Chase and Zio must be waiting, anxious to hear the details of my mission.

Well, aren't they in for a surprise.

"Atmosphere restored," the *Reliant* announces at the same time as the indicator to the right of the hatch switches from red to green.

Kieran lets go of my hand after he giving it a little squeeze. He straightens his uniform shirt and cracks his neck, a hint of nervousness crossing his face. I open the hatch and step out of the shuttle. As requested, Code Magenta is active, the lights dimmed and the shuttle bay empty, except for those three men about five meters away from the shuttle.

I hope nobody gets a heart attack, really.

As soon as I'm half out of the shuttle, Chase takes a few fast steps forward, a concerned look on his face. "About time. It looks like we might get company soon—" He stops dead in his tracks, so abruptly, Zio barely avoids running into him. Guess he's seen there's somebody behind me.

His eyes widen. Reaching one hand back for Zio, like he needed somebody to stabilize him, a strange, chocked sigh breaks from his throat, a soul so full of loss, pain, and love, it brings goosebumps to my skin. "Kieran." The apple in his throat moves up and down, hard. "Is that really..."

I move to the side, revealing the man they believed dead for the last thirty-five years.

For the longest two seconds, nobody moves. Not Chase, not Zio, not my dad. All three of them stare at Kieran as if they weren't sure whether their eyes were playing tricks on them.

Kieran lifts a hand. "Gentlemen. Rumors of my demise were greatly—" He doesn't get any further than that. Zio and Chase burst forward as if propelled by a rocket. Chase reaches him first and wraps his arms around the other man's shoulders in the tightest embrace possible, if he wants to let Kieran breathe, that is. He only opens one arm to welcome Zio into the hug. "You son of a gun," he whispers, his voice cracking. "You freakin' son of a gun."

His words must've triggered something in Kieran. He closes his eyes, shoulders heaving with one big breath before he relaxes into the embrace of his two best friends. A peaceful expression settles on his face, a first since he came back from the realm. And boy, does it feel good to see that.

Step by slow step, Dad comes over to me. "I'm really seeing this, correct?" He lays one hand on my shoulder and squeezes, as if he needed to assure himself I—this situation—was real.

"You are, Dad. The Quaneez realm was quite interesting."

"No kidding," he murmurs, then shakes his head. "Unbelievable. Captain Wildason, like on the day he left… It's hard to make sense of it."

Somebody in the triple-embrace, probably Kieran, exhales so forcefully it makes all of them laugh.

"Are you telling us you can't take a simple hug anymore?" Chase loosens his pseudo-death grip on his friends and pulls back a bit to look at Kieran. Tears shine in his eyes—actually, all three of them are teared up, but in a good, soul-soothing way.

Kieran lets loose a wry smile. "Excuse me, I didn't spend thirty-five years in that realm to be smothered to death the minute I leave."

Zio steps out of the hug, looking like he'd learned ghosts were real. "Obviously, that will be a story worthwhile to listen to." He makes a hand gesture up and down Kieran's body. "At least one of us has aged well."

"Well, we always knew too much of that soda…" Kieran lets the sentence trail and winks at the other two.

Chase snorts. "Excuse me, I'm still in excellent shape. If you weren't just resurrected from the dead, I'd take you to the gym to prove it."

Something in Kieran's eyes sparkles. "Nah, not a good idea. I'd really feel bad kicking an admiral's butt…" He flicks a finger at the pips on Chase's collar. "Does that mean I have to call you sir now? Both of you?"

Zio lifts an eyebrow. "I'd be surprised if they didn't promote you to admiral or higher the second command knows you're alive. Then there shouldn't be a problem with young you showing the old admiral what he has lost to the last decades. And to Lubbecks," he adds under his breath, but exactly loud enough for everybody to hear.

"Zee, don't rain on my parade," Chase puts both hands on his hips. "I—"

"Gentlemen, please." I hold both hands up as I step closer, using them to physically separate Kieran from the others. Don't we all know that once they get going… "I think we all agree we're happy Kieran is back. Butt-kicking details will have to be evaluated later."

Behind me, Dad clears his throat, and I get the hint. "Kieran, you remember my dad, Tom Thorburn?" I make a swiping hand motion and step aside.

Dad holds a hand out to Kieran. "Captain Wildason… I don't know what to say. I'm thrilled to have you back."

Kieran takes his hand and shakes it. "Admiral Thorburn. Believe me, I'm at least as thrilled to be back."

"I never got to thank you for what you did for me. I owe so much to you, least of all my career." Gratitude shines in his gaze, as Kieran's flicks over to me.

"It was all my pleasure. And I believe I'm the one to thank you, since it's your daughter I owe my life to." The look he gives me says *several times.*

"Which, by the way," Chase cuts in, "is a story I would like to hear. Most importantly and urgently though, we need to know what the

Quaneez said. Were you able to communicate?" He turns toward me, expectation in his gaze.

"The Essken," Kieran corrects his friend. "They're called the Essken."

Chase whips his head around, surprise coloring his tone. "You spoke to them?"

"Well, what else did you think I was doing in there for three decades?" He cocks an eyebrow at the other man as if the last thirty-five years were a walk in the park and not a continuous trauma.

Dad blows out a puff of air. "And you, too, Nonie?" When I nod, he works a hand through his hair. "It can be done. Our people can talk. Not all is lost."

"Bridge to Thorburn." Dad's Hablamate lights up.

"Thorburn here."

"Sir, the Pioneer *is requesting to rendezvous with us."*

"The *Pioneer*?" Kieran sucks in a sharp breath at the mentioning of his former ship at the same time as Dad raises an eye brow at me.

"Taro Magona?" he asks.

"Yes, sir. The Taro requests transfer of a certain individual, *as she said."*

We exchange a look. *Mashaule,* I mouth, and Dad nods.

"That's fine. Have them rendezvous with us, Commander. I'm sure we'll have lots to talk about."

Like a debriefing about everything that led to me catching Mashaule. I wonder though if she knows Kieran is back. Did her First Sense alert her? Did Zio know, before Kieran stepped out of the shuttle? His sense isn't as strong as the Taro's, but he could've felt *something.*

"Understood, sir. Bridge ou— Wait a moment." The comm goes silent, and Chase slams his brow down into a V.

"That's not reassuring. What's going on up ther—?"

"Admiral, three battle cruisers have jumped to our coordinates. They're keeping themselves out of weapons range."

For one tiny, short-lived second all are frozen, our breaths stuck, eyes wide. Then, Dad curses. "The rest of the fleet?"

"Reports coming in that all ships under observation have made a move toward known Quaneez space, sir. Every single ship has their weapon system

activated, but they're still holding fire."

We all hear the *for now* at the end of the sentence.

Dad curses once more. "We're this close to peace, dammit! If we start firing at the Quaneez after months of ceasefire—"

Blood drains from Kieran's face. "You can't fire at the Essken! I admit I'm out of the loop, but I know there was a ceasefire, and while I know the Essken want peace, I can assure you they will defend their home and their people."

Something Lorr said in the realm comes back to me. "The only reason why we haven't been wiped out by them like so many other species before is that Kieran was in their realm, being our ambassador. Without him, humanity would've been extinct decades ago."

The *Hope* shakes once. Twice.

My stomach roils. We all know these vibrations.

We're under attack.

"Bridge to Thorburn. Two ships have begun to fire at the nebula, the third at us."

"Shields up, defensive actions! Get us in-between those ships and the nebula!" Dad barks out. "Gentlemen, break's over, let's go!" He jogs toward the doors, and we all follow.

BoomBoom!

Several more hits shake the *Hope*, albeit less than before. We sprint out onto the hallway toward the bridge as another wave of shots brings the ship to a shudder.

"Are those USEF ships firing on us?" Kieran calls out as he follows in Dad's footsteps.

"Unfortunately," Dad throws over his shoulder. "All traitors listening to Humanity First—you won't know them, but—"

"Oh no, thank you very much, I do remember them!" Kieran grunts as we all get thrown against the wall.

"Dammit!" Chase yells. "Conolly to security! What the hell are you doing down there? Shield status?" He listens to the report and barks out more orders while we dart up the last part of the hallway before the bridge. My heart might arrive there before me, judging by its pace.

The doors to the bridge slide apart as Dad rushes in, followed by us.

"Report!"

Nobody besides me notices the small stumble to Kieran's step as he clears the hallway and enters the bridge. As if nothing happened and as if that had been his job all along, he positions himself to the left of the command chair as Dad takes a seat there.

The officer sitting at tactical turns around. Surprise flickers across her face when her gaze falls upon Kieran. To her credit, she has herself under control even though her cheeks turn red. "S-sir, all Humanity First ships have begun firing."

Chase takes position on the other side of the chair where he always stood for Kieran. "Could we please not refer to them as Humanity First's ships, because that's giving them too much credit. Thank you. Second, any motion from the Ess—the Quaneez?"

She shakes her head. "Not yet—" Something beeps on her console and she checks it. "I take it back. All areas have Quaneez battlecruisers popping up out of nowhere. They haven't fired yet—"

"But they will," Kieran murmurs. "Unless—" He whirls around. "Admiral, could you put me on a fleet-wide override priority one channel?"

The bridge officers who had not yet noticed the additional new person on board turn to look at the man who requested a fleet-wide communication channel be opened in the middle of a battle. Not a single one is unaffected when they recognize Kieran. A murmur goes through the bridge, an awe-filled sense of recognition.

Kieran's cheeks turn the slightest pink, but he keeps his focus on Dad.

"Captain, all we did was talk for the last years, and it led nowhere with these people. I doubt—"

"With all due respect, Admiral. Maybe they need an outside perspective. I spent thirty-five years with the Essken, sir. And from what I was told," he shoots me a glance, "my name still matters to a degree. I beg you, let me have five minutes. They won't matter if I fail, but if I don't—"

"They might turn the tide." Dad gives a tight nod. "All right. Steinbach, you heard the man. Priority one, override, fleet wide." Then he turns toward Kieran. "Do what you can, Captain. Our fate rests in your hands."

Chapter Twenty-Four –
SHAPING THE FUTURE

"Channel open, Captain. You're live, fleet wide." Steinbach gives Kieran a thumbs up. Hats off to Steinbach, looking at him, you wouldn't know a long-thought dead captain was on his bridge, giving orders.

Kieran acknowledges this with a nod. Straightening his uniform shirt in typical Kieran-manner, he looks straight at the view screen displaying fleet-wide movement and weapons' activity. Most of the dots representing USEF ships are red, *in active battle*. Firing onto the Quaneez—or each other.

"USEF Fleet, this is Captain Kieran Wildason. Hold fire. I beg of you, hold fire!" With the last word, another impact rattles the *Hope*, as if to show defiance to his request.

I cringe, but Kieran isn't deterred. He takes two steps forward, so that he is slightly in front of my dad. "I ask you to listen, to listen for a moment that might change our fate. I appeal to your loyalty to your species, to life, and ask you to trust me. To listen to me for a few minutes."

Boom! BoomBoom! Hope tilts to the side, the internal Grav Stabilisators compensating without delay.

Kieran takes in one fast, deep breath. No time to lose, or we will have doomed ourselves. "I realize it must seem odd seeing me here. After all, I was believed dead. My story is a crazy one, but it comes with hope for humanity. I spent the last thirty-five years with the people we call Quaneez. And no, I was not kidnapped. I chose to meet them on the day I vanished. I entered their realm due to an accident, and, until today, had no means to return. While I was with them, I got to know them. I got to understand them, and I promise you they want peace as much as we do."

He begins to pace, once in a while dropping his gaze to the ground, a lost quality in his eyes, as if in his mind he were back with the Essken. "Their world differs from ours in all counts. It's a realm separated from the universe we know, where our laws of physics don't apply. Neither does our understanding of communication. Quaneez don't have speech. They communicate telepathically or by scent. Colors play a role, too."

The two officers in the back, tactical and communication, exchange a shocked glance. Everybody's glued to Kieran's lips. He's playing it smart, humanizing them, explaining, not calling them Essken. Even though it's just a name, it's new to humanity. They need to hear the *Quaneez*, whom we have eared and fought for over four decades, don't want them harm. Kieran is sacrificing some political correctness in favor of a clear message.

"When we attacked their world, we didn't do it on purpose, but they didn't understand that. To them, we reek of aggression, and to them, we don't listen to what they have to say—just like we feel the same about them." Kieran stops and looks straight into the camera system integrated into the view screen. "And make no mistake, it's us who started this war. Whenever we hail them, it causes them pain and they perceive it as an attack. Our... terraformed colonies are wreaking havoc on their realm." The short hesitation and phrasing tell me Kieran knows more than he wanted to share. Smart move. Tell Humanity First Tau-radiation destroys the Quaneez realm, and I bet we could start a countdown to them using it as a weapon in no time. "They acted in self-defense, just like we did."

Boom! Another hit rattles the *Hope*—but coming to think about it, none have for a while. Maybe there's hope, after all...

"So please, stop firing onto the Quaneez. Stop firing onto each other. Let the weapons rest. Enough women and men have died. We're only hurting ourselves. There's a way out of this, and it is holding fire and learning to listen to each other. Even if you have been firing on USEF ships—" Kieran looks back at my dad, who gives the shortest nod. "Even if you've been firing on USEF ships, please stop and know that we will try to work with you."

My dad stands up, but stays a step behind Kieran. "This is President Thorburn. I stand behind what Captain Wildason has said. You stand down, we are willing to work with you. We're all on the same team."

Another *BOOM*, but then—blissful silence. The bridge officers exchange hopeful glances.

Kieran crosses his hands behind his back. "We all want the same. Peace. We all thought we were defending it by decimating the enemy. Now it turns out the best defense is a step back. Please trust me on this one. I promise you won't regret it."

For one split second the screen turns static, before a smaller window pops up, overlying the left upper quadrant of the battle projection, showing the image of a blonde woman in her late fifties, early sixties. She looks into the camera, wearing a face-splitting grin. "Commander Thaler here, *USEF Expectation*. Good to have you back, Captain. We're taking care of the problem on our end over here."

Thaler—wait, that's Thaler from the *Pioneer*! Of course! And yes, she has gotten older, but it's definitely her! She steps aside—and reveals who must be the Captain of the *Expectation* sitting in the command chair behind her.

With three security guards aiming their weapons at him.

Oops.

Kieran salutes, a spark in his eye seeing his former pilot. "*Commander* Thaler. Appreciate the initiative." They share a moment that speaks of the years of service together before Thaler disconnects the call.

Another moment later, tactical announces. "*Expectation* has her weapons powered down, sir."

"*Mercury* here." The image of a younger captain in his thirties pops up, replacing Thaler's. "Captain Wildason, thrilled to see you alive and in one piece. *Mercury* standing down, awaiting your orders." With a curt nod, he disconnects the call.

"That was one of ours," Chase whispers for Kieran to hear. One on our side. Au contraire to Thaler, who, apparently, had to convince her superior to follow USEF's orders.

Somebody else chimes in, a woman in her late forties, early fifties maybe, red hair tied into a bun on top of her head. One of her eyes is blue, the other deep brown. "Captain Rozell of the *Homebound* here. How do I know you are who you say you are and what you say is true?" Captain Rozell isn't quite looking at Kieran in a hostile fashion, but I wouldn't say she was friendly either. Definitely closer to the Humanity First-side.

"Not one of ours," Chase whispers under his breath, confirming my theory.

Kieran spreads both arms. "I can only give you my word, Captain. I'm the same Kieran Wildason who left for the mission in the Kanouse nebula what feels simultaneously like this morning and decades ago."

The female captain crosses her arms in front of her chest. "It sounds quite unbelievable, and sorry, sir, but your word means nothing to me. You could be a holographic projection designed to—"

Something in her words together with her look makes it click inside my brain: Holographic projection. Her hair. The eyes! "Jazmine," I hiss-whisper under my breath, loud enough for Kieran to pick up on, but not enough for it to be transmitted. "It's Jazmine!"

Kieran's eyes go wide with understanding. "Jazmine?"

Rozell stills. "Yes?" Her eyes narrow as she tilts her head in slow motion. "I didn't know we were on a first-name basis."

"Your father is—or was, I apologize, I'm not up to speed—Admiral Rozell?"

"Yes, but—"

Kieran folds both hands behind his back and steps even closer to the view screen. We got this. "You were a little kid and interrupted your father on a holo-call with me. Your stuffed animal Pocky had been in the wash. I told you how to fix him."

The other captain's cheeks blush as Kieran holds her gaze, waiting. Waiting.

After a small eternity, her throat works on a hard swallow. "You… you look exactly like you did in that Holo."

Hallelujah if that sentence wasn't a homerun for Kieran! Dad looks back at me, one eyebrow raised, like *how did you know that?* I'll add it to the pile of stories to be told later, like—

A sharp, unnatural sting shoots through my chest, of the kind I've felt before. It comes with the sensation of doom, of *something* shifting. I gasp and press a hand to my heart, but the gesture goes unnoticed. Everybody is focused on Kieran.

"I know. Tell me about how I still look like I did three decades ago." Kieran motions down his body clad in a uniform a few decades out of fashion.

I breathe out hard and drop the hand pressed to my chest. The sensation is still there, but weaker. I look over to Zio, but unlike the last time my First Sense was triggered, he doesn't seem affected. Maybe I'm overreacting. Over-sensitive. I straighten my shirt and force my shoulders back into a straight stance. Focus, Thorburn. Trying to avoid war here.

Rozell pulls her eyebrows down. "Time works differently for the Quaneez?" She might be a skeptic, but there's some curiosity peeking through. These people are USEF-trained scientists after all. Yes, everybody has a different political opinion, but reason should work on a USEF officer.

"Everything works differently for them. I think both our people have been assuming too much of the other one, namely that we're similar. We're not. In the weeks to come, I will hopefully be able to phrase it better, because believe me, switching realms in either direction is quite traumatizing." He winces, then continues. "We're not much alike, only in our values and the pursuit of peace. And Captain, you have nothing to lose holding your fire. The element of surprise is gone, and either the Quaneez will be able to match your attack, or they won't. Holding your fire at least gives peace a chance."

Rozell stays silent for a good five seconds, then lowers her chin. "I'll take that into consideration. *Homebound* out."

"Madrigal. *Reunion*." The image of a man looking close to retirement age appears on the screen before Rozell's has snuffed out.

Somebody taps me on the shoulder from behind. "Lieutenant Thorburn?" The person whispers my name, and I twist back.

"Yes?" I face an ensign, maybe a few years older than me, holding a PAD in one hand.

She keeps her voice low. "This just came in, U-One, and for your eyes only." Handing me the PAD, she nods. "That's all. Sorry to interrupt."

I take the PAD. "N-no problem." That's a first. Urgency one, I can honestly say I've never received a message that important. Or one for my eyes only. I swallow hard, glancing up to the view screen and, who was it? Somebody from the *Reunion*, who has been talking for the last fifteen seconds or so.

"… and while I can't say I always see eye to eye with the higher-ups, you're right. It doesn't cost us to wait, but it could cost us dearly if we didn't. We're powering down." He hesitates. "And I'd be honored to meet you in person one day. *Reunion* out."

I'm about to log into the PAD when tactical whistles through his teeth. "*Reunion* powering down weapons, sir. Actually, so did the *Homebound!* Oh, and the *Excalibur*. And the *Prometheus. Revelation. Europa. Dedication. Heracles.* The—" He twists in his chair, looking at Kieran and my dad. "To make it short, ninety percent of the fleet have powered down their weapons." He rechecks his readings as more and more red dots turn grey on the view screen. "Ninety-three. Ninety-six. Ninety-eight. One hundred percent."

A collective deep sigh goes through the bridge crew. Holy Sun and Stars, this is really happening. I let the hand holding the PAD sink down. It's happening. We're not going to start shooting at each other. Or the Essken. We're not.

Everybody powered their weapons down. Everybody.

Kieran whirls around toward tactical. "Quaneez movement?"

"Stopped completely, Captain. The Quaneez are still holding fire."

Letting out a shaky laugh, Kieran turns back to the view screen. "Thank you, USEF community. Humanity is deep in your debt. I'm very much looking forward to meeting each and every one of you who made today possible, who turned their back on war and destruction and invested in the future. I'm deeply honored to be part of this team. Wildason out."

Steinbach cuts the channel—and the whole bridge explodes into cheers and claps, yells and happy laughter. Chase holds out a high five for Kieran, while Zio keeps an eye on everything from the back, grinning like an imbecile. If his First Sense is anything like mine, this needed to happen. Was supposed to happen. It feels right on so many levels.

But speaking of: A sense of foreboding, and not the good kind, rises when I lift up the PAD. It recognizes my fingerprint, and after a short flash, aka retinal scan, it unlocks for me. Around me everybody is celebrating, yet I feel nauseous somehow as I scan over the message displayed. It's from the Taro.

Held up for rendezvous. We'll meet as soon as possible. Something is off. Lieutenant Thorburn, do not trust anybody. Stay alert. Listen to your First Sense.

That's... vague. I click the PAD off and drop it onto a console to my right. *Something is off*—well, duh, that much I knew. I felt it. But okay, I can follow her instructions. Stay alert, be on the lookout for *something off.* Whatever it is though, I know in the bottom of my heart and thanks to my First Sense that this here, right now, is not it.

This is supposed to happen.

And boy, does it feel good.

Everybody is celebrating in one way or another. The guy on navigation is hugging the officer on tactical. Steinbach is laughing out loud at something some other ensign said. Dad slaps Kieran on the back, like a happy father-in-law, which is so weird, because he's younger than Kieran, but of course looks much older—and doesn't even know yet what's going on between us. That's going to be an interesting conversation when it happens.

Kieran laughs a beautiful, light laugh. It latches itself to my heart and opens it up.

Breathtaking.

As if he'd heard my thoughts, he turns around toward me, his smile even wider and even more beautiful for me. He takes one step—

And stops, confusion flickering across his face. Chase and Dad both shake hands, and Trip lays another hand on Kieran's shoulder, squeezing it. Neither man notices Kieran's attention is not on them, but me.

His smile fades ever so slowly, and when it's gone, reality hits me in the face with a sledge hammer. *Captain* Wildason. *Lieutenant* Thorburn. Or worse, soon it might be *Admiral* Wildason. And still *Lieutenant* Thorburn.

For one short, painful moment as our gazes connect, I see the other Kieran in him. The older one. I see his desire, his urge, his need for me—and like a wall between us, the captain's pips on his collar.

A look of longing passes between us, and an ache opens up in my chest.

Kieran may be back in the present, but *us*... We can only exist in the past.

USEF HOPE, September 14th, 2295, right outside the Kanouse Nebula

The tension is awkward as a yeoman walks Kieran and me from the bridge toward the D-deck and the guest quarters. Dad, Chase, and Zio stayed on the bridge to negotiate whatever agreements needed to be made with the Humanity First renegades, but there was no need for Kieran and I to stay.

Both of us are in need of a shower, some rest, and... well. Good question.

I know what I need.

I know what he needs.

But being in the same time has made our lives more complicated. Add the Taro's ominous warning, and *complicated* might only be the beginning.

We both stay silent as we turn the last corner toward the guest suites. Kieran's back is stiff like a log, hands clenched to fists by his side. My stomach is churning with acid, and for the first time in forever I feel like my one constant, my one fallback feel good fixer-upper is being ripped from me: that Kieran and I are *us*, whenever we are.

Looks like I was naive—or no, rather unsuspecting. Other Nonie and Old Kieran are the prime example, but I never expected this to happen to us here in this timeline. And it's different, since Kieran here is young—but he still outranks me.

We are still inappropriate.

The yeoman halts in front of a door. "Guest suite A for you, Captain, suite B for you, Lieutenant." He motions to two doors across each other.

Kieran nods curtly. "Thank you, Yeoman. Appreciate it."

The guy nods and walks down the hallway. Both our gazes follow him until he's turned a corner.

Once he has, Kieran swallows so audibly, it breaks the silence. "Would you mind coming to my quarters for a moment?" He moves closer to the door which opens thanks to facial ID.

"I'd love to," I whisper. Unease blossoms inside my heart. Come inside to do what? I have an idea, but I no idea what's going on in Kieran's head.

He takes me by the hand and leads me inside with three quick strides. "*Hope*, lock the door."

Click.

Kieran holds on to my hand like a bench vise.

But he stays completely still otherwise.

His breath come out harsh once… twice… three times.

"Kieran?" My voice might or might not have wavered the slightest bit. Actually, it did. Noticeably so.

Kieran whirls around, drops my hand, and cups my cheek with both his palms. "Nonie." My name is a caressing breath across my cheeks. Soul-soothing, like his touch.

I close my eyes and hold onto his wrists, like I wanted to make sure he didn't take his hands away. "Yes?"

He leans his forehead against mine. "You've been thinking the same, haven't you? Our ranks?"

I nod. I can't speak, or else I'd give away how much the expectation of the upcoming conversation hurts.

One shuddering breath later, he whispers. "I don't care. I don't care what USEF says. I lost thirty-five years in the realm. I'm not going to lose you." He brushes his lips across mine, and holy Sun and Stars, does that tender touch light up the fireworks in my stomach. My pulse kicks into overdrive as the atmosphere changes around us from strained and heavy to light, heady and… hopeful. The kiss only lasts a moment, but it cracks me wide open.

He pulls back the slightest, his breath feathering across my skin. "I won't take the promotion. And after you brought me back from the realm, they might promote you to lieutenant commander, and it's not unheard of for those two ranks to *mingle*." With the last word he kisses me once more. "And if they throw the fraternization regulations at us, we'll come up with something, I—"

Turning my face to the side, I place a kiss on the inside of his wrist. "I'm not under your direct command. I'm with the FBTI." And even if I'd be stationed wherever Kieran is going to be, he's not going to be my direct superior. That should be fine, right? Right?

"FBTI?" He smooths his thumbs across my cheeks.

"Federal Bureau of Temporal Investigation." I look into his eyes, those beautiful mesmerizing eyes.

"Ah, of course. Temporal Investigation. I do want to hear all about that. Feel like there might be a couple of surprises in it for me."

"Like the *Pioneer* being their ship now and the Taro commanding it?" Or the Taro messaging me to be extra careful? What if the Temporal War isn't over? Then Kieran is going to be in for one heck of a surprise, more than he bargained for.

He whistles through his teeth. "Yeah, exactly like that. But, priorities: We don't have to worry about fraternization then. It's settled." He glides both hands down my back and pulls me closer. "For a moment there I was worried."

"Me, too." I place my hands on his chest and feel his heart skip a beat.

His gaze softens. "It's been so long, Nonie. So long that I held you. So long that I felt like this. Felt alive." A small chuckle breaks free. "I'll have to talk to your dad though, which is beyond weird, because he's your dad, but also, he's Tom." He shakes his head, but then his gaze turns mischievous. "At least I need him to know what I feel for his daughter." One of his hands works its way under my shirt. Skin on skin—I gasp. Nothing is better than Kieran's skin on mine. "We—"

"Door lock overridden," Hope announces a millisecond before the door opens.

We dart apart, like two school kids caught doing something forbidden, and while I'm sure my face is looking like a tomato, Kieran's isn't.

It's not his happy face though either as he turns toward the man entering his cabin. "What—"

"Captain Kieran Wildason and Lieutenant Nonie Thorburn?" The man looks from Kieran to me and back, then down onto… a holo-projection hovering at chest level. *Without* a PAD or wristPAD—and I can't see what's on the projection, like he was holding a sheet of paper I couldn't read from the back. That's new. Something else about him is odd. For one, he isn't wearing a uniform I know. Grey with red lines over the shoulder—never seen that. For another, I dunno, something about him feels weird. Not very precise, I get that, but something is off.

Lieutenant Thorburn, do not trust anyone.

Not that I needed that advice, but I take it, inching closer to Kieran, wishing I had a weapon.

To Kieran's credit, he's perceptive, and he knows me well. Like me, he shifts his weight into an inconspicuous fighting stance. "Yes? And you are?"

The look he gives us is full of disdain. "My name doesn't matter. My authority, on the other hand, does. You are accused of several severe violations against the one major timeline and are hereby arrested for the crimes you committed. Be aware, that when you are found guilty, punishment will be your removal from the timeline."

Kieran and I suck in a sharp gasp. What—

A green beam of light shoots out from *somewhere* in his direction, bifurcating halfway between him and us, one beam hitting Kieran, the other one me.

My chest explodes in red-hot pain, like somebody had set me on fire.

Kieran chokes on his next breath, goes down on one knee—

I stumble—

And then, nothing.

About the Author

Micky O'Brady is a pediatrician-turned-writer living in beautiful, dry Southern California with her husband and two critters (one son, one dog). Micky loves to write YA thrillers and sci-fi with a romantic twist, mainly because she wishes her life had been such an awesome mix of action and cute guys when she was a teen.

When she isn't up at around 3 a.m. (with a cup of tea, Earl Grey, hot) drafting stories she can't get out of her head, she can be found at a martial arts dojo, though maybe not at 3 a.m. She holds a first degree black belt in Krav Maga and a second degree black belt in Judo, and is convinced every girl should know how to kick some butt.

Micky also is a firm believer in the healing powers of Nutella eaten straight from the glass and in the magic that can happen on a rainy day, as long as there are fuzzy socks and a cup of hot tea involved.

Her previous publications include a doctoral thesis and several medical articles as well as a medical book about emergency communication. None of them are as fun to read as her YA novels though. Her first YA-novel, THE PRESIDENT'S DAUGHTER, and its sequel TRIAL BY ICE, are published by Curiosity Quills and available through all major retailers, such as Amazon, B&N, Kobo, and Smashwords.

Through Snowy Wings Publishing Micky is the author of the YA-sci-fi romance BETWEEN WORLDS, a super-cool contemporary romance-slash-pro-wrestling-story PLAYING WITH #FIRE, as well as another sci-fi romance, TIME WARPED, and its sequel TIME BOUND.

9 781952 667732